Raise the Flag
and
Sound the Cannon

RAISE THE FLAG
AND
SOUND THE CANNON

The Northernmost Battle of the Civil War

The Confederate Raid on St. Albans, Vermont
October 19, 1864

A Historical Novel

Donald J. Davison

Shoreline

Edited by John Vatsis
Graphics and author's photo by Robert Kertesz
Colour photos by Donald Davison

Published by Shoreline
23 Ste-Anne, Ste-Anne-de-Bellevue, QC H9X 1L1
shoreline@sympatico.ca   514.457.5733   www.shorelinepress.ca

Printed in Canada by Marquis Imprimeur

Dépôt legal: Library and Archives Canada
and Bibliothèque nationale de Québec

Library and Archives Cataloguing in Publication

Davison, Donald J., 1932-
Raise the flag and sound the cannon : the Civil War—
October 19, 1864 at St. Albans, Vermont / Donald J. Davison

Includes bibliographical references.
ISBN 978-1-896754-63-5

1. Saint Albans (Vt.)—History—Raid, 1864—Fiction. I. Title.
PS8607.A9573R34 2008   C813'.6   C2008-903631-X

DEDICATION

This book is dedicated to Carl E. Johnson of St. Albans, Vermont, and to all those tireless archivists who devote their time and energy to North America's heritage along both sides of the border between Quebec and Vermont.

ABOUT THE BOOK

The author has written this book to entertain and to increase the awareness of the circumstances surrounding the raid on St. Albans. While this book is not purported to be a history book, it tries to illustrate the role that Canada played in this conflict.

If you would like to communicate with the author, please e-mail him at donalddavison@sympatico.ca. Errors or omissions can be corrected or included in succeeding editions.

Cover illustration from: *Frank Leslie's Illustrated Report on the Raid,* New York, 1864. Courtesy of the Vermont Historical Society, Montpelier.

CSA is the abbreviation for Confederate States of America

ABOUT THE AUTHOR

Donald Davison was born in Hudson Heights, Quebec, and attended Macdonald High School. He then earned a BCom from Sir George Williams College, where he was editor of the *Georgian Weekly* newspaper. He received his MBA from University of Western Ontario, and became an Accredited Financial Counselor. He has two children and lives in Knowlton, Quebec, where he enjoys singing, outdoor activities and photography.

Donald Davison is the author of *Take Control of your Money* (published in the U.S. and Canada by Productive Publications, Toronto, and *Banished,* a biography. *Raise the Flag and Sound the Cannon* was adapted and produced as a musical comedy, 'Chickasaw: The Elixer of Love' in 2007 by the Knowlton Players.

He is working on a second novel, *Sadie the Lady.* It is a historical fiction tale of horse racing at Saratoga Springs, New York.

PREFACE

"We have had to use Cousin Joe's forcible expression, a 'Raid from Hell'. For about half an hour yesterday afternoon I thought that we should be burnt up and robbed. But I hope you don't imagine I was one moment frightened, though the noise of guns, the agitated looks of the rushing men and our powerless condition were startlingly enough." (1)

This book is a novel based upon the raid by Confederate soldiers, called Rebels, on the mercantile banks of St. Albans, Vermont, October 19th, 1864, towards the end of the Civil War.

The Rebels, the family names of the St. Albans townspeople, the Governor and Mrs. Smith, the posse, Chester Goodenough, Henry Hogan, Alfred Kimball, and the Canadian law officers and magistrates are real. One of the real-life principals in this story is a bankrupt English solicitor, John Rumsey. The author has Rumsey's diary from 1842–1849. While his story is a true one, his actions, from the moment he meets his old friend Patrick O'Toole and embarks upon a career selling patent medicine, are fictitious. Nearly everyone else is fictitious and was created in order to give the book some compassion and continuity.

The Vermont governor and his wife give a dinner for Rumsey, Minnie Green, Ben Potter, and Ben's parents after Rumsey's and Ben's release from the Montreal jail. The dinner is fictitious.

The Rebels escaped on roads and trains that existed in 1864. While we know where the Rebels were arrested, very little is known of what happened during their escape. This story attempts to recreate what the Rebels might have done, but it was never confirmed. These assumptions are particularly important when trying to recreate what happened to those who got away and were never heard of again.

I conducted extensive research along the border from the historical museums in St. Albans, Enosburg Falls and Richford, Vermont, to Stanbridge East and Knowlton, Quebec.

It was Dale Porter of the St. Albans Museum and the U.S. customs officers at the Franklin border that suggested I meet Carl E. Johnson and read his book, *The St. Albans Raid, October, 1864,* that he published in 2001.

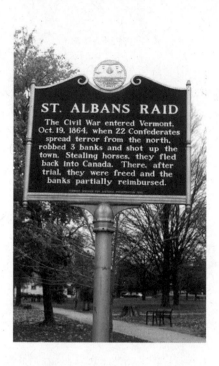

ST. ALBANS RAID
The Civil War entered Vermont,
Oct. 19, 1864, when 22 Confederates
spread terror from the north,
robbed 3 banks and shot up the
town. Stealing horses, they fled
back into Canada. There, after
trial, they were freed and the
banks partially reimbursed.

**Photo courtesy of Peter Flood.
Author's note: There were twenty-one
men. Huntley was aka Hutchison.**

As I was pulling away from the border, one of the officers looked at me closely and whispered in my ear, "You really should meet this fellow Johnson. He's a retired policeman, you know!"

Carl turned out to be a fine historian and a wonderful host. He introduced me to downtown St. Albans, the 'Raid' on North Main Street and the town's historic cemetery where many of the families of 1864 are buried.

It was in The St. Albans Raid, 1864, that I found the quote for the beginning of the preface. It is from a letter from Mrs. Anne Eliza Brainerd Smith to her husband, John Gregory Smith, Governor of Vermont, on October 20th, 1864.

CONTENTS

Maps:

INTRODUCTION

The setting is St. Albans, Vermont, during the American Civil War (1861 -1865). Mid 19th century America was in a period of transition. Huge immigration from Europe in the first half of the century was followed by rapid industrial expansion during the second half.

Lifestyles were simple. Evening church services were the only diversion in town. There were no cars, phones or lights. Patent medicines were the principal method for curing the effects of various maladies, but not their causes. St. Albans was suffering the loss of many of its men who went to the War.

When Robert E. Lee's Confederate Army lost the Battle of Gettysburg in July 1863 and General Ulysses Grant became leader of the Union forces in the spring of 1864, the tide of the Civil War turned against the Confederate States of America.

By the fall of 1864, the president of the Confederacy, Jefferson Davis, in Richmond, Virginia, was getting desperate for money to pay for munitions that were coming in part from Europe. Extreme measures were needed, such as raiding Union banks close to the Canadian border for the stronger union dollar.

It is into this situation then, that Lieutenant Bennett Young leads twenty Confederate soldiers into St. Albans to rob their mercantile banks. He enlists at gunpoint a patent-medicine man, 'Doc' Rumsey, to look after his wounded. The raid is a story stranger than fiction....

In 1864, what is now called Quebec, was then called Canada East. By 1791, after the American Revolution, farmland south of the St. Lawrence and east of the Richelieu Rivers running east to the Maine Border was surveyed for settlement by Loyalists from the United States. This area became known as the Eastern Townships. South of the border, in 1791, Vermont became the 14th of the United States.

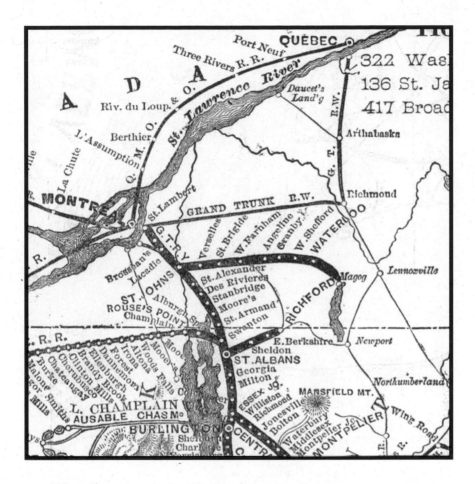

Grand Trunk / Central Vermont RR 1879. Courtesy of CNR

The Rebels used the trains to get to St. Albans and had planned to use them for their escape thereafter. The above map was drawn several years after the raid, when two important lines were built: the St. Albans-Richford line in 1871 and the Waterloo-Magog line in 1877. The Central Vermont and the Canadian Grand Trunk controlled most lines.

John Gregory Smith, Governor of Vermont in 1864, was the owner of the Central-Vermont Railroad and had moved the workshops and head office to St. Albans when he acquired the line in 1855. His family lived in St. Albans at the time of the raid.

Canadian National is the current owner of the Grand Trunk and the CV RR. (Currently, the New England Central runs the CV.)

RUMSEY'S ENTRANCE

Quebec, Wednesday, September 5, 1863

Rumsey stepped off the gangplank of the steamship that had brought him across the Atlantic, feeling relieved that he was once again walking firmly on solid ground after a month at sea. John felt a wave of excitement rush over him as he took in his new surroundings. This sense of elation did not last, however, as the cruel realities of life once again set in. John thought about his recently deceased wife, his bankruptcy, and his children, whom he was forced to leave at home in Britain.

He looked up at the battlements of the old City of Quebec and realized that his life in North America would be completely different from the one he knew. His days as a solicitor from a prominent family of noted physicians and surgeons would fade into memory. His bankruptcy involved spending clients' funds and his own family's as well. He had been desperate when clients wouldn't pay their bills. Eventually he couldn't cover his illegal withdrawals and had to confess to his father and to the county what he had done. His wife went into seclusion and never recovered. She died a few months later.

Rumsey was sent to the county of Buckinghamshire's debtor's prison. Fortunately, his sister Margaret, in High Wycombe, was made the foster parent of his two young girls. While in prison, his sister set about rescuing him. After a year she was able to arrange for Rumsey to be given 'transportation to America'. This move saved his life because he was dying of pneumonia in the cold and damp prison. Before he took the train to London en route to Southampton, Margaret was able to visit him.

"John," Margaret whispered through the bars, "I know you meant well and you've suffered enough, but I really feel that you should start over, otherwise you'll die in prison. I can look after the girls until you become established. I know how hard it must be, bearing the burden of bankruptcy, moving to a new country. You know that Father is still unforgiving. He and Brother James are doctors and very proud of it.

They cannot reconcile their embarrassment. I feel differently. I can provide a small pension to help you. You'll never have the ability to recover quickly if you don't accept some financial help. I know you're a proud man, but be practical. Write to me as soon as you get to Canada and tell me to which bank I should direct the drafts each month. Someday, when you're settled, you can pay me back."

His sister's help overwhelmed him and left him speechless. After giving him some additional funds, Margaret stood up, blew a kiss to her tearful brother and quietly left the prison, leaving him alone to mull over his fate.

Once in Canada, Rumsey stayed in Quebec City long enough to make travel arrangements to Montreal by train along the southern shore of the St. Lawrence River. While Quebec was the capital of the United Province of Canada, Rumsey felt that Montreal, further west along the St. Lawrence, had more potential, being a more commercial city. He had heard that the government in Quebec City would be moving to Ottawa, just west of Montreal, in a couple of years. This would reduce the population and possible job opportunities.

Montreal, Friday, September 7, 1863

John Rumsey took the Grand Trunk Railway's Richmond to St. Johns to Montreal train and arrived at the cavernous Bonaventure Railway Station at the foot of Great St. James Street in downtown Montreal. He had lost quite a bit of weight during his incarceration, and looked almost cadaverous and much older than his 45 years. His trademark gray eyes, long nose and chin remained, but his gray, full-front, frock coat, vest, leggings and boots, cane, and topper had all seen better days. He was even down to the last two of his beloved detachable linen collars that weren't frayed or permanently soiled. Linen collars didn't clean well, much to Rumsey's chagrin.

During the voyage overseas he had realized how stooped he was getting. He began to take on the posture of a defeated man. Margaret had scolded him, "John, for heavens sake, keep your head up! Now remember that when you land in America."

So he had practiced trying to look as successful as he had felt in the past. It wasn't easy for him. His confidence and self-esteem had been badly shattered. On the deck of the ship he practiced standing tall and walking with his chin up. He practiced being what he used to be, a successful British solicitor. Still, mirrors were things to be avoided.

Rumsey hailed a cab to drive him to a proper hotel. He found himself being carried along Great St. James Street, the main business district, to the St. Lawrence Hall Hotel - the best one in town. When Rumsey stepped down from the carriage, he realized that he might have made a mistake. He could no longer afford such luxury. After one night, he knew he had to move.

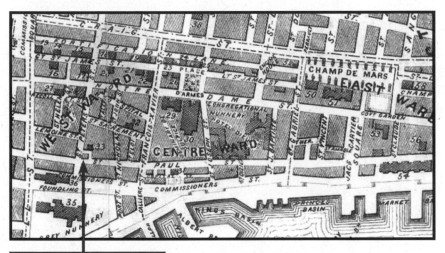

Goodenough's Coffee Exchange House

Vieux Montreal, 1859

The concierge understood John's plight. With a knowing smile he said, "I suspect the Great St. James Club up the street would not be appropriate until you are established, sir. The alternative on Great St. James Street would be the Ottawa Hotel." Then he paused and looked more closely at him. "Then again, to live more modestly for awhile, you should consider Chester Goodenough's Coffee Exchange House. Just walk one block west to St. Peter Street, then down a few blocks to St. Paul Street. The inn is right there on the corner. "

Rumsey decided to walk. He found the Exchange House beside a small square at the corner of St. Paul Street where the coaches made their turns. John stared at this rundown old building. All the gray brick and cobblestones were wearing out; the wrought iron signpost was broken and had lost its coat of arms. There had been a time when Goodenough's

17

was rather fashionable, serving the coach trade before the railways came to town, but all that had changed in the last decade. Now Chester Goodenough needed any kind of business to survive. Guests were few and far between. While Rumsey felt that Goodenough's was beneath his social station, he was encouraged that at least Mr. Goodenough was glad to see him.

When Rumsey signed the register, Mr. Goodenough complained about the lack of business.

"I can't even afford to make repairs! How I miss my family crest on the signpost. How the mighty have fallen!"

Old Mr. Goodenough was long past retirement, but he had to keep open his hotel, being his only source of income. He was a typical exchange house proprietor, red faced from doing all his own cooking, pouring cider at all hours, managing the change of horses, keeping the water troughs full, and receiving tired passengers. While he was burned out, overweight and bald, his brown eyes were alive with humour and could always find the bright side of things. Close friends called him "Sunny" Goodenough.

Rumsey spent the following day getting acclimatized to his new life, and starting to venture out onto the streets of Montreal. He found that Goodenough's was only a block away from the harbour and the city's beautiful boardwalk. Ah, how he loved the fresh air on the river, the halyards clicking away on the ocean-going vessels, the trains shunting back and forth on the quays and the steam from the railway engines. Best of all was the view. The mighty St. Lawrence, according to Mr. Goodenough, had more water flowing down it to the sea than any other known river in America. What a sight, John said to himself.

Rumsey marvelled at how trains from all over the United States and Canada ran right up to the docks all year long. Ever since the Victoria Bridge had been built in 1859, the railways would come across the St. Lawrence River to the city and to port side. While the trains were slowly taking over in 1864 and the investors were building terminals in the west end of town, the hotels of the day still faced the harbour around the Bonsecours Market between Commissioners and Great St. James Street. If only I could afford to travel, sighed Rumsey.

The boardwalk gave him peace and tranquility. He was away from the fetid smells of Great St. James Street, the horses, the wagons and the yelling of the draymen. Anyone stepping off a curb was in danger of serious injury from runaway wagons with their wild horses on a wet cobblestone street.

Each day, no matter what John was doing to find a job, he always reserved a few moments on the boardwalk, where he could sit down and enjoy poetry, his lifelong hobby. Verse would give him a moment of peace … his only entertainment. He loved to sit and read poems from Tennyson, the poet laureate of England. It was during moments like this that John would think about his wife who had passed on.

The Departure

And on her lover's arm she lent,
And round her waist she felt it fold,
And far across the hills they went.
In that new world which is the old,
Across the hills and far away.

After a particularly discouraging and demeaning round of ceaseless enquiry for legal work, he left for the solace of the river. Each day he saw a dog sitting on the little square in front of the Exchange House. Every morning the dog would be there. Rumsey would notice him again when he was seated on the boardwalk. Each time the dog just sat there staring at him very quietly.

He wondered what kind of a dog it was. It was certainly not a pure-bred, like Margaret's setter at her home in High Wycombe. This one looked part chow, German shepherd, collie, and retriever. He was about two feet high and had long brown hair and pointed ears.

Rumsey stared at the dog and the dog returned his gaze. Neither blinked. Finally he motioned for the dog to come closer. He looked deeper into his eyes and found the dog had a rather intelligent look about him. In fact he seemed to frown, smile, cry, and laugh. This made Rumsey chuckle. To his astonishment, he was sure that the dog was laughing back! These moments occurred every day.

Rumsey would try new expressions and even comments. The dog would look at Rumsey in such a way that he seemed to understand Rumsey's positive and negative expressions, his indifference, encouragement, and so on. Usually the ears moved according to the dog's feelings. Positives mean his ears are up and negatives mean his ears are down. After awhile, John felt that he could literally read the dog's mind.

How in God's name can he react like that? Rumsey questioned no one in particular. Yet he became more convinced than ever that the dog understood him, but he thought, I better not tell anyone that. Then Rumsey sat back and recited a Williams Wordsworth poem to himself.

Daffodils

I wandered lonely as a cloud
That floats on high o'er vales and hills,
When all at once I saw a crowd,
A host, of golden daffodils;
Beside the lake, beneath the trees,
Fluttering and dancing in the breeze.

Ah, the late Wordsworth will be missed, Rumsey thought. But now we have Lord Tennyson."

As the days progressed he enjoyed having the dog accompanying him around the city. When he returned to the Exchange House, the dog stopped, sat in the little square and waited until he came out the next morning. With winter approaching, Rumsey became very concerned about this strange dog that he had befriended. He should be fed and kept indoors during the cold months ahead. When he mentioned this to Chester Goodenough, he didn't get a straight answer. Mr. Goodenough just wasn't interested.

"Probably the dog was left off a stagecoach as it passed through town. It happens when some people want to lose their pets. The owners should have returned by now," he said.

If that was the case, something should be done. The answer came to him one night - why not call the dog 'Chester' after Mr. Goodenough? He might be very flattered. This was indeed the case, and finally a deal was struck, Chester could stay in his room as long as Rumsey cleaned up after him. Scraps could be fed to Chester without much trouble. Mr. Goodenough started to talk to Chester and began to accept him. In the hotel Chester was clean and quiet. He never barked! Unique relationships formed, 'partnerships', grinned John Rumsey, the solicitor. Conversations between Chester and the hotelier, and Chester and Rumsey became a regular event in the Exchange House, much to the dismay and puzzlement of the upstairs maid.

Rumsey didn't anticipate the severity of Montreal winters. The first thing he needed was a good overcoat. He had never heard of freezing noses, hands and feet. Fortunately his family's name preceded him and some solicitors were able to find research and copy work for him. With his modest wages he was able to purchase some new clothing from the clothier, Giovanni Primo & Son on Great St. James Street. Margaret's pension that he arranged to have deposited at the Bank of British North America up on Great St. James Street paid for his lodgings and food.

One day just as the spring of 1864 turned into summer, Mr. Goodenough confided in Rumsey that 20 young farm boys from Central Kentucky had just registered at the hotel.

Mister Goodenough leaned closer to Rumsey and whispered, "They are a little rough-hewn, but so far they haven't caused me any trouble. They're taking their meals here and paying in advance every week. I have no idea how long they plan on staying, but it's good money for me!"

Rumsey hardly listened. The United States and the Confederate States were the farthest things from his mind. Just as these farm boys stuck to themselves, so did Rumsey keep to himself. For some reason, Chester was not happy. He would lie with his nose buried between his outstretched paws, ears down and eyes up. Chester wanted no part of them.

As the summer was ending, Rumsey became more anxious to spend time along the harbour. The boardwalk was a very popular place to meet friends in the summer. One of the attractions that he greatly anticipated was the aroma of roasting chestnuts when the weather turned colder. For a penny, he could have his daily luxury. Then, he would sit down on a bench by the Kings Basin and watch the ferries arriving from and departing for the south shore of the St. Lawrence River.

The Boardwalk, Friday, September 9, 1864
One day later in the summer, while he was sitting by the Basin, a voice rang out from among the passersby.

"John ... John Rumsey?"

John looked up. To his surprise there stood his old Irish friend, Patrick O'Toole, whom he hadn't seen since the previous fall when he had tried to help him sell patent medicines. According to John's diary:

"This being a country in which great things sometimes come from little beginnings, I suggested to a poor Irish servant, the vending of a corn medicine. I gave him a recipe, a fine name for it and an elaborate account of its merits. I mixed up the first fourteen bottles, the Queen's Printer gave publicity to it and after sending the bottles among Les Canadiens, my Irish friend is now practicing his profession in the widespread and free soil of the Yankees."

John had advised Patrick about the difference between the native French population that have historically been known as 'Les Canadiens' and the new British and Scottish immigrants that were calling themselves 'Canadians' after the Act of Union in 1841 that enforced the difference. "Be careful Patrick. Know your customer!" he laughed.

Patrick, very enthusiastic, started to sell the tinctures along Notre Dame Street on his way to the Bonaventure Grand Trunk railway station. He was heading for the free soil of the Yankee. Rumsey was quite jealous. Now there was O'Toole with his head held high, wearing a checkered sports jacket, twill pants, a string tie, tweed cap, and a sparkle in his eyes.

"Patrick my boy, I never thought that I'd see you again."

O'Toole sat down with a flourish and grinned at him. "I've just returned to pay off some old debts and to pick up some things I left behind last year. I thought I'd take the time to look for you. I'm so glad we've met, John. I wanted to thank you so much for helping me. Remember how you made my patent medicines? Well, the tincture of your medicine started to sell so well I figured I'd try my luck in the United States. The trains go all the way down the Hudson River now. So I took off for Albany, the New York State capital. It was a wise choice. I found an apothecary shop on Market Street. The proprietor, Phillip Schoonmaker, a fine old gentleman, claimed he could make up my tinctures and find a printer that would produce my advertisements.

"The corn medicine you prepared sold well. But there is a new medicine that Mr. Schoonmaker told me about. Some folks had come to Albany from as far west as Oklahoma and Ohio to escape the ravages of the Civil War. They brought with them some plums from the Chickasaw tree they claimed could cure almost anything. While he hadn't mixed up any formula yet, he had some plums to offer me if I wanted to give it a try.

"I knew I had to start. I realized that selling benefits of a medicine to a lady was more important than describing obscure formulas. So what would I have to do to sell a new medicine like the extract from the Chickasaw Plum? I had seen other patent medicine men with dancing bears, dog and pony shows, tricks, cards, and even freaks. While a few of them jingled little bells, most of them missed the added dimension of sound! So to attract attention I needed my own kind of jingle to rise above the hustle and bustle of the street. John, you know how I love to sing Irish songs. Well, I decided to write a song that I could sing to advertise the sale of my tinctures, Patrick's Finest Tinctures. When I tried to sing my new jingle, people started to talk to me. The more I sang, the more people would stop. It worked.

"John, why don't you forget your past in England and start life over? Sell patent medicine. You love writing and poetry. Why not sing your own medicine jingle, as I do. You write the words and I'll write the music for you."

Rumsey looked over the river for some time, trying to imagine himself as a salesman. Then he turned to O'Toole and confided, "Nothing else has worked."

O'Toole laughed and proclaimed, "John, from now on its 'Doc Rumsey's Finest Tinctures'. Anyone can be a doctor. Who's to say you are or not? Stand properly and stick your chin out. You look, therefore - you are."

So they started to think about a new song to sell Rumsey's tincture. "Everyone I've met here complains about the lack of energy, indigestion, and listlessness. Why not call our medicine the Chickasaw Revival Tonic," John suggested. O'Toole grinned, "First, what are the benefits? Let's start thinking of some." Patrick then took his pen and started to write furiously. John looked over his shoulder and fussed, "Patrick, how can you say these things? Who's to say what works and what doesn't? This is ridiculous!"

The Brand of Great Renown

Chickasaw is a pure and powerful tonic. Chickasaw is a corrective and alternative of wonderful efficacy in disease of the stomach, liver and bowels. This tonic prevents fever and ague and bilious remittent fever. It fortifies the system against miasmas and the evil effects of unwholesome water. It invigorates the organs of digestion and the bowels. It steadies the nerves, and tends to prolong life. It cures dyspepsia, liver complaint, sick and nervous headache, general debility, nervousness, depression of the spirits, constipation, colic, intermittent fevers, seasickness, cramps and spasms, all complaints of either sex and certain rare oriental diseases.

"Now the next step is to write a new song to sell this medicine." Patrick started to laugh. He was having fun!

"All right. Let's give it a name for what it really does for people. Let's call it the 'Chickasaw Revival Tonic Song'. John started to laugh.

Now Chester was worried. He had never heard singing before. These two men were acting a little crazy, especially the way they laughed at each other over their rhymes. Chester was glad to see that other people seemed to think the same way.

The Chickasaw Revival Tonic Song©

My name is Rumsey.
That's Doctor Rumsey,
A physician from Britain, that's where I gained my fame.
I bring this potion
From o'er the ocean
So hark, as I impress on you its memorable name.

It's Chickasaw Revival Tonic,
Cures all ills from mild to chronic!
Try it now and feel euphoric!
Chickasaw Revival Tonic.

Have a little tincture, madam,
For what ails you in the winter, madam.
Coughs'n colds'n sneezes simply melt away!
When you're feeling horrid, madam,
Just rub it on your forrid, madam.

24

Reinstates your lovely smiles and keeps those frowns at bay!
Try my special potion, madam!
Apply it as a lotion, madam!
It banishes all itches from feet to arms to head.
Disorders abdominal, madam?
Fainting spells abominable, madam?
Chickasaw will fix them all and keep you out of bed!

Chickasaw the great Revival Tonic.
Chickasaw the brand of great renown.

© Graham Hardman

John complained to himself: After all these years of being down, here was this smiling cocky Irishman telling me to look and act up. Euphoric be damned! Here I am being asked to act like a doctor ... and sing! O'Toole gave me a few singing lessons and loaned me a pitch pipe to ensure that I sing in the right key.

"John, it's not how well you sing, but just plain singing that counts. In fact if you are not too good, the ladies might sympathize and be more receptive!" So they sang. Chester howled. He lifted his head and bayed like a wolfhound. They were startled. He howled only when they sang.

"He must love to sing! The ladies will love it. I can't believe that Chester is actually a singing dog," laughed Patrick. The more they sang, the more Chester howled. The more he howled the more people stopped to stare at them.

John found that singing was his own breakthrough, too. He could never stand up in a crowd and start to sell something, but singing was a completely different approach. If he could sing, he could sell. He didn't have to reveal his true personality. He didn't have to act naturally ... he was acting when he sang!

"I can wire my apothecary in Albany for the Chickasaw Plum that is called *Prunus Angustifolia*. Remember, what is in it is a big secret!"

The Ingredients (Confidential)

Cod Liver Oil
Dried Prunus Angustifolia
Glycerin

Sugar
Licorice
Flavouring oils
Sarsaparilla
Alcohol (50% by vol.)

"People only care what the tincture can do for them, anyway. Don't confuse them with too much. Keep it simple … repeat and repeat that the medicine will make them feel better."

Rumsey looked crestfallen. "I have no money," he cried. "How can I possibly do all that you suggest?"

"John, you helped me to get started so now I can help you. I can lend you some money to order all the ingredients, produce the labels and tinctures and print an advertisement that you can hand out. With your family's background, you are sure to succeed."

It was growing dark and quiet on the Boardwalk. With the sound of the trains and the ships' halyards growing quieter, Rumsey and O'Toole decided to call it a day. O'Toole offered Rumsey and Chester dinner back at the St. Lawrence Hall Hotel. During dinner, he confided in John that he should try the United States as he had done. "I think you should leave Montreal … try the widespread and free soil of the Yankee. It's only a few hours away!

"Try a smaller town such as St. Albans in Vermont. It's a growing railway town showing lots of promise. Take the train. You'll be there in no time. Only in America, they say, can you succeed, one tincture at a time! Monday we'll find an apothecary shop here in town and make arrangements for a shipment of *Prunus Angustifolia* to Montreal. When you get to St. Albans, don't advertise right away. Get some money in first. Once you are settled, wire me. We can discuss how you can pay me back and how we can work together. Who's to say where this may go?"

The wine and turkey had made Rumsey mellower than he had been in years. The glow was giving him a sense of confidence. He looked down at Chester, then to Patrick and replied, "One tincture at a time?"

Chester sat and listened quietly, blinking his eyes from time to time. When Rumsey had returned to Goodenough's that evening, he said to Chester, "Tomorrow will certainly be a new day. Ah! *Prunus Angustifolia,* from oe'r the ocean. Can I remember the verses? Have a little tincture, Madame?"

Rumsey snored that night. He had dreams. He could just see himself, a pitiful old man, selling a fool's opiate to innocent people. There was his family standing on the street watching. They were sneering and shouting at him. "Stop selling quack medicines, for goodness sake. Be what you are, a British gentleman of the establishment, otherwise Burke's Peerage will erase you! Go back to law immediately!"

Yet, John Rumsey now had a plan. He was committed to starting a new life by reviving the townspeople of St. Albans. Chester looked up at how restless John seemed to be in his sleep. He blinked thoughtfully and then he, too, went back to sleep, but his ears stayed up.

Piper's Apothecary, Monday, September 12, 1864

John Rumsey arrived with Patrick O'Toole to talk about a foreign substance called *Prunus Angustifolia*, extracts of some plums from the midwest of the United States.

"I work with an apothecary shop in Albany and would like to have some of this extract delivered to you. The balance of the ingredients for our new medicine is listed here on my notepaper. Unfortunately, I have to return but my colleague, 'Doc' Rumsey, will follow up. I'd like him to learn the mixing for subsequent orders. He must be allowed to help you, Mr. Piper. Doc has a good background in medicine. Don't you, Doc?"

Rumsey muttered something that no one could hear.

Now that the initial order was made, they would have to wait while the order was telegraphed to Mr. Schoonmaker in Albany. O'Toole said, "Hopefully it won't take more than a week or two. The direct railway connection via Vermont will certainly speed things up. Remember, I have to order the tinctures, the labels and the feature sheets. Delivery of these items could take about ten days. So let's say we meet again on September 22nd"

"Everything should be here by then," commented Mr. Piper.

Piper's Apothecary, Thursday, September 22, 1864

O'Toole was back in Albany and Rumsey was at Piper's door. They were in business. Mr. Piper let Rumsey into his back room to help with the mixing, as per their arrangement. Because Rumsey was apparently familiar with medicines, Piper didn't mind opening up the back room to him. Piper even let Chester into the back room.

With the labels and circulars due from the printers at any moment, Robert Piper was happy with the transaction. With everything paid for by O'Toole, the shipment of 100 tinctures should be ready by Friday, October 7 and on a train for St. Albans, Wednesday, October 12.

* * *

YOUNG'S ENTRANCE

Montreal, Friday, September 23, 1864

A clean-cut looking young man, who claimed to be a 'Gentleman from Louisville,' had just stepped off the Quebec train at the Bonaventure Station. It had been a long trip from Virginia. He introduced himself as the Reverend Christian Clement Clyde of the United Christian Circuit from the neutral state of Kentucky. He smiled benignly and clutched his Bible for all to see. As a minister he was well dressed with a full-front frock coat and a beige, velvet waistcoat. The only bit of apparel that could give him away as someone who was not what he appeared to be was his insistence on wearing an old 'lawman's' hat with a flatter top and wider brim than a normal topper or traditional clergyman's hat. The hat was his attempt at looking 'Kentucky' in the eyes of easterners.

The Reverend Clyde described his anticipation of converting many country folk in Canada. His work was a missionary one. "A much needed revival of the Christian ethic!"

St. Lawrence Hall Hotel, Monday, September 26, 1864

No one could mistake southern gentlemen on the streets of Montreal. They had a way about them that put them above the crowd. They walked with such grace and dignity, with clothing to match from the new southern textile mills, and the pedestrians on the street quickly bowed to them in passing. The British might have their woolens but the south had their cottons! After all, they were supplying over two-thirds of the world's supply. Their vests and full-front frock coats were in bright colors, and they always sported a gold-tipped cane.

Jacob 'Jake' Thompson, former Congressman and Secretary of the Interior in the James Madison administration, walked with dignity up to the entrance of the hotel followed closely by two attentive assistants, former Senator Clement C. Clay, from Alabama and George Sanders of Virginia. Little did the local people realize that these dignified 'fancy' gentlemen were Confederate Rebels. It was the topper hats and the gold-tipped canes that impressed the locals. While the lightweight and brightly coloured clothing made the members of the Beaver Club shiver, they accepted them for what they thought they were: southern gentlemen on diplomatic missions.

Jake Thompson was the oldest of the three. His beard was short and curly. His face was a little heavy and looked more like a bulldog on the prowl. He didn't laugh easily and one did not argue with Jake without feeling the fear of the Almighty breathing down your back.

Clement C. Clay was taller and slighter than Thompson. He had a full beard and looked older than Jake. With a very straight back, he fit well into his southern genteel clothing, giving him the look of the perfect southern gentleman. The way Clay pulled out his gold watch-chain and the manner in which he touched his nose with his silk handkerchief made him out as a man of obvious culture.

George Sander, of Virginia, was younger than the other two, shorter and thinner than Clay. Nearly clean-shaven, he was always grooming his small mustache. George was a dapper man by northern standards. He laughed easily. Mr. Sanders reported to both Thompson and Clay.

Despite their genteel façade, these southern gentlemen were spies. Thompson was the Commissioner of both the Montreal and Toronto offices of a clandestine operation of the Confederate Army. For the last two months Thompson's deputy Commissioner, Clement C. Clay, had been running their mission in St. Catharine's on Lake Ontario. From the safety of neutral Canada, he had been reviewing and planning operations for robbing and burning towns along the Canadian border. With diplomatic missions in Halifax, Toronto, St. Catharine's, and Montreal, the Confederates called themselves members of The Provincial Army of the Confederate States of America. Their criminal activity was disguised as legitimate warfare. These soft-spoken men were paid to cause havoc in the Union, but also to create breaches in neutrality that might bring Britain and Canada into conflict with the North.

The hotel doorman quickly opened the door for such gentlemen who seemed to be on important business. The manager rushed up to Commissioner Thompson. "A gentleman has been waiting for you all day. He is seated in the corner underneath the potted palm."

Thompson turned to gaze at the young man, who was reading a Bible. He was impeccably dressed in light southern clothing, typical of what the commissioners wore. Tall, sitting erect, clear blue eyes, clean-shaven, and obviously quite young, this gentleman looked like the minister that he claimed to be.

Thompson turned to his two colleagues and whispered, "My God, this can't be the young officer from General Morgan's 8th Kentucky Cavalry that Secretary Mallory wired me about. I need an experienced soldier that can lead raids - not a minister to lead a congregation in hymn singing." The man seated in the corner was the man who called himself Reverend Christian Clement Clyde.

With some misgivings, Thompson left his companions and strolled across the lobby to meet Young. The lieutenant jumped up, recognizing the politician.

"Why Commissioner Thompson, what a pleasure to meet you. Secretary Mallory spoke so highly of you."

All of a sudden Thompson was flattered. "Oh, really?"

The young man continued, "We have so much to talk about.…"

Thompson leaned forward and whispered, "Not here. Follow us upstairs and we'll talk privately. This is no place for a serious chat."

So, making no introductions, Thompson led the way silently up the grand staircase to the mezzanine and along the carpeted hall to his suite. When they entered, only then did Thompson introduce Young to his Deputy Commissioner, Senator Clement Clay and George Sanders.

"Tell us about yourself, sir."

"Certainly, Commissioner. While I have been acting as the Reverend Christian Clement Clyde of the United Christian Circuit of Lexington, Kentucky, my real name and rank is Lieutenant Bennett Young of the Confederate Eighth Cavalry, where I served under General John Hunt Morgan. My regiment raided with General Morgan in Kentucky, Indiana, Missouri, and Ohio.

"Unfortunately, many of us were caught and sent to prison at Fort Douglas outside of Chicago, but some of us escaped and made our way to Canada and the mission here in Montreal to look for some guidance and money to return to Richmond. We met Chaplain Cameron, a fine man who helped us considerably. He agreed that I should try to get back to Richmond, and advised me that one person had a better chance of surviving the hazardous journey than a whole platoon did. He suggested that the rest stay here in Montreal and await instructions via the mission office. So, I took a boat to Halifax and eventually a slow steamer to Wilmington, Delaware. From there I was able to reach Virginia and report to President Davis in Richmond."

Thompson was skeptical of this extraordinary story, but first of all, he needed to settle down this enthusiastic young officer. "Lieutenant, the Confederacy is losing. Last June, Lee won his last battle at Cold Harbour and in July, Jubal Early nearly made it to Washington. Since then it has been one loss after another. Sheridan is chasing Early all the way back up the Shenandoah, and few battles have aroused more bitterness than this one. Sherman has just captured Atlanta! General Bragg hasn't won anything since Chickamauga last year and Lee is tied up in the siege of Petersburg against Grant. I also regret to tell you, but your General Morgan is no longer with us."

Young stared at him, "What do you mean?"

Thompson paused for a moment. "General Morgan was killed at Greenville, Tennessee, just a few weeks ago on September 3rd."

Young sat down and tried to recover. Morgan was his idol. He rode for Morgan. "I would have ridden anywhere for him," he whispered.

Thompson broke out into a soft smile while his companions looked on sternly at Young's emotions.

"Lieutenant Young, this is war and you had better be prepared to lose men … some family, some friends and some leaders."

He waited a few minutes and then continued, "I assume you are familiar with the New York operation? One group was to set all the hotels on fire, another to take control of the police department, another group was to seize all the federal buildings and municipal offices, and another was to set free all the prisoners from Fort Lafayette. The final group was to capture General John Adam Dix and throw him into prison. Are you aware of what happened to the plan?"

Thompson whispered, "The north found out about it. Too much time and too many messages had passed since the plan was established last March. So the order was scrapped. However, I have an old friend who still wants to burn down the hotels as close to the federal election next month as possible. Who's to say? We'll have to wait and see."

Thompson leaned closer to Young and asked quietly, "So tell us, Mr. Young, what is it that Richmond thinks you can do for us? I hear that Secretary Mallory expects great things."

"There is an old chemical invented in Constantinople in 670 A.D. called Greek fire that Richmond has told us to copy and use against the Union." Young confided the composition to them.

The Ingredients (Confidential)

Sulphur
Naphtha
Quicklime

"It worked well against northern riverboats on the Mississippi this year. It looks like water and when exposed to the air, it ignites into flames. An apothecary can make it up and put them into small tincture bottles. Greek fire can be very potent."

"Yes, we're familiar with it." Thompson was cautious. "I've heard that it's very unstable. You put the sulphur and naphtha in first, then pour in the quicklime or siphon in the elemental phosphorous and cap it quickly. The apothecary might get suspicious once he knows the formula. So keeping the Greek fire a secret is just as important as keeping yourselves from getting burned to death."

Young resumed, "When I was here in the spring, I saw how we could raid border towns and escape back quickly to neutral Canada. I told the President that I could round up 20 good Kentucky cavalrymen whom I had helped escape from prison to run raids out of Canada. In fact I told him that I had a good sergeant who is familiar with the Greek fire that was used on the Mississippi River. His Secretary of War approved of my plan and gave me a Lieutenant's commission. He told me to bring the horrors of war to the people of the New England states bordering on Canada, and to avenge Sheridan in the Shenandoah. That, gentleman, is my story and Richmond's strategy."

Commissioner Thompson was silent for a moment, and then he turned to all three of them and said, "Gentlemen, that's all very well, but where do we go from here?"

Deputy Commissioner Clay broke in to say, "Lieutenant Young, we agree with what you want to do. So I'd like to ask Agent George Sanders to tell you a few things that are important."

Sanders looked closely at Young and said, "Twenty men should be enough to raid small Union towns. I was thinking of St. Albans,

Vermont. It's a town about 14 miles south of the Quebec border. The settlements along the Missisquoi River all use St. Albans for their banking. There are a number of banks in the town, some state and some federal. Because St. Albans is in a strategic location, there should be good money in the bank vaults.

"Lieutenant Young, the Union election is fast approaching on November 8th. If we can stage a raid before then, hopefully we can discourage people from voting for Lincoln. We prefer the Democrat, the former General McClellan."

Clay laughed and continued "McClellan was a fool as a general ... and will be a fool as a president!"

Young replied. "All my men are here in town. We can arrange a meeting with Agent Sanders for tomorrow afternoon and in a few days we should be on our way ... once we make the Greek fire, of course,"

"Young, here is enough money to buy the chemicals for the Greek fire. This money should be sufficient to order and fill ten small tincture bottles per man. The Secretary and this office are putting a great deal of trust in you! Be sure of what you are doing."

Clay looked closely at Young and scowled. "Tomorrow evening, you can look over our stock of weapons we can distribute to your men."

Sanders followed. "We have Richard Mason 1860 .44 caliber army pistols. All the cylinders hold six cartridges; the pistols are quite heavy and are 14 inches in length. There is plenty of Sycamore FFG Smokeless Black Powder that has been made into gunpowder for you. The bullet heads and cartridges are here, as well. You have to load the gunpowder, swage or twist the bullets into the cylinders and place the caps on the ends. I have about three extra cylinders for each of your men. That provides 24 shots. For a bank robbery, that should be enough. Remember, you must hide your pistols in your pouches. Sticking the revolvers inside your belts could look fearsome. You do not want to raise any suspicions. I'll be here to help those who haven't loaded a gun before. With luck, I'll not be needed!"

Young interrupted. "We should try to find an apothecary to provide the chemicals and bottles for the Greek fire. We could make them up in our hotel rooms, if we don't burn down the building. Mixing can be tricky."

Evening was upon them and the steward had entered the room to light the gaslights. "Lieutenant Young," Thompson advised, "I think that we should finish the subject of the Greek fire, the revolvers and bullets tomorrow. Let's celebrate your venture by going down to dinner. Before we dine, we have a tradition in this mission. We sing 'The South Shall Rise Up Free' - sort of our national anthem!"

The South Shall Rise Up Free©

The bugles sound upon the plain,
Our men are gathering fast,
You would not have your friend remain,
And be among the last,
Cheer up, cheer up, my southern flow'r,
There's joy for you and me,
While right is strong and God has pow'r,
The South shall rise up free,
While right is strong and God has pow'r,
The South shall rise up free!

© Benjamin Tubbs. (2)

As they entered the main dining room, they were shown to a corner table surrounded by red velvet drapes and plush carpeting. They were impressed by the white linens, crystal and sterling silver cutlery. They talked about everything other than the Confederacy. They laughed, told stories and finally opted for the buffet.

Young retired to his room with its clean sheets, his new pair of long winter underwear, a bowl of fruit, and a bed canopy. All he needed was Righteous Rachel from the tavern of the hotel to help him get to sleep! On the following day, he would introduce Agent Sanders to his men, and then he'd go to the apothecary and start ordering the Greek fire. His plan to raid St. Albans was born.

Life is good, Young laughed to himself.

* * *

PLANNING

St. Lawrence Hall Hotel, Tuesday, September 27, 1864
Young met again with the three commissioners to go over some of the final arrangements before George Sanders was to meet the 20 Rebels later in the day. The guns were ready and available in Sanders room. George was to supervise issuing the guns and the ingredients for the bullets.

Young looked closely at the three of them and lowered his voice. "I don't want to take any more chances than I have to in completing this raid. Regarding our discussion last night, do any of you know an apothecary here in town that could make and move explosives?"

"I do," Sanders replied. "I've noticed this old British soldier down on St. Paul Street who could be sympathetic to us - like many of the British here in town that I've met. His name is Robert Piper. He set up his business a few years ago and seems quite established. I'll wager we could get him on our side. I'll bet he's for the South! Money talks. He can fill the tinctures and put them securely into his own cushioned shipping cartons that he calls his egg crates. Once that is accomplished, the key is how to get the cartons to St. Albans without blowing up! If Piper doesn't know a way, I'll eat your lawman's hat, Young!"

Thompson looked skeptical. "We're putting a lot of responsibility on a stranger. Lieutenant, go see Piper. Let's make this approach carefully. I can understand Piper making the explosives. However, transporting depends on what he has to say. Talk to him and report back as soon as you can."

Piper's Apothecary, Wednesday, September 28, 1864
Young left the St. Lawrence Hall Hotel early in the morning and walked down Great St. James Street to the courthouse, then south on St. Gabriel to St. Paul Street. There across the street was Piper's Apothecary. Robert Piper was busy making a new patent medicine from Oklahoma that a British gentleman had ordered. Young decided to be as casual as possible. So he waited in the shop without sounding the little bell to bring

Piper out from the back room. Eventually Piper noticed him and apologized for not seeing him earlier. Young couldn't have been more reasonable. Piper was ready to listen to him.

Lieutenant Young got right to the point. "Sir, I'm not sure whether I should introduce myself to you as whom I truly am."

"Of course you should, sir. That's the only way we can do business. I'm an old military man and can deal with whoever you may be."

"It's not exactly who I am that matters, Mr. Piper ... it's who I represent. I've just arrived from Virginia, having run a United States naval blockade. Remember at the beginning of the Civil War, the two Confederate diplomats, James M. Mason and John Slidell, as well as their personal secretaries, who were arrested by naval gunners of the Union and taken off the British Mail Steamer, *The Trent*? Remember how the British government nearly went to war over the incident? Did they not send 20,000 soldiers over to Canada? Are they not still here, defending the Canadian frontier?"

"Yes, they certainly did. They certainly are!" cried Piper rising to the bait. "I guess you know my sentiments. The Confederacy is getting the wrong end of the cricket bat. If you rode the blockade, sir, I take it you are Confederate?"

"To many travellers, I call myself the Reverend Christian Clement Clyde of the United Christian Circuit of neutral Kentucky. But Mr. Piper, to be honest with you, I am a Confederate cavalry officer, sir. We in the Confederacy have been concerned that the Union is looking north for resources to fight the war. We believe that action may be taken soon to move troops this way! We believe that St. Albans may become the military headquarters for this campaign. Piper's eyes opened wide. Young smiled, hoping that Piper would believe such a ridiculous story.

"You see, sir, I'm the commanding officer of a special force that has been sent to Canada to help defend it from such an incursion. It is in our best interest to try to soften the underbelly of the Union and to protect our good and faithful friend, the United Province of Canada."

"Well, what can I do to help you sir?" Piper had bitten.

"Thank you Mr. Piper, we appreciate your co-operation. I can assure you that what we have in mind is entirely confidential and militarily most secret. You will never be compromised. You will be called only what you truly are - an apothecary! In fact the Confederacy has asked me to make sure that we offer you a contribution to the well-being of your business here on St. Paul Street. We would like to order ingredients for a munition that will be used in our action against the garrison in St. Albans. Remember, not a word to anyone, it's a most military secret."

"Certainly, I'm sure I can help."

"We would like to order and pay in advance for 200 four-ounce tinctures of Greek fire. It is composed of sulphur, naphtha and quicklime. The proportions and mixing instructions are here for you. Now, I want to assure you that price is not an issue. Delivery and secrecy are the issues. So please add a premium to the price to ensure that these issues are accomplished. The Commission office will accept the bill." Young gave Piper his most confidential and trustworthy look.

"Certainly, sir!" Piper never questioned Young at all.

"Now, while we are discussing the transaction: secrecy is one thing, delivery is another. How would you propose to deliver this shipment safely and securely to St. Albans?"

"Sir, I have already ordered extra tinctures as the result of another order that I made just recently. Tinctures take the most time to purchase, especially 200 of them! So, I should have everything ready for mixing by Tuesday, October 4. Might I suggest shipping by rail? All my shipments come and go by train because this method is faster and safer than any other way. I suspect that we could consider a train on Wednesday, October 12. I am in contact with the Grand Trunk shipping agent, Edgar Montpetit, on a daily basis. While I could choose a variety of shipping points, I prefer to use Montpetit right here in the harbour, just across Commissioners Street from my shop. He supervises shipments directly from the rail lines at the harbour to the connection at Point St. Charles for the south-bound trains. I could go to the freight sheds at Point St. Charles or even to the baggage office on Bonaventure Street, but there could be problems. Using the harbour line via Point St. Charles to the Victoria Bridge is the easiest and safest way. I can carry each case across the street directly to Montpetit and the railway boxcar."

"But how do we get past customs officers?" asked Young.

"I'm preparing to ship some patent medicine to St. Albans. It's called the Chickasaw Revival Tonic. While my shipments usually go straight through, both countries rely heavily on import duty to finance their governments and would impose some tax on the shipments. That's all these customs men are after. Someone should go along to smooth the way, as they say. Now if I labelled your shipment explosives, I'd never get past the Canadian customs office in St. Johns or the American office in Highgate Springs. The shipment would just be taken, with no questions asked. So, why don't we package your shipment as a patent medicine? If you agree, Lieutenant, shouldn't we give the medicine a name?"'

Young started to laugh. He was in the medicine business. Then a thought came to him. "Why not call the medicine the Chickamauga Spiritual Elixir, sort of a communion wine you might say. Chickamauga was a victory that General Bragg had over the north last fall. We can toast him every time we throw the Greek fire at the enemy," he laughed.

"We could send the Chickamauga Spiritual Elixir care of the Reverend Christian Clement Clyde of the United Christian Circuit at the Tremont Hotel in St. Albans. This would allow you and your men to proceed across the border without the fear of being arrested. The explosives would not be traced to you. Now how does that sound?"

Young left immediately for the hotel to tell Thompson about the plan. It took only a few minutes to tell the story, get approval and return to Piper. The deal was struck. An estimate was made of the cost, profit and delivery and a cheque was issued from Molson's Bank on Great St. James Street. Piper would handle ordering, mixing the items and making the shipping arrangements with Edgar Montpetit.

"I don't want any problems so I want to witness the mixing and delivering with my ordnance officer, Sergeant Huntley."

Piper smiled to himself. "Big orders often seem to bring this insistence, but I can't blame you. This order is a tricky one!" He turned to Young and said, "That's fine."

"Making the arrangements with Montpetit shouldn't be a problem, but I think it would be wise to keep him ignorant of the contents of the Chickamauga tinctures. In fact, I could claim that the tinctures were delivered to me in bulk for packaging and shipping only. In this way we are both innocent. Besides, I want to be in Montpetit's favour after this episode is over. He could travel with the shipment to ensure that the cartons will be delivered. Now I want to emphasize a vital point: I can't guarantee that the Greek fire won't explode en route! That's the risk we both take."

He continued. "Let's assume that Montpetit does agree to our proposal. Freight boxcars are often attached to passenger trains when it's convenient. I can arrange for this shipment to be attached to a morning train to St. Albans. Montpetit could be very useful at the border. He could humour the Canadian inspectors in St. Johns and pay the duty to the American inspectors at Highgate Springs. After all, the cartons contain 'medicine'! Remember, a great deal of strategic goods are passing through this port of entry to supply the North, so the customs agents have to co-operate. You could pick up the shipment at the baggage office and Montpetit could return to Montreal by train, none the wiser. However, Lieutenant, you may have to provide some consideration."

"Yes, I think that is a good idea."

After the agreement, Piper closed up his shop and left for the harbour and a little chat with Montpetit, while Young left for the hotel to report to and pick up George Sanders.

Sanders and Young left the St. Lawrence Hall Hotel on Great St. James Street and made their way over to and down St. Peter Street. The buildings here were older.

"What a contrast to the soft velvet curtains and liveried waiters in the hotel," Sanders complained to Young.

This had been his fortune since the war started. Clandestine work meant dealing with questionable people in funny places. This time it would not be whispers and messages passed furtively on dark street corners, but a confrontation with 20 young military men from the Confederacy, many from good Kentucky farms, some with money, education and opinions of their own.

Sanders, being from Alabama, complained to himself: I can't stand Kentuckians. They talk too much and have strong opinions on both sides of the War. They love slaves, but will not fight for them! They think the State is holy ground and should be neutral. They think the Kentucky River that flows between Frankfort and the Ohio River is holy water! Kentucky … neutral? Piffle!

Bennett Young glanced at him with a brief smile. "Come sit on this bench. I want to tell you about my boys before you meet them. They have been fighting for several years and have become a rough bunch. Alcohol and women are popular, so you may want to straighten them out a little bit. Making them missionaries may be difficult.

"I have enlisted most of them into the 5th Confederate State Retributors. All the names have been duly forwarded to the Confederate War Department, but despite this attempt at military identification, keeping them under control could be difficult. No one seems to take this exercise seriously. They just laughed at the title."

"Break them up!" said Sanders. "Put them all into smaller groups. Control is much easier this way. Assign leaders. Call them sections 1, 2 and 3. Give some of them nicknames. Give them identification. Loners may be the hardest to manage, so let me know about them."

Young leaned over and talked quietly to Sanders.

"Bill Huntley, 37, is from Georgia and a member of the 4th Georgia Infantry. Secretary Seddan used him to deliver sealed orders to our mission here this year. He's a plumber and knows munitions, like Greek fire. We've travelled together. He can be a loner, but he is mature.

"Squire Turner Teavis, 22, was with Morgan's 11th Kentucky Cavalry, and was captured with me in Ohio but we escaped together from Camp Morton. Turner is a Jessamine County boy.

"Charles Swager, 22, is from a prosperous Louisville family whose living was made on the Ohio River. Charles is also from the 1st Kentucky Cavalry, but he's restless and outspoken

"Marcus Antonius Spur, 20, from Morgan's 8th Kentucky Cavalry, escaped from Camp Douglas. Marcus shoots first and asks questions after, but he's from a good family in Fayette County and well schooled for his age. I like him.

"Tom Collins, 22, is from Madison County. He's a college graduate who was a captain in Morgan's 11th Kentucky Cavalry. His father is a retired trader from along the Ohio. Tom wants to be a doctor. He's pretty smart, and a natural leader … provided he can get along with his men.

"George Scott, 21, is from Jessamine County and Nicholasville. He was with Morgan's 8th Kentucky Cavalry. George is a strange person. He keeps to himself.

"Alamanda Pope Bruce, 23, is from Boyle City and from Morgan's 6th Kentucky Cavalry. Bruce is a quiet and hardworking young man.

"James Alexander Doty, 24, is from Garrard County, was with Morgan's 6th Kentucky Cavalry and escaped from Camp Douglas.

"Joe 'Granpappy' McGrorty, 38, was with Morgan's 6th Cavalry and wounded on General Morgan's last raid. He's the oldest of the group and everyone looks to Joe for leadership. Can you imagine - a Texan from Donegal?

"Sam Lackey, 23, a Virginia graduate, was with Morgan's 6th Kentucky Cavalry. Sam is a Lexington man whose father is a fireman on the railroad. He is a real free spirit, laughs and talks a lot, but don't get him started on religion!

"Caleb McDowell Wallace, 26, is from Woodford County and was with Morgan's 5th Cavalry. Watch out, he is the nephew of John J. Crittendon, the former U.S. Senator from Kentucky.

"Bill Moore, 22, from Anderson, Kentucky, rode with Morgan's 5th Kentucky Cavalry. He escaped from Camp Chase in Ohio.

"Samuel Simpson Gregg, 22, is a neighbor from Jessamine County and rode with Morgan's 8th Kentucky Cavalry. He keeps to himself.

"William Thomas Stone Teavis, 24, is Squire Teavis's older brother, who was with me in the 8th Kentucky Cavalry. He's a Nicholasville boy who speaks and shoots well.

"Louis Singleton Price, 22, was with Morgan's 8th Kentucky Cavalry and escaped from Camp Douglas. Louis is from a good family in Lexington. He is a smooth talker, but I don't trust him.

"John Moss, a strange and lonely man from Quantrill's Irregulars. He has real experience. He's quiet, but I like him.

"John McInnis, 21, was with the 36th Alabama Infantry and escaped from Rock Island. He doesn't seem to fit in with the Kentucky boys, but I trust him.

"Homer Brown 'Lean Bean' Collins, 22 is a recent addition to the group. He has no military experience, but he has enthusiasm.

"Dan Butterworth, 24, was with the 1st Confederate cavalry. Another loner from Central Kentucky. I don't know much about him.

"Charles Higbee, 38, is from Fayette County, a university graduate and related to the Teavis boys. He rode with Quantrill's Irregulars. Charlie accompanied Quantrill and Andy Blunt to Richmond, Virginia, to raise a unit of Partisan Rangers in Missouri. He was at Quantrill's ransacking of Lawrence, Kansas, last year. I like Charlie. He is a good leader. Claims he'll practice law after the war.

"That's it, George. Those are all the men. As you can see, many are from around my hometown of Nicholasville in Jessamine County."

Sanders thought for a moment and whispered to Young, "Lieutenant, Deputy Commissioner Clay has given me $1400 in notes from his bank in St. Catharine's to pass on to you. I'd cash the bank notes right away and ask for gold coins in return. Get small denominations so that you can give small amounts to each man. Tell the men to use it for travelling and lodgings. Never use cheques or greenbacks if at all possible. Most of them are counterfeit. Gold and silver coins are never questioned. So remember when you rob the banks, look for the gold and silver coins in the vaults."

Young thought about the money. "Gold coins are heavy. Can horses manage to carry such weight?" Thompson wasn't listening.

"Don't worry about it. If Senator Clay agrees, I'd suggest you divide up the 20 men into five sections. Then give $200 to each section leader and keep the same for yourself. The leaders in turn can give their men $50 each."

With the money issue settled, they rose and moved quietly into the coffee house to meet everyone. The dining room was crowded, noisy and full of pungent tobacco smoke. The men had been drinking, smoking and sweating from the warmth of the room. No one had shaved or looked after their beards. The barmaid, Righteous Rachel, seemed to flirt with everyone she could. Righteous didn't like you touching her when she was serving, but when she put down her tray ... look out!

Sanders nearly choked on the tobacco smell. "What kind of tobacco is that? No southerner in his right mind would tolerate such smoke."

'Grandpappy' Joe McGrorty slowly stood and smiled in a very congenial way. "Why that's genuine Virginia burley leaf. It was brought to Canada and cultivated here on a private estate. They call it 'estate tobacco'."

"Estate Tobacco? Would you mind explaining yourself, sir?"

With a twinkle in his eyes, Joe replied, "Sir, that's private stock from the uh, uh ... Chateau Laprairie. It's grown amongst the Chateau's renowned grape vineyards. You'd love it." Joe stood there with a straight face, blew a smoke ring straight at Sanders, belched and sat down. Young hushed everyone and introduced Sanders.

George spoke out. "This is going to be a long meeting and it's nobody's business but ours. So pay attention. I want you to know that I'm not impressed with you as much as your leader, Lieutenant Young,

43

seems to be! We have serious business to attend to and none of you look up to the challenge."

Dead silence and intense eyes looked at him. George stared back. "Lieutenant Young has advised you of our intentions to attack the Union from neutral Canada. Are you all clear on this mission?" A chorus of cheers and agreement answered him.

"Deputy Commissioner Clay has asked me to take charge of this plan and to see it through to success. Lincoln is going to the polls next month against his former general, the retired George McClellan, whom he fired two years ago. If we can start harassing and prompting uprisings in the north, it might discourage northerners from enlisting and voting for Lincoln.

"Confederate dollars have dropped in value to dangerously low levels. So, how do we get Union dollars? How do we weaken the north's banking system and cause inflation? One approach is to print northern bank greenbacks and flood the north's banking system with them. Oversupply is one way to cause inflation. The value of northern dollars has to drop. Commissioner Thompson and Deputy Commissioner Clay are working hard on this angle. The only other recourse is to raid the banks in small towns close to the Canadian border. Stealing the silver and gold reserves make it difficult for those banks to continue operating. They simply don't have enough reserves to cover the redemptions or demands on the deposits. This leads us to St. Albans, Vermont. The city is just south of the border. Trains go there daily from Montreal. We want you to steal their horses, rob their banks, burn down the town, and then run for the border. A retreat of 14 miles can be covered easily in an hour or two. Once in Canada, you are safe. Canada is neutral.

"Our office is providing funds, two guns, two satchels and Greek fire for each of you. Go to the hotel after this meeting Go up to my room on the mezzanine. I'll give you your revolvers, ammunition and Moroccan leather satchels. While all the ingredients are provided, such as the cartridges, caps, bullet heads, and bags of gunpowder, you'll have to make your own bullets.

"Finally, do something with your guns. Sticking two big guns in your belt with your ammunition draped around you may look smart but you'd be recognized a mile away as a rampaging Rebel."

A Richard Mason 1860 .44 caliber Army pistol. Some claim that this one was Bennett Young's pistol that was seized by Canadian authorities after the St. Albans raid. Photo is courtesy of William and Bruce LaBelle of Champlain, New York.

Young had been studying his notes carefully and making notations. He stood slowly to address the Rebels. "I want to break you up into five sections. I have put down the names for each section, which is to be commanded by a sergeant. First of all, I want Tom Collins to lead section number one into a bank. Tom was with me in Louisville and we escaped together out of Chicago. No one knows maps better than Tom."

Section #1 Bank
Tom Collins Sgt.
Turner Teavis
Marcus Spur
Louis Price

"Section number two is to be led by Joe McGrorty. Joe is our most experienced soldier. He has spent his whole life in uniform. Joe, you're to take the second bank."

Section #2 Bank
Joe McGrorty Sgt.
James Doty
Caleb Wallace
Alamanda Bruce

"Section number three is to be commanded by Bill Huntley. Bill is an ordnance expert out of the 4th Georgia Infantry. Even though Bill is not from Kentucky he can roll a cigar better than all of us. Bill, you take the third bank."

Section #3   Bank
Bill Huntley Sgt.
John Moss
Dan Butterworth
Bill Moore

"Section number four is to be lead by Charlie Higbee. Charlie served in Quantrill's Irregulars. Charlie, rustle up the horses."

Section #4   Horses
Charlie Higbee Sgt.
Sam Gregg
John McInnis
Wm. Teavis

"Section number five is to be commanded by Sam Lackey. Just let Sam flirt with the ladies on the St. Albans Green and we'll all look innocent. Sam, you're to guard the horses."

Section #5   Guards
Sam Lackey Sgt.
Charles Swager
George Scott
Homer Collins

"I'll begin distributing the money just as soon as I can cash the Commissioner's cheque. So tomorrow morning I'd like to meet here with the sergeants. Each person gets $50 for travel expenses. I'll explain at that time how we are handling the Greek fire. I'll give you the tinctures in St. Albans from my hotel room the night before the raid."

Young's Plan of Battle for Monday, October 10, 1864.
"We'll start leaving for St. Albans. Sgt. Collins will go with me first so that we can study the town and plan our escape routes. We'll check out hotels, banks and stables. The Greek fire has been ordered to arrive by Wednesday the 12th, just to be sure. If there are any holdups on the shipment we have a week to deal with it.

"Take the trains, drift into town and take rooms. For heaven's sake, look like respectable citizens, don't look like Rebels running from the Wilderness! First take the Grand Trunk Railway to St. Johns. Transfer to The Montreal and Vermont Junction Railroad to the border at Highgate Springs. Custom officers may speak to you in St. Johns and Highgate Springs. Be patient, they're looking for tax income not Confederate soldiers. As I've said before, don't take any chances. Keep the guns and bullets buried deep in the saddlebags.

"Once you are across the border, transfer to the Vermont & Canada Railroad which will take you to Swanton and St. Albans. You should be there before supper. Even though you are in sections, don't travel or stay together. Break up and above all be ready when you are needed. Take your time and space out your travel over a period of days.

"Consider various options that are open to you: stop in at Leonard Hogle's Hotel in St. Johns or the Lafayette Hotel in Philipsburg, take a train all the way to Burlington and double back, stay in Montreal until the 16th if you prefer. Whatever your plans are, make sure that you tell your sergeant. Drift into St. Albans by Monday the 17th in a manner that will not raise suspicion.

"There are three hotels and some rooming houses. Stay on North Main Street where all the banks and hotels are. Or you could stay in a hotel or rooming house just across the street from the railway station. It is very close to North Main Street. Then focus on the Green in the middle of town where everyone congregates. Here is the plan:

1. Check in to your hotel.
2. Go directly to my room at the Tremont Hotel.
3. I want to know where you all are by 5.30 p.m. on Tuesday, 18th.
4. I'll tell you where your sergeants are staying.
5. Contact your sergeant.
6. Await orders and keep in touch with your sergeant.

"I want you to follow my plan to the letter. If you don't co-operate, you will not be part of the raid and must return the money, guns and Greek fire to me immediately.

"Tuesday evening, the 18th, after supper I want to meet with the sergeants to study the individual section responsibilities. The sergeants will then contact you before midnight.

"Tuesday, October 18th is Market Day. Prepare and study your jobs and locations. The most important issue will be arranging for the horses and ensuring they are all saddled and bridled by 1.00 p.m. on the 19th, the day of the raid. The town will be busy, crowded and few will notice our activity.

"On Wednesday morning, October 19th, the shopkeepers will have finished their morning trading, will be depositing their receipts in the banks before lunch, and by mid-afternoon many will be taking naps. Each sergeant will be responsible for checking out his area of responsibility during the morning hours and meeting with his men by lunch.

"If anyone asks you what you are doing in St. Albans, say that you are all members of the United Christian Circuit and waiting to go on a fishing trip with the Reverend Clyde. I'm travelling as the Reverend Christian Clement Clyde. I intend to persuade the ladies that they have nothing to fear from either my friends or me. So a little Bible study and preaching may keep the ladies from prying into our affairs too much.

"Wednesday afternoon at 1:00, we take the horses and take them to the Green well before 3.00 p.m. The horses should be all bridled and saddled. If you are late I'll shoot you dead!

"At 1.30 p.m. the guards will assemble on the Green. At 3.00 p.m. we raid the banks. This stage shouldn't take more than 20 minutes. So, you must be back at the Green by no later than 3.30 p.m.

"At 3.30 p.m. we mount our horses, shoot off a few rounds and throw the Greek fire at the buildings. Then we gallop straight up North Main Street for Swanton and Highgate Springs. Depending on how successful we are, we might raid the Swanton banks as well.

"Act like you are all members of the United Christian Circuit as long as you can. Just remember that I'm your benevolent disciple, the Reverend Christian Clement Clyde. We must seem like we have a purpose for being in town. While we have come to spread the gospel we are also looking for a little fishing on the side. Don't loiter or the people will get suspicious. After the raid, be quick to tell everyone that this was a military exercise to get even for the Shenandoah. Then tell them that we are all members of the 5th Confederate State Retributors. As we leave, we are all to sing 'The South Shall Rise Up Free'."

Everyone looked at each other and started to find their sergeants. While no one said very much, Sam Gregg went over to Bennett and stuck his chin out. "This is serious stuff, Bennett. Show me my money and pistols. I ain't moving until I have my tools."

Piper's Apothecary, Monday, October 3, 1864

"How do you like the labels, Dr. Rumsey?" enquired Piper. "We have to state the alcoholic content and the essential ingredient, the *Prunus Angustifolia.* I have produced 100 four-ounce tinctures that I'll be labelling this weekend and preparing to ship next week. In addition, here are the fact sheets to show people the features as you outlined them to me. I'd like to suggest that we ship the tinctures via rail to St. Albans. I can do that right here on Commissioners Street. All I have to do is cross the street from the back of my shop and deliver the cartons to Mr. Montpetit of the Grand Trunk. Mind you, shipping by rail can take time ... let's say a week. Trains aren't as regular as we think they should be out of Montreal."

Rumsey had listened to Piper and started to hesitate when it came to the railways. "Why can't I take the shipments in the baggage car of my train? Then everything would arrive at the same time."

"Well, if you're willing to carry the four cartons down to the Bonaventure Station a mile to the west of here and stay with the medicine until St. Albans, it might work, but the medicine could be stolen. Too many people come and go through the car during the trip. The baggage cars are for passenger baggage, not for four cartons of commercial products. The rates are higher. Customs officers may not accept this route. Dr. Rumsey, why don't you relax and travel without that responsibility? We'll ship it as soon as we can, it won't take that long. Remember, the boxcar is bonded and sealed so no one can steal anything. I suspect we can arrange a shipment by Wednesday, October 12th."

Rumsey left Piper's, satisfied that his tonics would be in St. Albans in a few days. He had nothing to worry about. All he had to do now was get ready for the trip. He and Chester could just enjoy themselves.

Piper's Apothecary, Tuesday, October 4, 1864

Lieutenant Young and Bill Huntley walked along St. Paul Street from the Exchange Coffee House and turned into Piper's Apothecary. Piper was ready for them.

"Ah, Mr. Piper I'd like you to meet my ordnance officer, Sergeant William Huntley." They shook hands and got down to business.

Piper explained, "Lieutenant, Sergeant, the key to this process is the siphoning of the elemental phosphorous so that the boiling concentrate is not exposed to air."

With that said, he proceeded to show them how to mix the lime and sulphur and prepare the tinctures to receive the hot phosphorous. Not much was said, they all worked quietly. Slowly the first tinctures were filled and capped. Young smiled and Huntley's eyes kept popping. Both of them sweated heavily. The air in the shop was far from fresh. Piper kept talking about the possibility of an explosion, which scared Huntley half to death. After the 200 tinctures were ready, Piper labelled and put them into cartons. He had prepared them so that the tinctures didn't rattle or hit each other en route.

Both Young and Huntley couldn't wait to get out of the shop. Piper was finally alone with the Chickasaw and the Chickamauga medicines, 300 tinctures in all. There were 50 tinctures in each carton, totaling six cartons. Piper then addressed the cartons to St. Albans: Chickasaw to Ethan Potter and the Chickamauga to Reverend Clyde. All Montpetit had to do was be there to ensure delivery to the depot at St. Albans.

While Piper had arranged with Edgar Montpetit for shipment on the morning train to Vermont, Wednesday, October 12, Piper had not talked to Edgar about going along for the ride.

Edgar Montpetit had a jolly countenance that made him a pleasure to deal with, when he was in a good mood. When he became excited, his face turned red and his eyes became bloodshot and glassy. His anger looked like the buttons would pop off his vest and his flat railway man's hat would lift off into the air. It was hard to reason with Montpetit when this happened.

"My concern, Edgar, is that the U.S. border agents will want you to pay duty. I can provide the funds for this moment, but you will have to go along for the ride."

Montpetit surprised him with, "That shouldn't be a problem,"

4

READY

**Point St. Charles Station,
Monday Evening, October 10, 1864**

A few years earlier, the Grand Trunk had built a grandiose Victorian railway station at the junction of Great St. James and Bonaventure Streets in the west end of Montreal. The railway was running all their passenger trains from there. All trains headed due west until they reached the St. Henry yards. Travelling to Toronto, the train kept going straight west. However if the train was travelling across the St. Lawrence River, the tracks switched south to the Point St. Charles Station and then across the Victoria Bridge to the Eastern Townships, New England and the Atlantic.

Young and Collins were the first to leave. Young told the others at the Exchange Coffee House to wait until tomorrow to start making their moves down Great St. James to McGill, Wellington and finally to St. Etienne Street and the Point St. Charles Station. There would be less conspicuous there than at the Bonaventure Station.

Once on the train, Young started to tell Collins about his plans.

"The best way to hurt a Yankee is in his pocketbook. Because the prices of silver and gold have risen dramatically since the start of the Civil War, our strategy is to steal all we can of it. Gold has risen from $20.67 per ounce at the beginning of the War in 1861 to $47.02 per ounce today in 1864. That's over double the value. Can you imagine how the banks would feel if we took their precious gold? Then there is silver that rose from $1,292 in 1861 to $2,939 today. Without their reserves, the banks can't operate. They have to have a certain percentage on hand in the event that customers demand their money back on their deposit accounts. Without the reserve, the federal government could close the banks. The smaller state banks have more room to maneuver but I wouldn't put my money with them, they don't have the financial support that the federal banks do. So our prime purpose is not so much to avenge the Shenandoah, nor burn down the town, nor upset the politics of Lincoln, it's to get as much gold and silver as we can to support the banking system in the Confederacy.

"Now, how much can we carry, you may ask?" Young grinned and took out his notebook. "We all have new Moroccan satchels. How much can a satchel take and a horse carry? I've always felt that I could pack 35 pounds easily on my back. So, how much am I carrying?

Gold is $47 per Troy oz. (12 oz. per lb.)
12 oz. x 35 lb. x $47 = $19,740.
20 men x $19,740 = $394,000

Silver is $2.92 per Troy oz.
12 oz. x 35 x $2.92 = $1,226
20 men x $1226 = $24,528

"Now, which metal would you go for? Our strategy is to take as much gold as we can, then silver, then cash or what they call greenbacks. The secret is in the horses. Can they carry the weight? We may be carrying two full satchels each. A horse galloping up a long hill may tire easily. In Vermont, a good horse means a Morgan Horse. No relation to our revered leader, of course. So when our men are looking for horses in the public stables and in particular the stable of the Governor of Vermont, who happens to be living in St. Albans, they have to look for the short, stubby, powerful Morgan horses."

Before they knew it, they had transferred trains twice and were arriving at the St. Albans station. Young turned to Collins and bade him good-bye and good fishing! Young went up North Main Street to the Tremont Hotel, the leading hotel in town. The Tremont, built in 1820, rose with dignity, a solid four-story brick structure with nearly 80 rooms, many overlooking the Main Street. The building could offer the best panoramic view of the town from the gallery on the roof. This hotel is where the refined people stayed.

Collins followed but turned quickly into the American Hotel, a little older and a little less fancy than the Tremont. It had great balconies overlooking the Main Street, but the hotel was only two stories high and had fewer rooms than the Tremont. While the hotel had not aged well, its clientele were less discriminating than those at the Tremont. They were more comfortable here. Tomorrow Young and Collins would rent two horses and begin their review of the town and the countryside.

St. Johns, Quebec, Tuesday, October 11, 1864

Charles Higbee, John Moss, Sam Lackey, and George Scott took the afternoon train and arrived in St. Johns about one and a half hours later. Hogle's Hotel was just across the street. The desk clerk noticed something different about the visitors.

He turned to one of his customers and spoke softly. "They look just like all the other travellers, except their accent is distinctly southern … and they walk gently! Like ladies! You'd think they were carrying perfume or something … but those guns in their belts and the strap of bullets scare me. Apparently they are all going fishing with some minister down in St. Albans. They stopped to see the town as tourists and will make their way in a few days to St. Albans. I see that they went straight to the tavern. I wonder what their minister would say to that...."

Bonaventure Station, Tuesday, October 11, 1864

Rumsey opted for the opulent Bonaventure Station for his and Chester's grand departure. Chester had never seen a steam engine before. Despite all his bravado to Rumsey, this was too much. His basic instinct told him to mark his territory … and so he did, much to Rumsey's surprise.

"Chester, you are on the platform of a modern train station, this is not someone's back yard or camp site!"

John carried Chester onto the train. They settled down and began their journey, turning south at St. Henry, stopping briefly at the Point St. Charles Station before finally crossing the St. Lawrence River on the new Victoria Bridge. John was surprised at the size of the river and the large bridge. He held his breath. Chester just shut his eyes.

Rumsey had his Grand Trunk railway map in his lap that showed him each stop along the way to St. Albans. The train reached the south shore of the Saint-Lawrence River at St. Lambert and proceeded on its way to St. Johns. John and Chester changed trains at St. Johns for the Montreal & Vermont Junction Railway and headed south to the border. Train travel was unique and swift. John could never have made this trip in such short time on foot, by horse or stagecoach, or on a Chambly Canal boat.

The two of them arrived at the border point where they transferred to the last train, the Vermont & Canada Railway, that took them directly to St. Albans. The view was breathtaking: Lake Champlain and the Adirondack Mountains were to the west and the rising Green Mountains were to the east. Chester even looked out the window.

At moments like this Rumsey could become very poetic, much to Chester's annoyance. Vermont's scenery led John to hark to Tennyson again. Peace did not come to John often, but poetry could do it.

The Flower

Once in a golden hour
I cast to earth a seed.Up there came a flower,
The people said, a weed.
Then it grew so tall
It wore a crown of light,
But thieves from o'er the wall
Stole the seed by night;
Sow'd it far and wide
By every town and tower,
Till all the people cried,
Splendid is the flower.

Rumsey laughed and laughed. Chester just stared at him and blinked politely. John had forgotten what it was like to laugh at anything! He thought, What kind of an image should I convey to the townspeople? I'm British! Do Yankees really like British people?

The train had come and gone from Swanton and was now chugging into the new and expansive railway yards of St. Albans. The train stopped at a new, large red brick Victorian railway station very close to North Main Street and downtown.

Across the tracks from the station was the St. Albans House Hotel that had been built in 1840. It was called the 'railway' hotel. With the trains, the smoke and the foundry across the street, the ladies didn't like to be seen there. Travelling salesmen might stay there, though. Beside the hotel was a more modest building known as Willard's Boarding House, serving more simple people - trainmen, coachmen and workers from the shops. It was close to the stables of Gilmore and Field.

Rumsey, realizing that he was starting over, one tincture at a time, decided to continue his modest lifestyle and entered the boarding house. Chester walked beside him with his ears straight up. John had hoped for a private room with fresh sheets. Unfortunately he was shown to a room he had to share with a large man from Rutland who didn't like dogs. The window revealed a smoky picture of the local railway foundry!

John thought, While we have separate beds, the sheets are moth-eaten. Mr. Goodenough wouldn't be impressed. For fifty cents a night you'd think I could do better!

The following day John arrived on the Green and easily found Ethan and Elizabeth Potter with their son, Benjamin. He was able to introduce himself and Chester to this young couple, from near Green's Corners, who had recently established their own apothecary shop.

Ethan was delighted to meet him. "We received a telegram from Montreal yesterday, informing us of your delivery. Your revival tonic sounds interesting!"

Philipsburg, Quebec, Wednesday, October 12, 1864

The rain came pouring down just as the train came into the border station at St. Armand/Highgate. The fall season had not been a pleasant one. Consequently, most of the passengers that stepped out onto the platform became quite wet. Most then had to take open carriages off to Philipsburg in the neighbouring town.

By the time Squire Teavis, Louis Price, Dan Butterworth, and Bill Moore got to the Lafayette Hotel in Philipsburg, their cloaks were soaking wet, their hats pulled way down over their faces. The manager asked them what they were doing in town. No one knew what to say.

Dan Butterworth, being the oldest, lifted his head and began to speak. "Why, we are on a spiritual mission to tender to the needs of the farmers and their families starving for faith here in this region. We represent the United Christian Circuit from the famed beautiful blue-grass country of Central Kentucky. We have been spreading his Gospel throughout the St. Lawrence Valley. Because of our obvious success here, we have decided to explore the lifestyles of families along the Missisquoi River Valley to ensure that they are observing good Christian principles. We give lectures and provide personal advice and prayers wherever we can. Don't we, men?"

The other three just nodded their heads.

"In any event, we are here to recover from our arduous journeys over the last few weeks, to take advantage of your famous dinner table and eventually to proceed in a few days further south."

During the Civil War, it was rumored that half of all U.S. paper currency in circulation was counterfeit. Were many Canadian towns along the border busy printing money? Philipsburg was a town that could have been in the business, but no one would talk about it.

As a result, when these men stumbled into the Lafayette Hotel out of the rain, they appeared to the people reclining in the lobby, as counterfeiters. Their story didn't wash. It was hard to hide their guns and bullets. They were too proud of their guns to hide them in their Moroccan leather satchels. The manager didn't ask questions.

St. Johns, Wednesday, October 12, 1864

By lunchtime, Montpetit's train had arrived in St. Johns and was stopped for inspection by Canadian Customs. The officers were surprised to see Edgar in the baggage car, but didn't question his shipment. They didn't care. Having switched engines for the Montreal & Vermont Junction Railroad, away went the train due south to the border at Highgate Springs. Montpetit was having a pleasant outing. It was fun being a passenger en route to St. Albans. He had only been across the border once as a young man. Edgar was even able to doze off a little.

St. Armand, Friday, October 14, 1864

Montpetit had completely forgotten about customs at Highgate Springs. The officers jumped on board, reviewed Montpetit's manifest, charged him a modest fee and left. Edgar Montpetit was now in the United States safely en route to St. Albans with all his medicine.

By noon the train had arrived in St. Albans and Montpetit had to face an unusually anxious Lieutenant Young and a grinning and thankful 'Doc' Rumsey. It took only a few minutes to open the car and to deliver the medicine directly to Young and Rumsey. Everyone was happy. After all, it was only patent medicine! Montpetit stood there and slowly turned around to buy a ticket back to Montreal. He grinned because he still had most of the customs gratuity in his pocket.

St. Johns, Friday, October 14, 1864

Bill Huntley arrived and checked in to Hogle's Hotel as Dr. W.P. Jones of Troy, N.Y, a lecturer and administrator of mesmerism. The clerk noticed him because he looked seedier than the other guests. How could a ruffian like that hypnotize anyone, he grumbled to himself.

Essex Junction, Vermont, Friday, October 14, 1864

Marcus Spur and Alamanda Bruce took the train from St. Armand all the way to Essex Junction south of St. Albans. They decided to take the train back as far as Milton. Then they would hire a carriage to make their grand entrance into St. Albans. By nightfall when they reached North Main Street they were able to arrive in style.

"To the Tremont, driver!" Marcus cried out.

Young and Collins had been keeping an eye out for the two of them and had to control their laughter when the two aristocrats drew up to the curb at the Tremont.

* * *

AIM

St. Albans, Vermont, Friday, October 14, 1864

The Chickasaw Revival Tonic had arrived and the Potters were most impressed with the medicine, the ingredients and the labels. They were also impressed with 'Doctor' Rumsey. 'Doc' just didn't seem appropriate. When John offered to make satisfactory arrangements for the sale of the tinctures in their shop, the Potters were most receptive.

"While I must remember my sponsor in the profit from these sales, I want you to share in my venture as well. So, I promise to buy all future tinctures and medicine from you."

Ethan Potter told him the tinctures could sell for $3.00 each. Elizabeth cautioned him, "Doctor, nothing is known about this tonic. It is a great story about the Chickasaw plums from the midwest but there are no real testimonials!"

Elizabeth thought for a moment and seemed to make up her mind. "Maybe I should try it on Ben, who has not been feeling well for a number of months. I may have to spend more time with him, and winter is coming. Well, what have we got to lose?"

Then she turned to her new box stove to prepare supper. Rumsey was delighted at Elizabeth's offer to share their evening meal with them. Home cooking was an exception in his life - not for Chester, though, who picked up kitchen bits as he went along.

"Doctor, I'm so proud of my new stove. You know, it seems like yesterday that we all had to cook in open hearths, as our parents did before us. Everything was cooked in a hanging iron pot. Now I can stir a pot without burning my face and arms. No more ashes everywhere and no more big cast iron pots for Ethan to lift. Last year we converted the stove to coal burning. Now the stove gives off more smoke, but can you imagine not cutting and carrying all the wood?"

"Mrs. Potter, do you make your own bread?" Rumsey's eyes gleamed.

"Oh, no, I don't have a proper oven for baking. Bread is about the only thing we buy from a shop these days. My family loves my beans with bread for supper, Doc. I hope that is all right?"

Rumsey loved the smell from the earthenware pot. "Of course," he claimed.

A rumble could be heard outside and then the Potter's kitchen door exploded. Master Ben had arrived for lunch. He practically fell through the door he was so starved and anxious to play with Chester, who was becoming a good friend. Chester was a very quiet and polite dog that made friends slowly. He had never had the chance to befriend a teenager before. John was delighted for a variety of reasons. One of which was Ben's potential as a patent medicine man! He hoped Ben and Chester could become a great sales team.

Ben had a lot to say. "I've just come across the Green and talked to General Nason. He really is a nice man although he can't hear a thing. Did you know that he is an actual general? He wears his uniform and has the greatest grizzliest white beard you ever saw. A couple of folks told me that he walks and sits like he is at attention. Apparently he can sleep on the bench that way while sitting and reading the newspaper. Dad, how does he do that?"

Ethan just smiled and said he had no idea. Then Ben began to sing.

Fol, de rol, de rol, de riddle
'Twasn't so good as a cornstock fiddle.

Ben continued, "When General Nason was a young man, he lived in the country, where corn was being grown everywhere. His father taught him how to make a cornstalk fiddle. Apparently, when the stalk is green, you cut off about 12 inches with a sharp-pointed knife. Then lift a broad piece of the outer skin from end to end. Split this into fine threads. Strain them as tight as they will bear, by putting a wedge under at each end. You call this the fiddle part. Then make a bow the same way. Then you fiddle on it! Can I make one, Father? It sounds easy!"

Ethan just smiled.

Ben went on, "Oh, by the way, I just bumped into Mrs. Smith."

Elizabeth was speechless. She didn't know what to say and finally she blurted out, "You mean Governor Smith's wife?"

"Yes."

"What happened?"

"I don't know. I was about to run by her after seeing General Nason when she turned."

"Was she hurt?"

"No, I hardly bumped her."

"What did she say?"

"Nothing, but her maid sure did!"

"You mean Alice Butters?"

"Yes."

"Well … what did she say?"

"She just scolded me awful hard."

Elizabeth turned and glared at Ethan, who just smiled back.

Ben changed the subject. "Can I go out and play with Chester?"

"Ben, you must have your supper first."

"Oh, yeah, beans and bread?"

Then Ben turned to John and asked about Chester. "What kind of a dog is Chester, Doctor Rumsey?"

"Well, Ben, Chester is part shepherd, chow, collie, and retriever … I think!"

"So what does that make him?"

John said, "I've read that a shepherd is a strong, alert, direct and fearless dog. A chow is intelligent, dignified, aloof, and reserved. A collie is active, proud, timid, a bit frail, and marvellous with children. The retriever, by his very name retrieves things, is eager, alert, a hunter, friendly, and very trustworthy. You could say Chester is a little of all that."

Ben was impressed, but wasn't sure what to say next. He thought for a while then said, "Well, where did dogs come from?"

John thought for a minute and said, "I've read that no dog is native to America. They started out long ago as wolves that were domesticated in Asia. Then they came over the land bridge with the Indians about 15,000 years ago."

"What's a land bridge?"

"Ben, that's enough. Now eat your beans," said his mother.

Over supper, Ben said proudly, "I've just finished grade eight at school and I'll be 19 in five years. Father, I'm ready to start my apprenticeship. Could I start with Doctor Rumsey in the sale of his tonic?"

Ben rose from the table. He was quite tall, skin and bones at 14. His eyes were beaming. Ben was starting to be an adult in a hurry and had been growing too fast. Elizabeth had said that Ben had always been a bit shy, not unlike his father. But he had his father's quiet ease in dealing with the chemicals, as well as his mother's blue eyes and fair features.

Ben's eyes will break many hearts in the years to come, his mother believed.

Ben stood anxiously awaiting approval from his parents. Elizabeth and Ethan looked at each other. Elizabeth said, "Well maybe this would be one way to recover. Being active, with a goal, Ethan, helping Doctor Rumsey could be a good way to start Ben in the shop."

As Ethan agreed, Ben ran over to hug a very surprised John Rumsey. Even Chester seemed to approve. And so, the triumvirate of John, Chester and Ben was established. Ben would be a mixer with John, and then carry the tinctures to the Green where he could help John sing his song.

As Ben ran off with Chester, Ethan turned to John, "Where did the name of Chester come from?"

"When I first befriended him, I named him after Mr. Goodenough in Montreal. Chester was the hotelier's first name. I was having difficulty getting Chester allowed inside for the winter, so I felt that a subtle move was needed."

"I guess that settled that?" laughed Ethan. "I thought that you had named him after General Sheridan's horse, Winchester. Which reminds me of a favorite poem of mine, by Thomas Buchanan Read, that I committed to memory."

Sheridan's Ride

Up from the south, at break of day,
Bringing to Winchester fresh dismay,
The affrighted air with a shudder bore,
Like a herald in haste to the chieftain's door
The terrible grumble, and rumble and roar,
Telling the battle was on once more,
And Sheridan twenty miles away.

John Rumsey grinned and said, "Ethan, do you know any Longfellow?"

Ethan smiled at John and then looked serious. "Elizabeth, maybe we should ask Doctor Rumsey what he thinks of all the children's magazines that influence young people like Ben these days."

Without waiting for an answer, Ethan pressed, "It's so difficult to keep Ben sheltered from such influences and still raise him as a God-fearing young man! Our traditional values seem to be sweeping away and we can't do much about it. Here Doctor, look at these, *Robert Merry's Museum Monthly Chats* and all these Beadle's dime novels that he exchanges with his friends. Tell us, what do you think?" Both of the Potters looked at Rumsey expectantly.

John thought for a few moments, looked over the *Monthly Chats* and one of the dime novels, scratched his nose, adjusted his glasses and spoke. "There doesn't seem to be anything inflammatory or defamatory about these subjects and stories. In fact they sort of compliment the church's Christian teachings. The issues raised in the *Monthly Chats* are not political. I think your basic values are still present. Has Ben changed in any way over the last two years?"

"Well, no. In fact he is all that we want him to be."

John laughed "Well isn't that what's important? What I would do is just read with him. Discuss the chats and the Beadle stories. Don't let him shrink into another world all alone. Be with him, counsel him, confide in him. Be on his side."

Friday evening, October 14, 1864

Bennett Young and Tom Collins had been busy. The day after they arrived in town, they rented two good horses from Ed Fuller, beside the Tremont Hotel. They visited Swanton, Sheldon, Sheldon Springs, and Highgate Center. Slowly their circles brought them back to St. Albans.

Young was concerned with the escape routes they would have to take. "In town, the three main banks are clustered around the Green on Main Street. Running for the horses gathered there won't take too long. However, we'll have to watch out for the railway station and rail yards that are just west of North Main Street, where hundreds of men work. I wouldn't want these men turned loose on us. Escaping to the west would be asking for trouble.

"The hills rise pretty quickly to the east of Main Street. So riding up and over them, not knowing where we are going, would be slow, tiring and dangerous. That leaves travelling either north or south. The south pushes us further away from Canada. So up North Main Street is our only retreat. The only problems are that the telegraph wires will be singing in Highgate Center and Swanton, so we couldn't stay on the coach road. Eventually, we would have to head east to shake loose from a posse and head for the border through the woods and fields around the Missisquoi River. This approach leaves the Plank Road to Sheldon Springs as our only alternative.

"Section One is you, Tom. Which bank do you want?"

"The St. Albans Bank is near my hotel, the American. I can study the raid from there," replied Tom.

Young continued, "I'll let Joe McGrorty's Section Two take the First National Bank, since he is staying at the St. Albans Hotel around the corner, and let Bill Huntley's Section Three take the Franklin County Bank."

Young grinned at Tom, "The manager of the Tremont Hotel has a reservation for a Dr. W.P. Jones from Troy, New York, for Monday the 17th. That's Huntley! He's calling himself a Doctor for goodness sake. And I thought Reverend Clyde was crazy.

"The horses are all available behind the local hotels. Ed Fuller's stable is beside the Tremont with Warren & Eric Fuller's stable behind the American Hotel. Gilmore's and Sylvester's stables are behind the St. Albans Hotel and Willard's Boarding House. However, in Charlie Higbee's Section Four, the 'Rustle-uppers', we have only four men to rustle the horses. This means that one man has to handle one stable each: Higbee and Gregg could take the two Fuller Stables, McInnis could take Sylvester's and Will Teavis could take Gilmore's. That's pretty thin. It would mean four men to arrange, gather, bridle and saddle 21 horses the day before the raid. If we pretend to rent them on Tuesday, we can take them slowly and calmly up the street Wednesday after lunch. Then we can let the Keepers of the Green, Section Five, of Lackey, Swager, Scott, and Collins, look after them."

Young was enjoying himself. "The Rustle-uppers can say that The Reverend Clyde is sponsoring an outing, and that he'll be along shortly to pay the bill for the horses. While we are corralling them, I'll just saunter along North Main Street as if nothing was happening. I'll read my Bible and chat with the ladies. All I'm doing is waiting for my prayer meeting that I've promoted for the Green at three o'clock! I'll bring along the Chickamauga spiritual elixir to impress everyone. The folks will think it's a medicine when it's really Greek fire. I'll invite the whole town. Can't think of a better way to get everyone assembled for the Keepers of the Green. Hear ye, hear ye," Young laughed.

The Rebels had been drifting into town from the railway station. Charlie Higbee, Moss, Lackie, and Scott arrived at the St. Albans station from St. Johns a little hung over from the hotel's cider. They headed straight for the Tremont Hotel to report to Young. Later Teavis, Price, Butterworth, and Moore arrived downtown and found Young promenading on North Main. He urged them to go down the street to the American Hotel, register and await further orders. Joe McGrorty led James Doty, Homer Collins and Caleb Wallace to Willard's Boarding House. No one said a word and no questions were asked. That afternoon, Sam Gregg and Charles Swager walked up North Main Street and entered the American Hotel. Tom Collins was sitting in the lobby reading a Bible. They nearly spoke to him.

Order of Battle

The 5th Confederate State Retributors
Commanding Officer Lieut. Bennett H Young

Section One: St. Albans Bank
Tom Collins, Sgt.
Squire Turner Teavis
Marcus Spur
Louis Price

Section Two: The First National Bank
Joe McGrorty, Sgt.
James Doty
Caleb Wallace
Alamanda Bruce

Section Three: The Franklin County Bank
Bill Huntley, Sgt.
John Moss
Dan Butterworth
Bill Moore

Section Four: The Rustle-uppers
Ed Fuller's Stables, Charlie Higbee, Sgt.
Warren Fuller's, Stables Sam Gregg
Dennis Gilmore's Stables, Will Teavis
Sylvester Fields's Stables, John McInnis

Section Five: The Keepers of The Green
Sam Lucky Lackey, Sgt
Charles Swager
George Scott
Homer Collins

Schematic of Downtown St. Albans, 1864

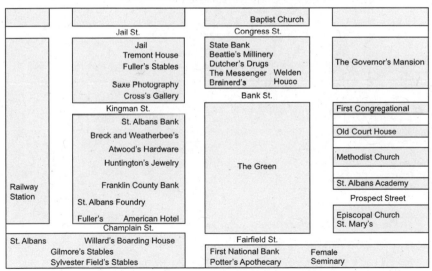

Saturday morning, October 15, 1864

Doc Rumsey was ready to sell his medicine. He had made a little table and a sign that read 'Rumsey's Finest Tinctures Co.' Ethan had suggested calling cards, but Doc Rumsey wasn't sure that his address at Willard's Boarding House was quite right for the occasion. He had spent the last several days with Ben and Chester memorizing the Chickasaw Revival Tonic Song. He confided in Ben, "Heavens. I can't sing! I don't know anything about medicine! How will I ever sell anything to anybody?"

Ben looked up at him and nervously tried to encourage him. Of course the wrong words came out, "But, Doctor, you have to sing something!" With that Rumsey started to shake. Chester blinked at John and barked. John stared back at Chester - and stopped shaking.

Elizabeth watched through the front window and prayed. Ethan turned and went back to work at his mortar and pestle. Their son had changed. Rumsey could be a blessing and Ethan had always wanted a dog around the house.

It wasn't a long walk. John hated the thought of the Green being so close. He wanted to take his time and postpone the fateful moment. He kept losing his breath and had to stop walking. Finally, they found themselves standing on the Green with their little table and tinctures. God knows whether Chester would sing along with him. John took a deep breath and started.

My name is Rumsey.
That's Doctor Rumsey,
A physician from Britain, that's where I gained my fame.
I bring this potion
From o'er the ocean,
So hark, as I impress on you its memorable name.
It's Chickasaw Revival Tonic:
Cures all ills from mild to chronic!
Try it now and feel euphoric!
Chickasaw Revival Tonic.

People stared casually at John, looked more curiously at Ben and continued walking. Some thought it quite odd.

"What's Master Potter doing here?"

Chester just stood and stared at the sky with his ears down. Some ladies stopped and stared. Some quietly greeted Ben. They listened but didn't venture forth. Propriety dictated that they make the first move. They didn't. They just swished on across the Green, some with hoop skirts to swish and some pulling down on their bonnets. John was so disheartened, his voice kept cracking and he could hardly whisper.

He left the field of battle wondering whether he would ever return. He was tone deaf, he was sure. He had lost the pitch pipe that Patrick O'Toole had given him and forgotten the keynote. He had even forgotten the two last lines of the verses.

Chester hadn't even staked out his territory. He trotted along beside John with his ears down, not uttering a sound. Every now and then he would look up at John as if to say something, then didn't.

"There you go being reticent again. For God's sake, Chester, say something," John demanded.

Ben loved every minute. He had never sung outside of church and school before. They returned to the shop. Then John and Chester left for their room and to their own thoughts.

Saturday afternoon, October 15, 1864

Later that afternoon Bennett Young returned for a stroll down North Main Street. While he was leaving the hotel, he paused to allow a young lady to pass through the entrance before him. She looked at him briefly and thanked him for being such a gentleman. Bennett tipped his hat and started to introduce himself. She scolded him for not observing the rules of propriety.

"How do you do? Sarah Stark, the schoolteacher. I just arrived in St. Albans. I see you read the Bible? You must be a religious man…."

Bennett was most impressed with Sarah's straightforward confident manner. "Indeed I am, Mistress. My name is Reverend Christian Clement Clyde of the United Christian Circuit. We represent the famed Reverend Robert Q. Breckinridge of the magnificent bluegrass country of Central Kentucky. I am travelling these parts to impart the knowledge and wisdom that I have attained from studying the Bible. Would you consider discussing this extraordinary subject with me?"

He is surely clean cut, must be clean living and in possession of a clean mind. He looks distinguished without one of those dirty beards, Sarah thought to herself. Then she said, "I would be willing to chat about the Gospels."

Young looked deep into her eyes and flashed his look of 'simple gentlemen from Louisville with good upbringing and lots of humility'.

Sarah Stark found herself walking with Bennett without realizing it. They even found a park bench on the Green before she knew what was happening. The two of them discussed the Bible for over an hour. Eventually, Bennett suggested that since the next day was Sunday, it would be a fine time to take another stroll. Sarah didn't object, and so it was arranged.

On returning to the hotel, Young spotted Tom Collins talking to Sam Gregg in front of the American Hotel. He motioned them to follow him to his room. Sam exclaimed, "I heard that the Union Army will be buying up most of the Morgan Horses this coming week, and all we can do is watch."

Tom Collins grinned at Sam. "The only consolation Sam, is that after we take the remainder, there won't be any horses for the posse. All money from the sales will be in the banks - and then in our satchels."

"Why don't we ride up to the Governor's Mansion at the top of the hill from the hotel and see what kind of horses they have?"

"We'll have to be more subtle than that. I'll stroll up to the house after church tomorrow and give the maid my calling card. It says 'The Reverend Christian Clement Clyde, The United Christian Circuit, Louisville, Kentucky'," laughed Young.

Sunday morning, October 16, 1864

Most of the churches in St. Albans were on the hill above the Green on and around what was known as Church Street. Such a cluster of churches was not unlike many found in New England towns.

While mornings for townspeople were spent in prayer, afternoons usually found most of them promenading on the Green. In existence since 1799, the park served many purposes for the townspeople.

John Smith, the Governor's father, and a former governor himself, had built a mansion for his family in 1852 out of fine Vermont Red Brick. When he passed away in 1858, his son, Governor John Gregory Smith, took over the family affairs. He had married a girl from the fine, local Brainerd family. The Brainerds had been partners with John Gregory's father in the founding of the Vermont Central Railroad.

With the mansion continuing to be the most prominent residence in the town, Mrs. Smith's new maid, Alice Butters, claimed, "The home is fine enough for Mrs. Lincoln to visit - if she ever has a mind to."

Bennett Young walked up Congress Street and found the Baptist church just across the street from the Governor's Mansion. How convenient, he thought to himself. He went to the service, kept to himself, listened attentively to the sermon and made a few notes in his own Bible. After the service, he chatted with the members of the congregation and commented on the fine sermon they had just heard.

As he was departing from the church, he suggested, "Come to think of it, you might like to attend my prayer meeting on the Green this Wednesday the 19th at 3.00 p.m. There will be extensive readings from the Book of John. You might find the experience a delightful complement to this service today and to the Reverend's sermon." With that, he left the congregation and walked towards the Governor's mansion.

The Governor's wife had just returned to the mansion from her own church service down the street when the front door bell rang. Alice Butters answered and quickly took Young's card to Mrs. Smith. She went to the door and asked Reverend Clyde what she could do for him.

"Mrs. Smith, I can't tell you how pleased and honoured I am to meet you on such a beautiful Sabbath day and especially at such a fine residence befitting the Governor of one of America's finest states."

Mrs. Smith commanded respect. She stood, listened and waited to hear what this man was doing on her doorstep. The lady staring at him was Mrs. Ann Eliza Brainerd Smith, the daughter of Hon. Lawrence Brainerd, of St. Albans, Vermont. Mrs. Smith was author of several novels, books of travel and other works. She was frequently chosen to represent Vermont women on a variety of social issues. The townspeople called everything she did a *tour de force.*

So it wasn't long before the phrase became her nickname usually accompanied by a quiet giggle. Bonnets would lean closer and someone would say, "How's ol' tour de force these days?"

On the doorstep, Mrs. Smith asked Reverend Clyde, "Speaking about fine states, tell me about Kentucky. As you may know, Vermont is very pro Lincoln. How is Kentucky?" she challenged him.

"Well, Kentucky is a fine farming state that is sort of split on the Civil War. There are a number of counties that call themselves Confederate."

"And how is the Reverend Clyde? Are you Confederate, sir? How is Central Kentucky, how is Lexington? I hear that those counties are aligned with the Southern Confederacy. She waited quietly for Young to answer.

Young started to stumble, "My church congregation, like many Kentuckians, have tried to avoid not just the fighting but the issues involved. I can assure you that not everyone wants to take up arms against each other. Farming is hard enough. To me, keeping the peace means keeping the land. Fighting the aggressor who wants our land is one thing, but fighting big military battles is another."

Young looked as saintly as he could, stared solemnly into Mrs. Smith's eyes and tried to change the subject. "I am on a holiday with some of my parishioners. We are planning a fishing trip up the Missisquoi River. I have just been to the Baptist service and saw that you live close by. I had heard of your fine stable of Morgan Horses. Not being too familiar with that type of horse, I was wondering if you would be able to show them to me."

Mrs. Smith continued to stare at him. This man was too well dressed, too smooth, too young, and too healthy to be a minister. Whatever this man was he was not of the cloth! "No, I don't think so. The stable houses our private stock of horses and the Governor and I are not accustomed to showing anyone, including travelling parsons, our estate."

"Yes, I understand of course. Before I depart, I was hoping that you might attend my prayer meeting on Wednesday at 3.00 p.m. on the Green. Would you like to read the lesson?"

"I'll think about it, Reverend Clyde."

With the Mrs. Smith mission accomplished, the Reverend Clyde left the Mansion and walked down the hill to the Green and his date with Sarah Stark. "Well, you can't win them all," laughed Young.

Sunday afternoon, October 16, 1864

Amongst all the strolling couples, Sarah Stark walked slowly with her Bible in hand. Young looked across the Green and marveled at her beauty. My, she looks attractive, a gathered full skirt, a matching virtuous blouse, gloves, sparkling blonde hair pulled back under her bonnet, and deep blue Nordic eyes. I could become serious about Miss Stark.

There was nothing timid about Miss Stark. She came right up to him and suggested they find their bench. She began to question him on all the Gospels, a challenge for Young. He tried to parry by asking questions of her. After about two hours, Young became anxious to change the subject and stroll up the street for a while.

"Miss Stark, I was wondering whether you might like me to talk to your students tomorrow? Then maybe ... dinner that evening?"

Sarah smiled, "Remember the rules of propriety! I really enjoyed our walk together. But I am anxious to get back to the hotel."

Young persisted. "By the way, I'm having a prayer meeting on the Green Wednesday afternoon. If you'd like to bring your students they may enjoy the religious experience." Sarah just smiled and passed through the hotel entrance.

Monday morning, October 17, 1864

While it had been raining 'Doc' Rumsey continued to rehearse his song with Ben behind Potter's Apothecary. This time he had a long talk with Chester. "Chester, you have to help me. You just can't be an innocent pet anymore. You just can't sit there. You have to pay your way, or else you may find you have another master!"

Now it was Chester's turn to be nervous. So they waited for the rain to stop. Then 'Doc' Rumsey set up his table and tinctures and he and Ben started to sing all over again.

My name is Rumsey.
That's Doctor Rumsey,
A physician from Britain:
that's where I gained my fame.
I bring this potion
From o'er the ocean,

Chester just looked at John. His ears were still down. He didn't sing or howl. John paused in his singing and stared at Chester with a severe warning look. "Start singing, damn it." Chester looked back rather sheepishly. Then all of a sudden the ears started to rise! He was ready! The sun was coming out. So John stared and started over.

Chester leaned back, lifted his head and started to howl. People had begun to return to the Green and they stopped and stared at Chester. Ben cheered. Soon the ladies started to gather with their friends and family to listen to what 'Doc' Rumsey had to say. They watched in wonder at his dog, Chester, with Master Potter. No one had heard of a singing dog before. Nobody questioned Ben. They sang their song all over again. This time everyone listened. They took his advertisement and started to read it. Chester sat proudly with his ears straight up. Ben was beaming. This time John remembered the last two lines.

Chickasaw the great Revival Tonic
Chickasaw the brand of great renown.

Their sales were precious few that afternoon, but people recognized him, listened to him and wished him well. Some stayed ... some bought. He was exhausted, but tomorrow was Butter Day, the market day for the region. There would be many folks here then. They'd be back.

John McInnis, Will Teavis and the others got off the afternoon train from St. Johns and went directly across the street. Some went to the St. Albans Hotel and some to Willard's Boarding House next door. By 5.30 p.m. they were ready to report.

Monday 5.30 p.m., October 17, 1864
The Reverend Christian Clement Clyde was holding court. The Rebels and their sergeants were all there to receive orders.

"The townspeople are growing restless." Sam said. "They're waiting for us to go on our fishing trip. So I keep saying that we're just waiting for a few more of our friends to show up. Now I'm getting nervous!"

Young wasn't really listening to Sam. He was preoccupied. He was ready to talk and didn't want anyone interrupting him.

"The Greek fire I want directed towards the banks, so give these tinctures of Greek fire to the bank sections. Tomorrow morning get an accurate count of the horses we can take. If there are shortfalls, we have to know about it as soon as possible. Charlie, that's your job. We need 21 good horses, bridled, saddled and ready to hit the Plank Road running. Charlie, you're Sergeant of the Rustle-uppers, what can we do?"

Charlie replied, "Fuller's stable behind the Tremont is half empty, but fresh Morgans may be arriving tomorrow. So we could get about six. Most of the horses look to be ready at Gilmore's and Sylvester's. There are about 15 from those two stables."

Justin Morgan
Courtesy of the American Morgan Horse Association

Young cautioned them all, "Remember, the horses need to be reserved tomorrow. Then the horses need to be saddled and bridled Wednesday morning. All of them have to be led to the hitching posts along North Main in front of the Green, Wednesday after lunch. Say to everyone you meet, we are going on a fishing trip and need the horses.

"Say I'll be along to pay the stables once we get the horses hitched up on North Main and finally counted. So be pleasant and reasonable with the stable proprietors on Tuesday. Then on Wednesday, stay calm with the horses and move them slowly. No one should be suspicious. We're just doing what we said we would do. Now remember, I have a prayer meeting scheduled for 3.00 p.m. That is a great way to get everyone on the Green.

"If we can't get 21 horses from the stables, then Sam, you and your boys will have to gallop up to the Governor's stable and grab what you can. We may have to take horses right off the main street. The saddling and hitching of the horses on North Main will have to be done by the Rustlers. Then we have to run.

"The original escape route to Canada is too dangerous. I have a new way that is a little different, but it will be a lot safer. We're going to take the Plank Road up the Missisquoi River and then we'll head through the woods to Canada. We may have to break up along the way, but don't worry about that for now."

"Remember we are all members of the United Christian Circuit. I have my Order of Battle. This is indeed a military operation! The history books will print what we have done. This is what people will remember."

Tuesday, Butter Day, October 18, 1864

Market days always started near dawn, with the fresh food all sold by about 10.00 a.m. Traffic on North Main Street was the heaviest of the week. But, also, this day the Union Army was in town to buy Morgan horses from each of the stables. While the Rebels couldn't do anything, they could at least keep their eyes open and their mouths shut.

One of the earliest local wagons to come into view down the Street was that of the widow Green. Minnie Green had just come down the Old Plank Road from her farm over Aldis Hill to sell her fall produce, such as apple pies and corn chowder, at the town market. Whenever she came to town, she liked to do a little shopping and to chat with her friend Mary Beattie in front of her millinery store. Mary hailed Minnie. They stood and shared the warm sun together. "Enjoy the sun while you can, Minnie. The 'waiting time' for the snow will soon be here."

"Waiting for me isn't the snow, Mary, it's another man. It's been a tough year since my husband, John, was killed at Sharpsburg on Antietam Creek, two years ago with the Old Brigade. He was with the 2nd Vermont lead by George Stannard, a man John really respected. 'When you follow George you never think of dying,' John said in one of his letters. Unfortunately, Stannard was promoted just before Sharpsburg and didn't lead them the day John was killed."

"Minnie, you should move into town or you might even rent a room at your farm to someone. Many of the other wives and widows are renting, too."

When Minnie left Mary Beattie, she proceeded to the offices of the *St. Albans Messenger*. Her mind was made up. She thought, I need to rent out a room. Maybe someone would see my advertisement. I'll place an announcement in Thursday's issue.

Back on Main Street, she met Elinus Morrison, who had just come down Bank Street from his room at the soon-to-be completed Welden Boarding House. Many of the town's more refined visitors were contemplating lengthy stays there. After all, it overlooked the town and was across from the Governor's Mansion. Elinus was a contractor from Manchester, New Hampshire, who was building the Welden House. He had just finished the railway yards for Mr. Smith.

"Why hello there, Widow Green! I hear that Miss Stark is looking for a more economical room than can be found at the Tremont. I spoke to her on Sunday about coming to the Welden House. Unfortunately, it's a bit expensive for a young schoolteacher trying to get established. Why don't you talk to her? Maybe you could offer her a room at your farm. This way both of you could win, so to speak."

Tuesday afternoon, October 18, 1864

Henry B. Sowles, president of the St. Albans Bank, stood on the steps after lunch with his cutaway frock coat pulled back and both thumbs firmly planted in the pockets of his new velvet vest.

President of the First National Bank, Harold Bellows, had the bank chartered in February of 1864. Now the bank notes were supported by a new National banking system. Mr. Bellows sat in his chair trying not to look overstuffed, as he said to himself after the Butter Day deposits.

The cashier of the Franklin County Bank that had been chartered in 1849 had been working for the bank's owner, Orville Burton, since he had left school. However, as time went on, he was becoming more and more suspicious of Mr. Burton. As cashier he could see how Burton was not maintaining the reserve policy of his bank, leaving depositors at risk. Since it was a State-controlled bank rather than a Federal one, Mr. Burton had no government guarantees backing the deposits. He wanted to stay a State bank because he was allowed to grant mortgages on real estate, which federal banks could not do at the time.

Tomorrow, the 19th, would be Ink Day, so named by the clerks because they were so busy entering the previous market day's transactions that by the end of the afternoon their hands would be covered in blue ink. So today, North Main settled down after a good day of trading.

Huntington's Jewelry dealt in watches, jewelry, silverware, and fancy goods. "Being right beside the St. Albans bank is sort of an enticement for banking customers to spend a few dollars in my establishment," Charles Huntington would confide to his friends. He had extensive properties in town ... and let everyone know it.

Vernon Atwood's Hardware was a wooden building whose floor sagged badly from the barrels of nails that Vernon always had on display. He dealt in iron, steel, nails, glass, paints, and table and pocket cutlery. Jeweler Charles Huntington wasn't too happy with this lopsided wooden house that was his poor looking neighbor. His biggest worry was what would happen if Vernon's building collapsed? Would his store follow? But Vernon's store attracted a lot of customers. "I guess you have to be practical."

Breck & Weatherbee's Gents Furnishings was built right up against the other side of Atwood's. Sam Breck's building seemed to sag every time Vernon added another keg of nails. He thought of moving, but the location was too good to leave.

All three proprietors often met on the street after the market and discussed sales. What was good for one person was good for the other. Yet, today was a little different. The townspeople had all noticed The Reverend Clyde strolling with his Bible up and down Main Street, John Rumsey's trio trying to sell patent medicines on The Green, a growing number of Young's parishioners coming and going quietly up and down the streets of town and some of them calling into all the stables. Vernon looked to Charles and Sam for agreement. "Yes, today is a little different," they nodded.

They had heard that Young was going fishing with his parishioners. Vernon complained. "They seem to be an odd lot, fishing with Reverend Clyde. When are they going to leave? Where is all this great fishing they talk about? Probably be fishing along the Missisquoi. That's stupid because the water is down at this time of year. How come they didn't buy anything at my store? Most fishermen always go to local hardware stores to talk about the best flies and lures - and the best fishing holes in the area. It's part of their culture. Something doesn't seem right about them."

By late afternoon, the proprietors on North Main closed up their businesses and retired to their homes up the hill. The stables for the town never closed. Business had been brisk. Many of the men in St. Albans were leaving for Burlington and Montpelier on government and court business. Instead of the trains, which could serve them easily, some still preferred to go by horseback. Times had been changing, but old habits can be hard to break.

* * *

6

FIRE

St. Albans, Vermont, Wednesday, October 19, 1864

Chester didn't lick John's nose this morning. He just lay there with his nose between his paws and his eyes wide open. John finally got up to face another good day on the Green. He had spent yesterday evening after dinner counting his sales for the day, his cost and his share to the Potters and his own profit. Twenty tinctures at $3.00 apiece gave $60 in cash. O'Toole's contribution to the first shipment's cost of each tincture was seventy-five cents and his share to the Potters was twenty-five cents. This left a margin of $2 for himself. My God, $2 times 20 tinctures was $40 - all in one day. No wonder Patrick O'Toole looked so prosperous. Maybe there was a light at the end of the tunnel after all. Late into the night John kept seeing dollar bills flying by his eyes.

Going up to Potter's Apothecary was no longer a venture in fear and doubt for John. Now Ethan and Elizabeth Potter were becoming fast friends. Their son, Ben, couldn't leave Chester's side. Chester even ran after a ball, as long as Ben had thrown it.

"Ethan, I have a problem. Pretty soon I'll have to order more stock and labels. This all takes money. I owe Patrick $75 for the original order of the Tonic we made together in Montreal."

"John, you should be very careful. Let me arrange bank accounts for you and Patrick. In this way you can slowly pay off what you owe."

This was the first time that John could ever remember having control of his money. A little cash management by Elizabeth could go a long way. In fact, his day of reckoning with Patrick was no longer a confused pit in his stomach.

There is hope! John cried to himself. Even Chester looked as if he approved.

Both Elizabeth and John went next door to the First National Bank where they were introduced to Mr. Sowles.

After they returned to the apothecary, John helped Ethan and Ben with the mixing of the tinctures. By 11.00 a.m. he was on his way to the Green with a singing Ben carrying the tinctures. Chester trotted along with his ears down. "Ready to sing, Chester?" Rumsey grinned. Chester's ears stayed down. Rumsey couldn't figure out why Chester was not being more supportive. Chester usually kept close, and when John started to sing, Chester howled along. Before long the ladies were back and anxious to know how the Doc, Ben and Chester had spent the evening. Everybody liked them!

One tincture at a time, Doc Rumsey laughed to himself.

Young had risen early. He had breakfast and was stepping out for his morning stroll when he spotted Sara Stark leaving the hotel for her school.

"I wanted to say good-bye until we meet again. After my prayer service this afternoon, my congregants and I are heading up the Missisquoi Valley for a little fishing. I trust that upon my return we may have the opportunity to enjoy dinner together. You never know the kind of fish we might catch," he laughed.

Sarah laughed, too. "Make sure it's filleted. I don't like the eyes." With that said they both bowed and went their separate ways.

Young commenced his final day in St. Albans by reading his Bible and urging everyone he met to attend his prayer meeting at 3.00 p.m. He strolled slowly up and down the west side of North Main reading his Bible and occasionally staring at the windows of Saxe's Gallery, Breck & Weatherbee's and Huntington's Jewelry. Every now and then he would stop, stare into space, refer to his Bible and look thoughtful. Then, casually, the Rebels started walking up and down North Main Street.

Joe McGrorty and Sam Lackey were waiting at the station. Finally the last three Rebels - Wallace, Homer Collins and Doty - came to town. They all huddled right there in the station. They were late and they knew it. After an intense discussion all five Rebels walked up to North Main Street to join the others and prepare for the raid. No bedding down now.

Section Four, The Rustle-uppers, went to work. Charlie Higbee and Sam Gregg went to Fuller's two stables beside the Tremont and behind the American Hotel. They would wait for the new Morgan horses that they heard were being delivered from Shelburne, Vermont. If the horses didn't arrive by noon, they might have a problem. The other two men of

79

the section, John McInnis and William Thomas Stone Teavis, went to Gilmore's and Sylvester Field's Stables. After reviewing the horses they had ordered the day before, Teavis and McInnis retired to John's room at the St. Albans House. After a short while they went over to have lunch with Charlie and Sam

The other Rebels were nervous that some people might be getting suspicious. So they walked casually, nodding to the passing Reverend Clyde and staring into the shop windows, like any good gun-toting raider with bottles of Greek fire in his satchel might do.

The St. Albans Bank was located directly in front of the Green. On the sidewalk of Main Street, Tom Collins was talking to his men of Section One: Turner Teavis, Marcus Spur and Louis Price. Louis was losing patience with Tom's hesitations. He whispered, "Come on, Tom. I'll go in and say I'm looking for Reverend Clyde. For sure, Lieutenant Young won't be there! They all know he is gathering us all for a fishing trip. Gives us an excuse to promote the prayer meeting at 3.00 p.m. I'll go in and see how many people are working there, where the cash teller is, where the vault is and finally where the president of the Bank sits." Louis didn't wait for an answer. He just crossed the street. Tom didn't argue with him. But he still didn't trust him.

Joe McGrorty's Section Two, with James Doty, Caleb Wallace and Alamanda Bruce, sat on a bench on the Green and looked down Main Street at the National Bank. Joe was older and more experienced than the rest of his section. "I'll go in and enquire about banking services. I could say that I'm expecting a small delivery of funds to pay for the fishing trip that the Reverend Clyde is hosting. I'll say that I'm responsible for managing the holiday. So when the funds arrive I'll want to bank the money safely for a few days. That should keep them quiet!"

Bill Huntley of Section 3 wanted to study the interior of the Franklin County Bank alone. His boys, John Moss, Dan Butterworth and Bill Moore, lounged on the Green as well as Section 2 and watched Bill enter.

All was set. They ate a quiet lunch, everyone with his own thoughts. The skies were clouding over and it looked like it could rain at any moment. The variable weather had brought many of the leaves down, indicating that late fall had arrived.

Doc Rumsey, Ben and Chester had sung and howled their hearts out. They (especially Chester) had won the praise of the ladies. The more he howled, the more they bought the Tonic. Ben stood and smiled. He even got up the courage to say, "Have a little tincture, Madame?"

The Tremont Hotel, 1.00 p.m.

For Charlie Higbee, sergeant of the Rustle-uppers, the time had come. The Morgans hadn't arrived by noon at Fuller's. So he went in to see Young, who was casually eating his lunch with Turner Teavis and Bill Huntley, the other two Rebels residing at the Tremont.

"Lieutenant, we count 16 horses ready and saddled. But we're still short five horses."

"Charlie, don't worry." Young replied calmly. "First of all, The Keepers of the Green, Section Five of Sam Lackey, Charles Swager, Homer Collins, and George Scott are looking after the other horses that will be arriving on North Main at the Green. Keep as calm as you can. Take the saddled and bridled horses and walk them slowly up North Main to the Green and hitch them there. Above all, stay calm.

"Everyone is waiting for my prayer service and many will realize that we are off on our fishing trip afterwards. Keep that story going until we have all the horses. Secondly, wait until we have most of the horses hitched and ready to go. Then take Sam Gregg and mount two of the horses you have and gallop up to the Governor's Mansion. I'm sure they have a number we could use. Charlie, for heavens sake, don't get Mrs. Smith excited! Go straight to the horse barn behind the mansion and take the horses. Even if she screams, keep thanking her for letting you have her horses. Say the Reverend Clyde approved it. That will confuse her. Then hurry back to the Green. She could follow you back and blow the whole thing. If she does, it may be difficult keeping everyone under control until we raid the banks at 3.00 p.m.

"I'll wait until 3.00 p.m. then shoot off several rounds on the Green and declare that 'St. Albans is now in the Possession of the Confederate States of America.' Everyone will know our game. It will be up to Charlie's Section Four and Sam's Section Five to control everyone. Shoot bullets and throw Greek fire. I'll be there, too. Don't be afraid to shoot anyone. In this way, we keep everyone scared and confused. Keep it going until the sections get back from robbing the banks. Don't worry, it's my show! The Reverend Christian Clement Clyde will be preaching one memorable sermon," laughed Bennett Young.

The Green today, St. Albans

The Green, 1.00 p.m.

Doc Rumsey's trio had spent the entire noon hour singing on the Green, much to the amusement of all the Rebels who had been loitering around them. In fact the Chickasaw Revival Tonic Song was going well. They could actually sing it without forgetting the lines. John didn't even need Patrick O'Toole's pitch pipe. Even Ben was perfecting "Have a little tincture, madam?" Coming from Master Potter, the question seemed quite permissible.

Doc Rumsey had made more sales and befriended more ladies. He was nearly sold out. The bell on the Episcopal Church on the hill struck 2.00 o'clock.

John McInnis moved into Sylvester Field's Stables as casually as his nerves would allow. He was seasoned from fighting in Alabama and escaping from the Rock Island prison. So surely he could bluff his way here. "Good afternoon, my good man," John said to the first man to rise up from the hay. "I'll take those five horses we reserved now. The Reverend Clyde is anxious!"

The lad looked at him with a blank stare.

"I want payment now!"

John looked him up and down and said, "Obviously you are not familiar with the United Christian Circuit from Lexington, Kentucky. We are Christian missionaries who follow the teachings of the Bible. My word is my bond. If you have trouble with that let me speak to Mr. Field. The Reverend Clyde will be along shortly to make the payment - or would you rather that I go to Gilmore's Stables next door?"

By now the young lad was dazzled by McInnis and told him to go ahead. "I don't want any trouble from Sylvester. He'll be back from lunch in a few minutes." He helped John saddle and bridle the horses Not a Morgan in the bunch. In a few minutes, John had led three of them to North Main. He would return later and get the other two. All was proceeding well.

Will Teavis walked into Denis Gilmore's Stables and couldn't see anybody. Will said to himself, Where is everyone at 1:00 in the afternoon? Being Wednesday, people must be relaxing after Butter Day. There is old Gilmore dead asleep in the hay. He doesn't look like he will ever wake up. I'll take three of what we reserved and that are ready for us. I'll come back and take the other two later. Meanwhile, Mr. Gilmore slept on.

Warren's son, Eric Fuller, had just washed down the mounts in their stable behind the American hotel when Sam Gregg walked in. Sam was a bright young man of 22 years and seasoned in the Kentucky Cavalry. His problem was his accent. There was no way he could hide the fact that he was from Kentucky. "Those five good horses for the Reverend Clyde that we reserved yesterday? I need them right now. The good Reverend, whom you see strolling on the Green, will be over soon to pay you. We're off shortly after the prayer service. By the way, Whatever happened to the Morgan horses?"

"I have three ready and saddled for you, but we don't have as many Morgans as we thought because they are all out to our customers with business dealings in Burlington and Montpelier. There could be a couple of other good horses that we could let you have. They are nearly as strong as Morgans. But I'll have to wait for my father to return."

"Well," drawled Sam, "even a blind dog finds an acorn now and then. I really need those two more, though."

Eric asked, "Where are you going and for how long?"

Sam replied casually, "We thought we'd try the Missisquoi River above Sheldon Springs for a few days. They say that the springs are a welcome relief after a hard day of fishing. We'll take these three and I'll be back shortly." With that, Sam led the three horses out to the street.

Charlie Higbee entered Ed Fuller's stable beside the Tremont and found that his worst fears were realized. They didn't have a single Morgan. Like his brothers, Ed's best horses were all rented to local businessmen on trips out of town.

Ed claimed, "I do have the two that I had rented to the Reverend Clyde and Mr. Collins last week that I feel could hold their own. You could have them right now plus another one I have on hand. I heard you would be dropping by today, so I saddled and bridled 'em for you."

Charlie took them out to the street and called over to Sam who was fussing over the three that he had. There were only 14 horses hitched up on North Main. He needed seven more, not five as originally estimated at noon

The Green, 2.30 p.m.

When old Gilmore woke up, he looked up to see Will Teavis leading two more horses out of his stable without paying. He shouted at Teavis, "Stop, or I'll shoot you dead!" Will tried to calm the old man down by telling him about the Reverend Clyde. "I'm not listening. I just want compensation," demanded Gilmore.

Will Teavis murmured, "Take it easy, take it easy."

Gilmore shouted, "You have five of my horses. You sinner, how far do you think you are going to go?"

Teavis decided that he couldn't keep up the façade any longer. So he pulled out his gun and took a shot at Field. The shot missed but it stopped Gilmore cold. He didn't know what to do. Will walked out and calmly approached the Green with the two additional horses. Unfortunately, the fracas was heard at Field's next door. So Will Teavis was too late to fool anyone any longer. Not only was Denis Gilmore really mad, but Sylvester Field had raced out of his stable and was running up the street shouting after them, as well.

The total was now 16 horses rustled. They still needed five more. All the Rustle-uppers of Section Four - Higbee, Gregg, Teavis, and McInnis - now stood on the street. The Keepers of Section Five - Lackey, Swager, Collins, and Scott - stared down at them from the Green. They had only half an hour to keep up the game - and get more horses! So Charlie took the next step. He said, "Sam, you come with me, we're going to the Governor's Mansion."

Young, who had been waiting on the Green reading his Bible, ran over and ordered Swager and Scott, "Try to talk to Field and Gilmore. If they continue to argue, arrest them! The façade is over!" People were coming out onto the street to see what the shouting was about.

"Teavis, you and McInnis go across the street and take three horses that are tied to the hitching posts for customers and bring them up to the others we have assembled here. I don't care what people say. Shoot them. We can't hold off any a minute more. No longer are we members of any Jesus circuit!"

With that said, Charlie Higbee and Sam Gregg took off up Bank Street to get a pair of horses from the Governor's Mansion and to bear the temper of Mrs. Smith. The Keepers, Lackey and Swager, were rounding up the people at gunpoint and leading everyone to George Scott and Swager, who were waiting on the Green to corral them. They had tried to manage the raging Gilmore and Field, without success. Shots were fired into the air and gun smoke could be seen along Main Street.

Alice Butters, Mrs. Smith's housekeeper, could hear the gunshots as she was hanging up the laundry to dry. As she ran around to the front of the mansion, Charlie Higbee and Sam Gregg entered the stable.

Alice shouted, "Who, pray tell, are you?"

Sam cried out, "Leave us alone, we are members of the Provincial Army of the Confederate States of America. We are here to second your horses for our military action against St. Albans."

Alice was hysterical. She ran back in to the mansion screaming to Mrs. Smith, "The Rebels are coming! The Rebels are here! They're attacking us right now. They're taking our horses, Mrs. Smith? Mrs.

Smith, shouldn't we be raising our flag and sounding our cannon or something?"

Mrs. Smith was totally taken aback. The first thing she did was run for an old empty horse pistol, close all the velvet drapes and run to the front door with her hoop skirt swishing. "Yes, yes, do what you can!" By then Charlie and Sam had taken two horses and were leading them unsaddled out and down Bank Street to the Green. They got what they wanted, the saddles would have to wait.

Lieutenant F. Steward Stranahan, Mrs. Smith's brother-in-law who was home on leave from Custer's command, ran up the street in his Union uniform to help protect the mansion.

The Rebels were just leaving as he arrived. Mrs. Smith and Alice Butter were standing there raging at the Rebels from the front door. Alice took command.

"I'm firing the cannon, you raise the flag," she ordered a very surprised Lieutenant Stranahan.

The cannon hadn't been fired since the Revolution and had been plugged. The flag couldn't be found in the melee. So Mrs. Smith told Frank to guard the mansion. She was taking Alice down to the Green to see what was happening.

On the Green, everyone was screaming at the Rebels. By the time Charlie and Sam got back to North Main, John McInnis and Will Teavis were crossing the street with three unsaddled horses. The Rebels now had their 21 horses, some saddled, some not. It was 2.55 p.m. It was too late to check the stables for saddles and bridles, but the Rebels found a few blankets and some leather at S.S. Bedard & Co. on Foundry Street.

The Episcopal Church bell tolled 3.00 p.m. There was no longer any acting. Lieutenant Young was no longer the Reverend Christian Clement Clyde of the United Christian Circuit. Young stood up on the Green and fired off his pistol several times.

He shouted for all to hear, "This City is now in the Possession of the Confederate States of America," Young was beaming, glassy-eyed and very excited. It had been a long journey from his family's farm in Nicholasville, Kentucky, to the Green of St. Albans. His time had come. He was a leader who commanded all he surveyed. All would bow down to him now. He was on top of his world.

Many startled people had assembled first for the prayer service and then had been corralled. There was no longer peace in St. Albans. The northernmost battle of the Civil War was on. Yet no one seemed to understand. Many laughed at Young, which made him furious. He started to wave and shoot his gun again.

Doc Rumsey, with Ben and Chester, huddled nervously beside him, watched with increasing horror the reality of the Civil War being thrust upon an innocent town and the peaceful world they lived in.

The Academy, now the St Albans Historical Museum

Young, with Section Five of Lackey, Swager, Homer, Collins, and Scott had been corralling people onto the Green. No one could believe that this nice young man could turn out to be so evil and sinful. Using the Bible for a front to his activity could never be forgiven. For people who had lived with God and peace all their lives, this was the most shocking event they had ever experienced.

Just then, Charles Huntington left his store for the Academy up the hill on Church Street to take his children, Collin and Caroline, home. Young shot him for refusing to go to the Green. Even though Huntington had a bullet shot through his back and chest cage, he still had to go to the park. Many of the people on the Green came to his rescue and helped him to a bench, then tried to comfort him and stop the bleeding. Eventually Charles settled down and was taken home. He would survive, but recovery would take months of fever and rest.

The children were kept inside the Academy. Through the windows they saw the raid and watched as Mr. Huntington was shot.

Section Five kept up their shooting and then started to throw Greek fire at the banks and store windows along the street. Keeper George Scott went into the lobby of the American Hotel and threw a tincture against the wall. When nothing happened he ran back to the Green. A little smoke arose, but no fire. Something was wrong.

"Lieutenant, the Greek fire isn't working! We can't generate any fire other than some damn smoke!"

All the stores were shutting down along the street and people were running away. Store windows were breaking from the Greek fire tinctures and North Main was filling up with smoke. Between the shooting, smoke and breaking glass, downtown was in turmoil.

Mrs. Smith and Alice Butters arrived on the Green, demanding some answers. Mrs. Smith was half running, hoop skirt swirling and her new parasol swinging in the breeze. She was shouting and swearing.

The other Rebels who had brought the horses were coming back down the street, shouting, shooting and throwing Greek fire. There were now four Rebels on the Green and four attending the horses on North Main and watching Champlain Street for foundry or railway men who might run to the defense of the town.

Warren Fuller had just arrived back in town when he realized that all hell had broken loose. Being a man who ran a tight stable he was used to giving orders. So he looked for Young and demanded that he return the horses at once to everyone. Young laughed and took a shot at him. He demanded that Warren go to the Green. He took another shot. Warren pulled his own gun and tried to shoot back. He tried three times and to his dismay and embarrassment it never fired. So Warren jumped off his horse and headed off up the street. He wasn't going to let these rebels get away with it! The town needed to resist. So he stole around the back of the stores on North Main and made his way up Congress Street to the Weldon House, under construction. He knew that Elinus J. Morrison, the contractor, would help.

Morrison stopped the construction and told his men to get what firearms they could and to run down to the Green. It was a motley crew, but it was the beginning of resistance.

The St. Albans Bank, 3.00 p.m.

Tom Collins led Section One of Turner Teavis, Marcus Spur and Louis Price, bolstered by several pints of whisky, quickly across the street. The cashier was nervous from all the commotion outside, so he had forgotten to shut the vault. Business was being conducted as usual. So just as the Rebels entered, the cashier was able to run into the back office where a clerk was working and quickly barricaded the door. No sooner had they closed the door, when the Rebels kicked it in and it smashed back in their faces. the cashier was hit in the face and was knocked out cold. Tom Collins had his gun drawn and was pointing it at the clerk.

"Not a word from you, sir. We are soldiers of the Fifth Confederate State Retributors under the command of General Jubal Early. We have been instructed to rob and plunder your northern lands in retribution for what General Sheridan has done to our poor people in the Shenandoah Valley."

The clerk shouted, "That gives you no right to rob our bank!"

Just then the front door rattled. Someone wanted to come in. The Rebels had locked the door. Marcus Spur opened the door cautiously, peered out and found Sam Breck wanting to pay off a note. Marcus grabbed his money, $390. Then all of a sudden another young man appeared and Marcus grabbed his money, too, $210. Meanwhile, Teavis and Price were in the vault taking cash and looking for the gold. The cashier refused to tell them where the gold was stashed. Because the bags of silver were in plain view, they started to fill their satchels with silver and greenbacks. They took approximately $75,000 in specie and currency. Tom's whiskey breath was enough to stop a tomcat. At gunpoint he forced the staff to take an oath of allegiance.

"I solemnly swear to obey and respect the constitution of the Confederate States of America and to not fire on the men of that government in the town.

In addition I swear not to report this robbery until two hours after the men have left."

Because of the noise outside and their own nervousness, the Rebels were anxious to leave. A 12-minute wait was long enough, they were beginning to sober up. They overlooked $50,000 and $50,000 in uncut sheets of new St. Albans bank notes. Marcus Spur, who had said very little during the raid, gave a Kentucky holler. "Y'all will get what you deserve for the Shenandoah. Remember, the sun don't shine on the same dog's tail all the time!"

Collins looked at him and whispered, "Let's go, Marcus" No one said anything. The Rebels stormed out onto the street.

By now Mrs. Smith was hysterical trying to get someone to listen to her. Charles Swager couldn't resist a comment, "Mind your own bees-wax, lady."

"Don't you dare talk to me that way, you, you son of a gun, you scallywag," Mrs. Smith exploded, much to the surprise of everyone.

Young always kept himself in a position to see everything that was happening on the street and the Green. He saw Mrs. Smith howling at Swager. So he calmly walked over to her and introduced himself as a lieutenant of the 5th Confederate State Retributors.

Mrs. Smith told Young just what she thought of him. "I presume you have no soul, otherwise you would never have represented yourself to me as a religious man. You and your Bible ... hah! That's nothing but Billy Joe's Whiz-Bang. After all, your brain is only the size of a pea! You must be an extremely ignorant man to do what you did. Now here you are waving your pistol and shooting at people. Don't talk to me about being a soldier. My brother-in-law is on General Custer's staff. Now there is a soldier. You're just a common criminal. Don't ever think that you are any more than that. Now do the honorable thing, leave the horses and the bank's money and get out of town before we rise up in strength to crush you."

Young just smiled, knowing that she would probably say some-thing like that. "Lady, shut up and stand still. You are a prisoner, and don't ever think you are not!"

Mrs. Smith continued to rant and rave at them all over the Green with Alice Butters following closely behind.

The Franklin County Bank, 3.00 p.m.

Into the bank walked Section Three led by Bill Huntley, followed closely by John Moss, Dan Butterworth and Bill Moore. They were just customers, enquiring about the price of gold. Bill introduced his colleagues to the cashier.

"Sir, we do not deal in gold at this bank."

"You must have gold, how can you operate a bank without it?"

The cashier spotted Jasper Saxe and two other customers entering the bank. "Talk to them, they often deal in gold." Jasper told Huntley, "The price of gold at the moment for a transaction would be $47.04 a Troy ounce. While this price is considered at the top of the market, that's what we would want."

Bill Huntley accepted and a transaction was made. Thereafter the customers left the bank. The four Rebels followed. They stood outside for a moment and then stormed back inside. Bill's men stood by the door while he made his proclamation to everyone.

"We're members of the Fifth Confederate State Retributors. Hundreds of us in town have come to rob, plunder and burn the town down. Open the vault and bring out the greenbacks and species now!"

The unlocked vault was opened and the cashier was ordered into it. The other clerk tried to slip out the front door, but was caught by Dan Butterworth who pulled him back in again. "The last thing we need is someone running around outside saying we're robbing the place!"

The clerk was pushed into the vault with the cashier. Both of them shouted that they would die from lack of air if the Rebels closed the door on them. Huntley just laughed and told them to shut up.

"This is nothing compared to the way you're treating our people in the south." He slammed the vault door shut.

The four Rebels proceeded to stuff their satchels with silver and Franklin currency and quietly left the bank just as good customers would do. They took approximately $75,000.

Shortly thereafter two more customers entered the bank. With no one to serve them and hearing shouting coming from the vault, they knew that something was very wrong. They found the vault key still in the lock so were able to open the vault and free the two desperate men.

Orville Burton, President of the Franklin Bank, entered the bank later in the day. He was so distraught from what had happened, that he immediately closed the bank and filed for receivership. He said he would pay off all his honest debts. He declared that any money stolen would not be honoured when returned to the bank, because it was closed.

Fighting had developed on North Main from those who had lost their horses. Shots were fired but no one was seriously hurt. One of the townspeople, who was on North Main when the robberies occurred, ran to tell Captain George C. Conger. Conger, a Yankee, had been injured during the Civil War and had returned home. However, such injuries did not stop him from rising to the occasion. He ran up South Main recruiting anyone he could to fight the raiders. By the time he got to the square he had a few followers, but Young tried to arrest him. Conger refused to be taken and after a few gunshots ran across to the American Hotel and out the back door. Conger managed to get a rifle from a citizen and returned to the Green, but the gun kept jamming.

The First National Bank, 3.00 p.m.

Joe McGrorty led Section Two into the bank. He went immediately to the cashier. James Doty shouted, "You are all prisoners. Any resistance and I'll shoot you dead! We want control, then we will rob the vault."

Seated on one of the benches in the bank was retired General John Nason, nearly 90 and stone cold deaf. He had been a soldier during the War of 1812 and in command of the Franklin County Militia during the Canadian Rebellion of 1837. The General had become an institution downtown. Seeing the General nodding while he read the *St. Albans Messenger* was typical. During the robbery Mason just sat sleepily reading his paper. He had no idea what was happening around him.

Caleb Wallace wanted to shoot everyone in sight. So he turned to Alamanda Bruce, laughed and said, "Let's shoot the general. He's in his uniform. It would be quite normal to shoot a soldier dead!"

Alamanda looked at him and said, "That's a stupid way to become a hero. The Confederacy wouldn't be impressed! Come on, he's just a sleeping old man."

While James Doty put the clerk into the vault, Joe McGrorty declared, "We represent the Confederate States of America and have come here to retaliate for the acts committed against our people by General Sherman."

Just then a customer entered the bank, realized that a robbery was in progress and attacked Alamanda Bruce. Doty and Wallace promptly jumped on him. They were about to push him out the door when General Nason intervened. "Two against one isn't fair." He stood there looking at them with a blank look on his face. The General had awoken and was pulling at his sword. It was jammed in his scabbard.

Joe McGrorty and Doty pushed the clerk, a terrified young Josiah Martin, into the vault, grabbed as much cash as they could and found only sacks of pennies. They claimed they never found any gold. Finally they left, leaving General Nason talking to himself. They took approximately $55,000.

Total Take

St. Albans	$75,000
Franklin County	75,000
First National	55,000
Total	$205,000

The Green, 3.20 p.m.

By now all the men had returned from the banks and were running for their horses. During the last hour, pressure had built downtown. The Rebels had control for a while as the stunned populace looked on. The Rebels continued to look for more blankets, saddles and bridles in the stables. Slowly the reaction grew stronger and gunshots were fired at the Rebels, not by them. The Rebels tried to shout their Rebel yell and sing 'The South Shall Rise Up Free', but they were shouted down.

As they were running to and mounting their horses a shot rang out and Charlie Higbee was hit in the shoulder. He slumped off his horse and needed help to get back up. Young watched his key man bleeding badly and knew that something had to be done. He had seen this man, Doc Rumsey, selling his medicine on the Green. He concluded that he must have some medical knowledge so he enlisted him at gunpoint to look after Charlie.

"I'm not a doctor," Rumsey complained, but it was too late. No one was listening to him. All Young wanted was action, not words, at this point.

Young shouted, "Somebody give Charlie some money. He was looking after the horses and got shot."

Everyone was too busy to hear. So Young shouted over to Collins, "Tom, you got the most cash and gold from the St. Albans Bank. Put an extra satchel on Rumsey's horse. Charlie will need it to get help and maybe to escape from the posse. Give him about $75,000."

Young muttered to himself that the best way to keep loyalty in a man's heart is to keep money in his purse. "Rumsey, look after Charlie or you're a dead man. Get him help and then both of you return as soon as possible. Don't you dare steal any of his money."

Rumsey stared glassy eyed at the money and then glared at Young, "Steal whose money from whom? You are mentally unbalanced, sir!"

Then Young saw Ben staring with horror as to what was happening. Young shouted, "Squire Teavis, get the kid another horse from North Main. We'll take him, too! He'll make a fine ransom."

"Leave this young man alone, he doesn't deserve to ride with you. He's only fourteen," shouted Rumsey in anger.

Young told Rumsey to shut up. When Squire Teavis arrived with a saddled horse off the street for Ben, Young turned to Ben, "Stay close to me, son. I want to know where you are at all times." Then he whispered to Tom Collins, "I can't think of a better shield from the posse."

So Doc Rumsey was forced onto Charlie's horse at gunpoint and told to drape old Charlie across the back. Charlie was bleeding badly. As they were leaving, a voice whispered to Rumsey, "Take the soldier to the Widow Green's place on the old Plank Road. She's good at stichin'."

All the Rebels, Rumsey and Ben were now ready and were moving slowly up North Main Street. Ethan and Elizabeth Potter were hysterical at loosing their young son. They started to run after them with Chester barking and running beside Ben. There was no way Chester was going to be left behind. So Young turned and fired off a shot straight at Chester. The bullet hit Chester in the hindquarters. He rolled over on his side and started to yelp. Rumsey was forced to move on, calling for someone to help Chester. Fortunately, Ethan and Elizabeth Potter were able to reach Chester. Ethan lifted him up and cradled him. Then he and Elizabeth took him back to their apothecary.

With half the town following, the Rebels started to move off. Elinus Morrison had been at the corner of Congress and North Main trying desperately to supervise his men in defending the Green. As the Rebels started to move up the street they came right to Morrison's corner. Shots were aimed at Morrison, so he turned and ran up to Mary Beattie's Millinery Shop. He flung open the door and dived inside. When he put his hand on the doorknob to close the door behind him, Young fired at him. The shot passed through his hand and into his abdomen.

As the Rebels passed, some of the boys in the printing shop of the *St. Albans Messenger* could see Morrison falling back against the door, with blood everywhere. They ran down the stairs and along to Mary Beattie's shop to rescue Morrison. Mary was standing over Elinus Morrison screaming at Young and hollering for help. The boys tried to carry Morrison into Dutcher's drug store. Being a large strong man, he was heavy as lead to carry. The real problem seemed to be the amount of bleeding that they couldn't control. As a result a large trail of blood followed them into Dutcher's. Throughout all the commotion, Morrison was losing consciousness.

In the mid 1800s, the sight of blood was taken seriously. Bleeding usually meant either amputation or death from loss of blood or infection. Dr. John Branch, Sr. heard about poor Morrison and ran down Bank Street to help Mr. Dutcher attend to him. Morrison lay stricken on the floor of the drug store. Branch tried desperately to stop the bleeding and to stitch the wounds in his hand and abdomen. They tried to move him but Dr. Branch claimed that with such a loss of blood, he had better stay right where he was on the floor. A blanket was put over him and he was made as comfortable as Dr. Branch and Mr. Dutcher could make him.

By the time the Rebels had ridden north, Mrs. Smith and her maid were attending to everyone on the Green. The trauma and injuries needed attention. The telegraph wires were humming up and down the line as well as to the capital in Montpelier where Governor Smith was working. The local telegrapher from St. Albans wired him that Confederate soldiers had the town under siege. Governor Smith was torn between either returning quickly to St. Albans, or staying in his office to manage the affairs of the State. He was concerned that a conspiracy may have been forming to threaten the whole northern tier of Vermont. Even if he could return, the damage would have been done and the Rebels would have escaped. Therefore, he decided to stay. Lieutenant Stranahan remained in St. Albans to defend the Governor's mansion.

The Brainerd Block on North Main Street, housed the *St. Albans Messenger*. Beattie's Millinery and Dutcher's Apothecary were just down this side of the street. While those buildings can be seen in this picture, the original businesses are long gone.

The St. Albans Green

ESCAPE

St. Albans, North Main Street, 4.00 p.m. October 19, 1864
When St. Albans started to recover, they had to rely on certain military citizens to take charge. Captain John C. Conger had come out from behind the American Hotel to help enlist and direct the posse. Everyone with a horse and a gun was recruited. The smoke and noise from the tumult on North Main Street kept everyone either huddling inside or around safe corners. No one could see what was actually happening.

It appeared that Bennett Young had shot Elinus J. Morrison and hurt him badly. Some claimed that he had shot Charles Huntington in the back. While Morrison lay unconscious on the floor in Dutcher's Apothecary, Huntington lay on the Green.

Chester was having a bullet removed by Ethan Potter. Chester had never known such pain. There were no painkillers for man or beast except whisky, and Chester was not a whiskey man! So he howled and howled. Ethan was terrified that he may have to amputate a leg. He knew that Chester could die easily from this operation. Somehow Ethan removed the bullet with Elizabeth's help. While the stitching and bandaging went well without any more howling, Elizabeth feared that Chester's silence might be because he was either unconscious or dead!

Morrison was not so lucky. He was eventually lifted to a makeshift bed in the apothecary, but despite everyone's efforts to comfort him, he died two days later.

Mrs. Smith and Alice stayed until all the injured were looked after. Then they started slowly up the hill to the comfort of their own home. Their skirts had been soiled beyond repair but they had done what they could for everyone. Alice's apron was bloody and torn. They were exhausted.

To Alice's surprise, Mrs. Smith started to laugh. She turned to Alice and said, "You know something? I've never sworn so much in all my life!"

The Plank Road

The Rebels had been moving up North Main Street and were approaching the turn east onto the Richford Plank Road that would lead them towards the village of Sheldon. Young and the Rebels were in the lead, with Ben, Rumsey and Charlie Higbee, galloping along behind. It was difficult to saddle up a horse and gallop out of town without spilling dollar bills and coins all over the place.

By the time the Rebels started heading east, the town had been paralyzed for about an hour. Assembling a posse was difficult with few good horses available and most of the good firearms down with the St. Albans enlisted men in the Wilderness with the Army of the Potomac. Many of the men who were not enlisted were away on business in Burlington or Montpelier. While the military was being called up, it would take approximately 24 hours for them to reach St. Albans from Burlington.

In the meantime, Stranahan had been nervous about leaving the Governor's Mansion, Mrs. Smith and Alice Butters seemed to be looking after themselves down on the Green, Stranahan began to assemble as many military men as possible to back up Captain Conger - not an easy task with troops expected only the following day from Burlington.

Eventually, men did arrive by horseback and buggy, with pitchforks and shotguns, smooth bore and otherwise. Ed Fuller was the first onto the street to join Conger. He and his brother had a vested interest in getting their horses returned. In addition, Captain Conger's 19-year-old son, George, and a number of the local shopkeepers were arming themselves and trying to find horses. Conger assembled approximately 50 men ready for the chase.

The Widow Green's Farm

Minnie Green's market garden and farmhouse came into view just over Aldis Hill on the Plank Road out of St. Albans. As the Rebels charged on down the Plank Road, John Rumsey struggled behind. When he came upon the farm, he trotted onto the property and helped Charlie off of his horse. Minnie could see by the way the Rebels galloped and waved their guns that they were bank robbers, but she didn't know that they were Confederate Rebels. She couldn't quite understand Rumsey's role, especially with a sick man on his horse, but she felt that the least she could do was try and help him.

Green's Corners today

"We don't need any more shooting and killing," she muttered to herself. So she went out to help John Rumsey carry Charlie Higbee into her home. It was when he was lowered on to her bed, bathed in dirt, dust, sweat, and blood that Charlie tried to tell her that he was a sergeant and had been on a military mission for the Confederacy. Minnie was shocked. She looked at Rumsey and shouted, "Who are you? Are you a Rebel, too?"

John Rumsey tried to explain about being 'Doc' Rumsey, a seller of patent medicines. Minnie just glared at him and said, "If you lie down with dogs you'll still rise with fleas!"

Charlie had been given $75,000 in St. Albans National and Franklin County greenbacks and some gold coins by Young to try to take back to the Confederacy. So he quickly pulled out a huge wad of bills and offered Minnie $5,000 if she would look after him. He needed stitching, rest and transportation.

The sight of 50 - $100 greenbacks, wrapped neatly together, was something neither John nor Minnie had ever seen before. When Minnie recovered from the shock, she replied, "As long as you throw in some gold coins." Minnie stared wide-eyed at the money, paused and then replied, "Well, just call me Minnie. Forget the fleas!"

Minnie was beginning to feel better about this whole affair, especially with $5,000 hidden deep in her full skirt. With a quick attempt at combing her gray hair, she even turned to Doc and tried a little smile.

"Doc, would you like to try some of my famous Minnie's Green Mountain Corn Chowder? Many of my market clients ask for it every week. I have a big batch that's been waiting for my son to come home. It needs to be supped pretty soon! Oh, and I have some fresh vegetables and a little fresh apply pie." Minnie sort of whispered this in John's ear to entice him.

John hadn't eaten since breakfast, but with the posse on his heels and the image of Young's gun staring him in his face, he felt that he should move on. "Oh my, how I'd like that soup," cried Rumsey as he bowed his head to the Widow Green. He was beginning to feel very untidy in front of the lady. He hadn't changed his topcoat, striped pants and spats or had a bath since leaving Montreal.

He said to the widow, "I'm delighted to be in your fair home, madam, to assist this poor gentlemen, no matter how evil these men may be, and to ensure that your protection is secure. Yet I feel that I must complete my mission. You see, I am at gunpoint at the moment and they're holding Master Ben Potter as ransom. The leader of those Rebels wants me to report on Sergeant Higbee's condition or else he is going to find me and shoot me dead."

He looked as innocent as any 45-year-old bankrupt British solicitor could look who is trying to pass for a doctor. With that explanation given, John Rumsey bowed to the widow, tried to kiss her hand that was covered with Charlie's blood and slowly stumbled backwards out of her farmhouse.

What an interesting person, she said to herself. Although I don't like his long nose, he is clean shaven more or less, a gentleman to be sure, but what was that about patent medicines? She smiled and whispered to no one, Oh, well, the older the fiddle the sweeter the tune.

Then she asked herself, Now, what do I do with the cash? Everyone will know it's from the Rebels. I'll just have to think about this a bit more. At least there are a few coins.

Minnie took the cash from her skirt and hid it carefully deep inside a jar on the kitchen shelves. "You never know when someone might come snooping around," she muttered. Charlie slept on and off for two days. Minnie slept beside him as best she could. Whenever he woke, Minnie poured her Green Mountain Corn Chowder down his throat. It wasn't too hot. The odd bit of swearing changed to strange ramblings and then finally to thanks over and over again.

Ben kept falling behind, not being as experienced a rider as the others and despite Young's urging to catch up. Ben had been crying, not knowing what had happened to John and Chester. After going down the Plank Road, the Rebels veered off to the right and then took the Fairfield Pond Road due east to the village of Sheldon. Young had some idea about robbing the bank there, too. Ben feared that Rumsey would stay on the Plank Road and miss them entirely. So he devised a scheme. He would give John clues by leaving a trail of greenbacks that were so handy to the pouch close to his left hand. A little here and there and eventually the trail led down towards the Pond.

Ben rode onwards, fearful of being noticed, but the Rebels were looking straight ahead. They really weren't watching Ben. Another turn occurred at the other side of the Fairfield Pond, so Ben dropped a few more greenbacks.

John Rumsey trotted down to the cemetery at Green's Corners and saw the greenbacks. He laughed at how sloppy the Rebels had been. Then he realized that a perfect trail had been set for him. So off John galloped along the Fairfield Pond Road. So far he couldn't see any posse behind him on Aldis Hill. The time was fast approaching 5.00 p.m. and he could hear in his imagination, galloping horses, shouting and shotguns roaring from the top of Aldis Hill in the distance on the Plank Road. The Pond Road veered off the planks so John could see some evidence of the Rebels as they galloped east towards Fairfield Pond.

As John approached the Pond he saw a man standing by the Pond letting an old horse drink some water. John shouted, "Which way'd they go?"

The man answered, "To hell with you, they took my good horse and left me with this tired old clinker."

John didn't know what to say, so he galloped on, following the hoofprints and the greenbacks until he could see the Village of Sheldon in the distance.

Dear God, I pray that Ben is O.K, cried John to himself.

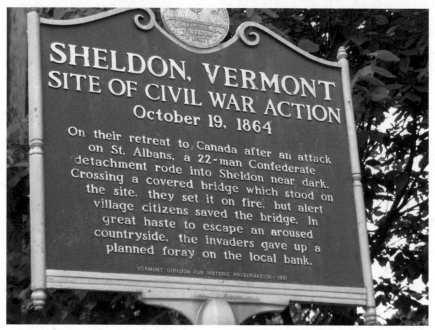

Plaque in Sheldon

Sheldon

Rolling hills and farms formed the landscape of Sheldon with Black Creek running through the village. Rumsey continued along the highway into town until he came to a turnoff to a bridge. It was here that he could see the rest of the Rebels. They were all down at the covered bridge over Black Creek. He turned down the hill and approached a greatly relieved Ben and a surprised Bennett Young.

Young was having an argument with a local farmer over the removal of a load of hay stuck inside the bridge. All the Rebels were very nervous and wanted to move on as fast as they could. Young said to his men, "Boys, burn it all down." The Rebels took out what they had left of their Greek fire and tried to burn down the hay cart and the bridge. The cart started to burn but the bridge only smoked.

Running down the opposite hill came the Methodist minister with a pail of water, urging the local townspeople to help him put out the fire on the hay cart. The Rebels threatened him, but he didn't take any notice. With everyone staying hidden from the raiders, the minister put out the fire himself, but he didn't remove the cart from the bridge. He wanted the Rebels to have a hard time getting over Black Creek. As Young was staring at the water, the minister shouted at him, "Why don't you part the water, just like the good St. Alban did in Roman times?"

Young looked up, confused. "When ... when did he do that?"

The minister replied, "On the way to his execution, just like the Venerable Beade said he did."

By then the Rebels with Ben had managed to cross the Creek with Rumsey struggling along behind.

"May I talk to you now, Mr. Young? " Rumsey shouted.

"No, just ride." Young replied.

Rumsey tried to complain but no one was listening. No one asked about Charlie. Ben saw that Rumsey was safe - sort of! More hills appeared on the other side of the creek, so the Rebels had to ride their horses up hills again. By now the horses were frothing badly. Their progress started to slow. Fortunately, the posse had still not caught up with them. No one looked back. No one talked.

The Pinnacle

Just as they arrived at the turn to North Sheldon at the Kane Road, Young called a halt. The autumn leaves were falling and many trees were bare. They could see down to and across the Missisquoi River at North Sheldon, the road leading up to Franklin. Then off to the east they could see the Pinnacle, a mountain rising in golden light on the northern horizon at the Canadian border, the legendary 'Happy Hunting Grounds' of the Abenaki, Huron and Iroquois tribes.

"We need to have a meeting. All the horses are tired and some of you are exhausted," Young shouted out to his men.

Bill Moore approached Young breathlessly and whispered to him, "Sir, I'm sure I saw some of the posse on the hill above Black Creek. We'd better hurry, I'm terrified!"

Young turned to the men and said, "Settle down, everyone. There are three issues. One, all of us with Doc Rumsey and the kid galloping down the road must be an awesome sight, kicking up a lot of dust that can be seen for miles. If you were on the Pinnacle, you could see our trail. Two, our horses can't go much further. The weight of the satchels is holding them down. Three, there is too great a risk in galloping through any town loaded down with silver and gold. It is vital that we bury the metal, remember where it is and get back there when the excitement settles down.... We have to break up."

Mt. Pinnacle, Quebec, from Vermont

Young turned first to Tom Collins, his youngest sergeant, but a smart man. "Tom," Young whispered, "I want you to go straight up the North Sheldon Road towards Franklin and then straight to the border. You have a lot of the silver and gold, so bury it as soon as you can. See that farm on the other side of the river? Go up that hill and into the woods bordering on the farm's upper fields. This way, when you go through Franklin further up, they can't pin anything on you."

Collins looked doubtful. "Shouldn't we try to get the silver and gold into Canada first? They won't arrest us! Canada East is neutral."

Young just looked at Tom and said, "How are your horses? Can they make all the hills between here and the border? Well, I doubt it, Tom. I wouldn't take any more chances. It will be dark by the time you get to the border. You have lots of cash. Despite what you gave to Charlie you could finance the six of you all the way back home. Tom, your goal will be to reach the railway due north of the border at West Farnham. Try to get back to Montreal and report to the Mission as soon as possible.

"Tom, you're the sergeant of the first group. Take Bruce, Lackey, Scott, and young Spur from your bank group. They are all good young Kentucky boys."

Collins gathered his men and they said their good-byes. "See you all in Montreal," Tom cried, as they pushed their tired horses down to the Missisquoi River.

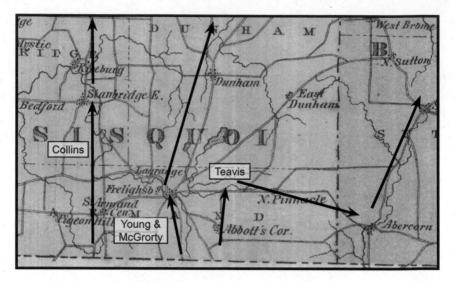

Rebel's Escape Plan: Canada East

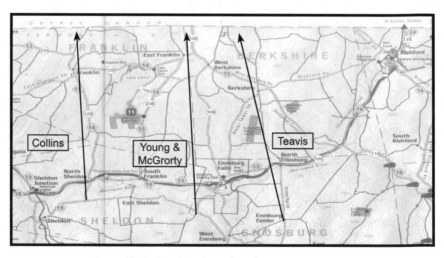

Rebel's Escape Plan: Vermont

* * *

TOM COLLIN'S RUN

North Sheldon, Vermont, October 19, 1864

Tom led his men down the long hill to the North Sheldon Bridge over the Missisquoi River. All of a sudden he was alone and in charge with his new men. Tom got along well with Young. He was one of the few Rebels who dared to call him Bennett. Both of them seemed to think along the same lines. However, now Tom had to lead his men without Bennett to back him up. Would they obey?

"This talk of cigars, we're just bank robbers. That's what we do - then that's what we are!" cried the oldest Rebel of the group, Alamanda Bruce. Alamanda, was a farm boy from Central Kentucky. Sam Lackey would laugh and say, "Don't let Alamanda get serious. When he does, he gets mad, most of the time."

Tom wasn't so sure of Samuel Lackey. Sam was from the same regiment as Alamanda, had been to college and had always wanted to be in the military. Sam had a good sense of humour. He was always kidding, even in the middle of a raid, and he was religious. George Scott and Marcus Spur were the other two. They left the talking to Sam.

"One thing about the ride down to the bridge, we can see if there is a posse or not." It was the only time Tom had felt safe since 3.00 p.m. that afternoon. Tom called out to his section, "It's been over an hour since we left, so a posse should be in hot pursuit. We can't see them anywhere, but just look straight ahead and move on."

"Sure and get shot in the back." roared Sam. He wasn't amused.

They reached the new steel bridge over the Missisquoi River and found that the village of North Sheldon was only a collection of farms along the road to Franklin. Because there were no telegraph lines in this part of the Valley, no one seemed to be concerned about five riders galloping north. They didn't stop to talk. In fact, it was approaching the supper hour and there were no churches to bring out the people for evensong. Twilight was falling. On they pressed across the road to North Sheldon and up the hills to the north.

Franklin Memorial, Vermont

Tom remembered what Young had said about the silver and gold. The horses were tiring badly now. He started to look for the wood lots and fields above the first farm in the valley. It didn't take long after the first hill to spot a good cluster of maple trees, and in they went. Tom led the way to a clearing in the woods that could be seen from the road. There was an old wagon road that had been overgrown with young poplars. They all got off their horses and started looking for their hunting knives to use for digging. The ground was sandy and easy to manage. Throwing down their Moroccan satchels was the toughest thing the group had to do. It meant leaving their treasure behind after all the fuss and bother of the last few weeks, but dig and bury their bags they did.

Franklin

"At least I feel more innocent now!" muttered Alamanda to Tom, sarcastically.

Not looking at him, Tom said, "Back on our horses. Keep going."

They quickly took off for Franklin. No one said a word. They all had some coins and greenbacks. Tom still kept most of approximately $30,000 in cash. The high land now levelled off to gently undulating farm country, but the light was fading quickly and they could barely make out the large lake off to their right. As they climbed up the side of Gates Hill on the left, the lamplights of Franklin gradually came into view. Down off the hill they came riding innocently towards the town. They didn't know what to expect, and wanted to get through town unnoticed if possible.

As they entered the town it became obvious that something was up. The Methodist church was just around the corner and many people could be seen slowly gathering their families there.

When the Rebels got to the corner, a lady dressed just like Mrs. Smith with a parasol and all, hailed Tom with her gloved hand. "Young man, who are you and where are you going?" shouted Mrs. Mary Cooms, obviously a leading lady in the community.

Tom stared and Alamanda brooded. Tom was in trouble, He was never very good at bluffing. His partner Alamanda was no better.

It was therefore up to Sam Lackey to talk them out of trouble. Sam just smiled benignly and said, "Why Madame, we are part of the Reverend Christian Clement Clyde's United Christian Circuit. The good Reverend has instructed us to proceed to Farnham in Canada East where we hope to assist in the raising of a fine Christian church for those hardworking neighbors of yours to the north in Canada."

Mrs. Cooms wasn't quite sure what to say. After a moment of silence, she looked up at Collins and said, "Well now, that's a fine cause I must say, but it's after 6.00 p.m. and you must be starved. I'd like to invite all of you to our chicken supper at the Methodist church. We'll be serving chicken, gravy, potatoes, and peas. We even have dumplings and cranberry sauce for those who care for that sort of thing. Surely you can take a few moments to replenish yourselves?" She smiled expectantly.

The Rebels were all weak from hunger. They hadn't eaten since lunch in St. Albans. Now it was Tom's turn to be tongue-tied. Before he could answer, Mrs. Cooms continued, "Oh by the way, The Honorable John K. Whitney, our loyal state representative is our special guest. He'll be speaking on our favorite subject, temperance."

By now all the Rebels were off their horses and pretending to be missionaries that they were not. Alamanda was the first to respond. "Mrs. Cooms, that sure beats the coosh and goober peas we had in the 6th Cavalry."

Tom looked quickly at Alamanda and then whispered to Mrs. Cooms, "That was before we persuaded him to join the Circuit. Poor

110

man was forced into a cavalry regiment. He didn't serve for very long ...
did you, Alamanda?"

"Didn't I not do what?" demanded Alamanda, raising his head.

Mrs. Cooms laughed and said, "Just as long as it wasn't for the
Confederacy. By the way, your accent is very southern. What state are
you all from?"

They all answered, "Kentucky, ma'am. It's neutral in the conflict."

Then Sam started to laugh. His accent was thicker than ever. "Why
ma'am, we're from Bluegrass Country. The grass that makes the bourbon
smooth, the girls fast and the horses beautiful." He laughed loudly.

Mrs. Cooms just stared at him. Now they were all nervous. They
couldn't shut Sam up! But they were all desperately hungry. Staying
meant listening to a sermon on temperance. They stood there with their
hats in their hands looking to Tom Collins expectantly. By now they
could smell the dinner wafting down the street. Mrs. Cooms was getting
a touch impatient waiting for an answer.

Tom finally told her, "No, ma'am, we have to carry on." He couldn't
risk their staying. If the posse were near they would be finished. The
clock was still ticking on them.

Marcus Spur asked, "Couldn't I just grab a couple of chicken
wings?"

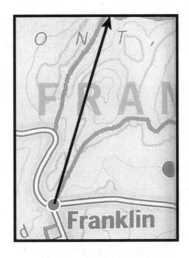

Collins's run to the border

Tom got back up on his horse and said, "Follow me or else I'll shoot you dead!" They followed. Marcus wanted to say something but didn't. Tom looked back at Mrs. Cooms and apologized for their hasty departure "We are truly sorry, ma'am. By the way, which is the best way to get to Canada? There must be at least three roads to follow from here."

"Keep going north, no matter what happens." she said. "You'll find a big turn in the road to the east to Morse's Line. However, by far the fastest way is to keep going straight north on Richard Road. It's a dark, steep and narrow valley. That way is quite hilly and wooded. Watch out! Horses have been known to stumble."

As Mrs. Cooms watched the men leave, she never knew that she had just helped five Rebels to escape to Canada. She shrugged her shoulders and turned down the street to the church supper and to listen to the Honorable John Whitney.

The five Rebels turned and left town as slowly as they dared. They kept looking back up the long hill to the south of Franklin and still couldn't see any hint of the posse. The horses were in better shape now much to the relief of the Rebels. They had been rested twice and the big hills were behind them. The turn on to Richard Road went smoothly but from then on the road was rougher and very dark. They had to walk most of the way to the border.

They knew they were in neutral Canada when the land leveled out onto the flat St. Lawrence River valley and the road sign indicated Eccles Hill Road. They kept on riding to the north knowing that they would never be arrested or shot at by a posse. Finally, at about 9.00 p.m., they arrived at the first town, Stanbridge East.

Tom called a halt to the ride. They dismounted beside the Pike River to water their horses and to talk. Alamanda turned to Tom, "The pressure is off now. Marcus and I want to go it alone from here. We're safe here in Canada, so there is no need to help each other anymore. We're tired and want to stop at Elder's Tavern just across the street. We can hardly wait to check in."

"I want to press on even if it means going all night to get to Montreal," Tom said. "At least let's try for the train at West Farnham."

Marcus said very quietly, "I have completely run out of energy and refuse to go on any further."

Even though Sam and George felt the same, they were not stopping, so they broke up. The three remaining Rebels, Tom Collins, Sam Lucky Lackey and George Scott started off.

Shortly after aiming straight up North Road to West Farnham and the railway to Montreal, they saw galloping horses in the rising moonlight, charging straight at them from the north. They had just crossed over the Pike River, had reached the little Puddledock Bridge and were horrified.

"Don't ask questions," Tom cried out to Sam and George. "They may or may not be a posse coming from the north, but don't take any chances. Throw away your guns and holsters and maintain the Reverend Clyde story about our missionary work. "

"Not our guns! They're our right arms," Cried Sam and George.

After a few seconds, George stated, "Tom, I'm on my own now. I have to look after myself, so I'm heading for the fields. Whoever they are, they're not going to take me or my guns!"

Before Tom could answer, George Scott had disappeared into the darkness leaving Sam Lackey speechless for the first time. He didn't know what to do. He just froze and stared at Tom. Tom grabbed Sam's gun and holster and along with his own, threw them off the bridge. Tom was determined to bluff it out. He had no choice, because the strange snorting horses were coming out of the darkness down the road in front of them. This was no posse, this was a company of the Canadian Militia just off the train from West Farnham. These were soldiers, commanded by Captain George Newcome.

Tom and Sam turned quickly and galloped back to Stanbridge East and hitched up at the Henry Bacon Hotel. They were just in time to look benignly at the soldiers and wish them well, when Captain Newcome rode up to them. Puffing and huffing, Newcome shouted, "Identify yourselves or risk being arrested. We mean business!"

Elder's Tavern, 1864 Stanbridge East, Quebec

A Justice of the Peace ran across the street and challenged them, as well. Tom desperately started on his missionary routine. "There's no need to get excited, Captain. My colleague and I are from Central Kentucky and represent the United Christian Circuit along with our pastor the Reverend Christian Clement Clyde. We're on our way to spread the Gospel in Farnham. You seem to be rather upset, sir...."

Newcome looked Tom straight in the eye and said, "Let's see what's in your pockets."

Tom looked at Sam. They didn't know what to say. They knew one thing, though. The game was up. They had too much cash. They were both searched and exclamations went up all around. "We have two Rebels!" cried the soldiers.

"On behalf of the government of Canada East, I arrest you for the bank robberies this afternoon in St. Albans," pronounced the Justice of the Peace.

Collins stood up and declared, "We are part of the 5th Confederate State Retributors acting on orders of the President of the Southern

114

Confederacy to avenge the horrible atrocities to the poor folk of the Shenandoah Valley by Phillip Sheridan. Captain, you cannot arrest us. This is a military operation and Canada East is neutral. You sir, are acting illegally. Watch yourself!"

Newcome didn't blink. "You certainly changed your story in a hurry! That, sir, is not for you to decide. The courts in Montreal will do that for us. In the meantime, you are arrested. Sergeant, handcuff these men. Form up three men under your command and take them to the fort in St. Johns. Forget the trains. Ride directly to St. Johns, even if it takes all night! It'll take you just as long to go to Farnham.

"Don't be fooled by this man talking about a military exercise. Take all their money and deposit it with the commander at the fort. Remember to get a receipt. Let's not waste any more time, we have a long way to go," Newcome cried. He hailed his men to proceed and off they went to Frelighsburg.

As they passed the corner of River and Maple, the proprietor of Elder's Inn ran out. "Captain, I'm sure I have two bad men upstairs. They have big sixguns and too much money on them."

Newcome beamed and his eyes glistened. He had three of his men charge up the stairs and arrest the Rebels right in their beds.

The sergeant told Marcus Spurr and Alamanda Bruce to get dressed, hand over their revolvers, give up all their money and get downstairs. On the street, Tom spoke to the Justice of the Peace. "As I just said, we are Confederate soldiers. The money that we took from the St. Albans Banks was in retaliation for the destruction of private property in the Shenandoah Valley by General Sheridan. Please telegraph our Commissioner in Montreal, C.C. Clay, and inform him of what happened. Ask him to do what he can for us."

Bruce and Spur were arrested, handcuffed by the Militia and sent off to St. Johns with Collins and Lackey and three highly armed soldiers. According to one of the arresting officers, who reported to Newcome, Bruce and Spur had badly chafed legs from riding bareback for six hours. He was concerned about their need for hospitalization. Newcome scoffed and told him to move on to St. Johns. "Men, lets move on quickly. Our orders are to proceed to the border as fast as possible."

George Scott watched the events in the town from the peace and security of darkness. He saw where the militia was taking Collins and

Lackey. Then he turned back on to the North Road and made his way to the West Farnham railway station - where more Militia waited for the Rebels. There would be five captured and sent to St. Johns.

Missisquoi Museum, Stanbridge East, Quebec

Pike River at the museum, Stanbridge East, Quebec

BENNETT YOUNG'S RUN

Jay Peak from the Missisquoi River

Enosburg Falls, October 19, 1864

Squire Teavis looked down on the Tom Collins group as it rode to the River and asked, "Will we ever see them again?" No one said a word. They could see Tom's group crossing the Missisquoi River and heading up the road to Franklin.

Finally, Young broke the spell, "Come on everyone, we're off to the next turn to Enosburg Falls."

Young counted 16 men left, including himself, Doc Rumsey and Ben. He would have to break up the men again. For the next 20 minutes he tried to figure out how to do that. Young looked down on the

Missisquoi River as the light was slowly fading, casting an ever-enriching soft golden glow on the hills. With the leaves mostly down by October 19th you could see the hills more clearly. Indian summer was here at last. To many Vermonters, this season is the most beautiful and tranquil time in Vermont. What could disturb this tranquility? Young grinned to himself.

Ah, who could ever imagine a charging posse chasing a simple group of young Kentucky farmers that insist their bank robberies were a military action?

Who could imagine converted farmers dedicated to the Very Reverend Christian Clement Clyde of the highly respected United Christian Movement? grinned Young.

It wasn't long before Young stopped again and called his men around him. "I want Charles Swager, Squire Turner Teavis, Caleb Wallace, Sam Gregg, with John Rumsey and the kid to come with me. That totals seven people including myself. Any more riding together and we could be spotted."

John Rumsey cried, "Why Ben and me? Why can't we leave, Lieutenant? You don't need us." John was practically pleading with Young to let him and Ben go.

Young replied, "Shut up and stay on your horses!"

John was furious. As they rode on he sought comfort in poetry:

The Charge of the Light Brigade

Half a league, half a league,
Half a league onward,
All in the valley of Death
Rode the six hundred
Forward, the Light Brigade!
Charge for the guns! He said:
Into the valley of Death
Rode the six hundred

"What are you talking about?" shouted Young.
"That's Tennyson."
"Any relation to the Venerable Beade?"
"They were English!"

Young didn't blink. "Now will you shut up and keep riding!"

Then addressing his men he said, "After we take the turn for Enosburg Falls, Joe McGrorty, Jim Doty, Bill Moore, and Bill Huntley will follow along at a short distance. Joe, you're in charge. Wait until we have passed over the bridge and have gone through the town to the north. Then cross the bridge and follow us. Our biggest problem is going to be the silver and gold that we have in our satchels. We should never go through any towns with these coins. It's too big a risk. We've spread the cash around, so each one of us should be able to manage on his own if he has to do so. The coins would be a dead give-away. It looks pretty hilly between here and the bridge. Let's bury them in the maple woods just over the next rise."

He counted his men again. "The Collins five are running for Franklin and West Farnham in Canada. Two groups totalling seven in one group led by myself, with Rumsey and the kid and four in the other led by McGrorty will leave shortly for Enosburg Falls, East Franklin then on to Frelighsburg and Waterloo in Canada.

"The remaining six led by Will Teavis with John Moss, Louis Price, John McInnis, Dan Butterworth, and Homer Collins will run further east on the Tyler Branch Road to the village of Enosburg Center, then turn north to North Enosburg on the Missisquoi River, Berkshire and finally overland to Waterloo. That's 22 and Charlie, wherever he is now."

Young took a good look at his men. Sergeant Caleb McDowell Wallace's uncle was John J. Crittendon, a former United States Senator from Kentucky. Young felt that he was a cut above the rest. Charles Swager was as outspoken as Wallace, but a little more restless. Squire Turner Teavis was a favorite of Young's and could get away with the odd cussing and arguing. Finally there was Sam Gregg, who didn't look like a Rebel, kept to himself and said nothing.

Once they got into the hills south of Enosburg Falls, they found a location just above the road on a hillock that was clearly seen from the road. Young called out to Charles Swager, "Take Rumsey and Ben down the road a piece and make sure that they don't see where we bury the loot." They all dismounted and followed each other in single solemn file through the field and up to the hillock carrying their satchels. Standing in a circle with their heads bowed, Young laughed and said, "Now I think would be a good time to have a reading from John 1"

Caleb Wallace didn't see the humor in this at all. "That's the most stupid thing I have ever heard you say, Young. Smarten up, for God's sake! This is serious stuff!"

No one said a thing. They all kept their heads bowed. Young was smart enough not to say anything and to just proceed. "All right, take out your knives and start digging. It's pretty sandy here."

Within a few minutes, the satchels buried, they moved on quickly. Young urged them to remember the hillock as a landmark for when they returned. So far there were no mishaps or posse. The bridge to Enosburg Falls was just around the next bend in the road. On they moved.

The second group, led by Joe McGrorty, was not far behind. They followed the lead in burying what they had in their satchels on the hillock. As they came around the final bend, the Town of Enosburg Falls could be seen in the distance. The approach to the bridge over the Missisquoi River was well wooded on each side. They slowed down to a more casual pace for the final advance to the bridge.

McGrorty's boys held back. Just then a shot rang out from the bridge. Young, thinking it was meant for them, jumped off his horse and headed for the bushes. Everyone followed. When they looked out they saw a dead cow on the road to the bridge, a young boy with a smoking shotgun and what looked like his father rushing up to scold him. The lamps of Enosburg Falls were lighting quickly as the darkness of night had fallen. Everyone in town seemed to be fussing over the cow. Once the poor cow was hauled away, the son was told to be more careful.

The lad returned to his seat by the bridge, shaking and crying from the goblins of the night. His folks had ordered him to defend the town from Rebels! "Guard the bridge," they had said. The townspeople had never been raided before so no one really knew what to expect. He never ever thought that anything would happen. In the darkness sounds can be exaggerated, and now he was nervous.

The Rebels still had to cross the bridge. Young was in a quandary. They had to keep moving. His first thought was to have Squire Teavis walk up casually and start talking to the young lad. He was closer to his age than the rest of them. He turned to him and said, "Turner, get out there and befriend that poor kid. Soften him up so that he won't be afraid of us when we approach. In the meantime I want to think about this a bit more."

Turner hesitated and stood frozen, unable to move.

So much for Squire Teavis, Young said to himself. This Reverend Clyde story is wearing a bit thin. Every time we mention the United Christian Movement, the Methodists and Episcopalians become very suspicious and I become more self-conscious.

"Rumsey, you need to earn your place with us. Right now I'm tempted to shoot you dead and bury you in that hill under The Pinnacle. I see that the first ridge is called Paradise Hill. How would you like to go to paradise?" Young leered at Rumsey and laughed. Rumsey cringed and muttered strange sounds. His eyes became glazed.

"So much for Rumsey," Young continued, "I have a great idea that could save us all from degradation and death. I want the Potter kid to stand up, take his horse and walk over and talk to the boy. Kid, take your time and don't be nervous! Befriend the boy and his father if he is still there. Talk about our group. Then call for Doc Rumsey. Doc, you go out and show your tinctures to the boy. Convince him that we are all part of a work group that is going up to West Berkshire to build a small plant to manufacture patent medicines. Get out there and save our lives. If you don't, yours won't be worth very much. Sing your damn jingle if you have to ... and kid, don't quit on us!"

Ben stood up and took the reins of his horse. He had never been so nervous in his life and his legs wouldn't stop shaking. Being thrust into an adult situation away from his parents was horrifying. If I fail, will these people shoot me to death? Ben wondered to himself.

The boy on the bridge saw something that he never expected. There was a boy of his own age slowly approaching the bridge with his horse.

"Hey," said Ben, "did I see a cow being shot?"

"Yep." The boy didn't know what else to say.

"You shoot it?"

"Yep."

"Well, that was something."

"Yep."

"What happened to it?"

"Who's to say?"

"I guess everybody will be eating well soon?"

"Yep."

John Rumsey broke out of the woods with his horse and advanced on the two kids and with his top hat, cane and old britches. He never felt more at risk in his life. He had 9 men, armed and hiding in the bushes, waiting to shoot him dead! Once he got his nerves under control, he walked up to the two boys and started to sing.

My name is Rumsey.
That's Doctor Rumsey.
A physician from Britain;
that's where I gained my fame.
I bring this potion from oe'r the ocean.
So hark as I impress on you it's memorable name.

"Good evening my good man. I've travelled from oe'r the ocean to bring this fine medicine, the Chickasaw Revival Tonic to the people of America. My colleagues and I are planning to build a sizable manufacturing plant not too far from here, in West Berkshire as a matter of fact. My father's estate bequeathed me a nice little property along a pleasant creek with fresh cool clear water that is ideal for producing this fine tonic. Would you like to try a sample of it?"

Ben declared the medicine was a marvel. "I've never felt so revived in all my life and I've been sick, very sick!" The younger boy was absolutely dazzled over this apparition of an old gentleman showing a tincture of his medicine to him.

The lad thought that the other men approaching up the road were there to deliver John and Ben to the home for sick people back in Sheldon. Eventually he recovered from his shock. His father had returned to see what the commotion was about and welcomed them to Enosburg Falls.

He asked John, "Have you and your men had any dinner? Oh, and by the way, have you seen any Rebels being chased by a posse?"

John replied, "You sure that you wouldn't like to try the tonic? Try it now and feel euphoric," laughed Rumsey.

Young approached John and whispered to him, "Shut up and get moving before you give the show away."

Then Young replied innocently to the boy's father, "No. We heard about the Rebels as well, but so far we haven't seen anything of them. We are behind schedule and anxious to get on before it becomes too late. We still have to bed down and aren't sure of what is ahead of us. By the way, how long does it take to get to West Berkshire?"

The father replied, "Oh, say, thirty minutes."

The group then walked their horses over the bridge, calmly got back onto their saddles and rode north slowly through the town.

The following group of McGrorty, Moore, Doty, and Huntley watched until the father left the bridge and went home. Then they broke out of the bushes and walked their horses to the bridge.

"Good evening, son," called Huntley, the oldest of the group in a fatherly sort of a way. "You must be getting hungry, sitting out here in the chilly October night. Have you seen my friends who have passed through town recently?"

"You mean Doc Rumsey? They're just ahead! They came by just a few minutes ago. It shouldn't take you too much time to catch up."

Bill didn't ask any questions and the men proceeded. No one in town noticed. They were all settling back to their evening meals, so McGrorty's section quietly passed through town and headed north.

The road to West Berkshire was hillier than the road along the Missisquoi River, and Bennett Young's horses were tiring again. It had been a long push. Every time they went over one rise there was always another. It was slow going. Eventually Young asked a farmer, who was just returning from his barn with a lantern, how long it would take to get to West Berkshire.

The farmer replied, "Oh, thirty minutes or so."

That frustrated Bennett. Is that all they can say around here? he asked himself.

Finally the lights of the village could be seen up ahead through the trees. It was only a few minutes before they came to the village. West Berkshire was a hamlet at the corner of two local roads. As they arrived, a horseman approached with a shotgun and aimed it straight at them. "This way," he said quietly.

Young thought that they were dead. Finally, he didn't object and motioned for everyone to follow. "What can we do for you, sir?" Young asked the rider nervously.

Before the rider answered, they found themselves behind a barn. Facing them, on horseback, were several men with shotguns.

"Where's the tobacco?" a voice whispered out of the darkness.

"The what?" answered Young in amazement.

"You heard me," the voice answered.

Then there was complete silence by everyone.

"Jake, I think we have the wrong men and the wrong goods! Who are you gentlemen, anyway? Where are you going?"

Young didn't know what to say, he was tired of the Reverend Clyde story. He finally said, "We mean you no harm, sir. We're just passing through. We don't have anything to sell to anyone. I won't ask you who you are, sir, and don't you ask me who we are," Young smiled.

"Then you better get going. We're waiting for some riders that are coming up from Boston. They have a consignment of certain goods for us."

"How long will it take to get to Frelighsburg?" asked Young.

The voice laughed, "Oh about thirty minutes on the low road. The other night a rider came through and asked, "Which way to West Berkshire? I replied, don't ya move a damned inch! Ha, ha. I nearly said, you can't get there from here. Ha, ha."

Rumsey stared at the shadow of this man roaring with laughter and turned to Young and whispered, "Is he crazy or something?" Nothing more was said.

The Rebels continued on their way, while the shadow continued laughing. After Young recovered from the insanity of the stranger, he remembered that they had to stay on the West Berkshire Road and stay left of the Pike River that flowed to Frelighsburg. The Pinnacle had been north of them. Now in the evening moonlight they could just make out its silhouette to their right.

This meant that they were crossing the border! As soon as Young was sure that the Pinnacle was fully on their right, he cried, "Men, we've made it, we're in Canada. The posse can't touch us!"

Former location of Windsor Hotel, Frelighsburg, Quebec

Windsor Hotel, circa 1905

"Freedom at last! On to Frelighsburg, cider, supper and sleep!" cried out Squire Teavis to the others.

Eventually, they made it to the village and the tavern. They hitched their horses to the rail at the hotel and took a deep breath.

It was now close to 9.00 p.m. They had been riding hard for five hours and cider and food were available from the tavern, so the men relaxed. Not Sam Gregg, however. He kept riding slowly through the village. The rest were making enough noise to distract anyone from noticing him as he quietly, almost nonchalantly, crossed the Pike River and turned up the long hill south out of town. He was just a shadow that disappeared.

It wasn't long before the town knew that they had visitors. The local bailiff, George A. Wells of Frelighsburg approached the gathering and asked the group, "Who is your leader?" After being directed to Bennett Young, he approached him.

"Good evening sir." stated Mr. Wells. "Just passing through?"

"Yes," replied Young. "I'm the Reverend Clement Christian Clyde. We're on our way to the train at Waterloo. How long is it to ride there?"

All of a sudden Young looked wild-eyed, pulled out his revolver and cried, "If you tell me thirty minutes, I'll shoot you dead!" Fatigue was taking over and he was beginning to lose it. Charles Swager, through impulse, pulled his revolver out as well.

Bailiff Wells realized that these men were certainly not religious men. He had received a wire that the Canadian Militia was sending a company of soldiers down to Frelighsburg from Montreal to apprehend the Rebels ... these men! We'll see how well they perform, Wells said to himself. So he decided to arrest them all.

Young was incensed and quickly changed their story.

"You can't do that, we are really soldiers of the Fifth Confederate State Retributors on a military mission for the Southern Confederacy. Canada East is neutral, and you know it! You simply cannot arrest us!"

Wells replied calmly, "Well, we'll just see about that. Robbing banks is frowned upon in Canada East just as much as it is in the United States and I assume in your Southern Confederacy. The Canadian Militia will be here shortly."

A rumble could be heard coming from down the road by the Pike River. All eyes in front of the tavern turned to look. The St. Albans posse was arriving. Captain George P. Conger rode up to Bailiff Wells and announced for the whole street to hear, "We represent the citizens of St. Albans, the stables and the banks of the town. We want these men. By orders from our government, we are here to take them back to St. Albans and to allow justice to be served."

Frelighsburg Main Street today

Conger then looked at Wells and said in a more friendly way, "We knew we couldn't capture the Rebels quickly because they were spread all over the Missisquoi Valley. I figured our best approach was to go straight to the border via the shortest route. We took the Richford Plank Road to South Franklin on the Missisquoi River, turned due north to East Franklin, along the Pike River and here we are. We want these men and our horses."

Conger and Wells stared at each other, both with hands on their holsters. Wells said, "Captain Conger, this is Canada East. We are neutral, but we have the right to manage our affairs in our own way. That means that if my government wants me to arrest someone, I will do my best to do just that! The Canadian Militia will be here shortly to take these men to St. Johns. You had better be careful or you could have a major diplomatic incident on your hands. Think very carefully."

Wells continued, "I can appreciate your feelings after what happened in St. Albans, the loss of the money, stealing the horses and the shooting of innocent people. Co-operate and you can still get what you want. The horses can be returned to you in St. Johns. We need them to get the prisoners to the jail at the fort. As for the stolen money and the men, the due process of law will look after that. Co-operate or you could lose everything."

Just then Capt. Conger saw Ben. He shouted, "What's Master Potter doing here?"

Young started to mumble.

Then Conger exploded, "Why you criminal, you took Ben Potter for a hostage! I'll have your neck for this." Conger continued to rage.

Wells turned to him and tried to calm him down. "Don't worry. When the militia arrives, I'm sure they will deal with Master Potter. These Rebels will have a lot to answer for, I can tell you!"

Ben stood there speechless with his blue eyes popping.

While Conger and Wells argued, they could hear the militia coming down into the village. Bennett Young was getting nervous, so he turned, jumped on his horse and tried to escape up the hill to the southeast of the village. Bailiff Wells took all the Rebels to his home in the town and told them to stay put until he returned. The posse would see to that. He then jumped on his horse and took off towards Saint Armand Center after Young. The St. Albans posse could only stand and watch. It didn't take Wells long to catch up with Young. His horse looked exhausted, because it had never been given water in Frelighsburg. The long hill above Frelighsburg was Young's undoing.

By the time they returned, the Canadian Militia led by Captain Newcome was arguing with Captain Conger nose to nose. Wells thought that he had settled everything. Now both sides were firing shots at each other, but everyone's guns were jamming. The posse had not had time to clean the bores of their pistols of the black powder residue left from the constant firing from the battle in St. Albans. The Militia had never fired their guns in action before and had never been told to clean them! It's difficult to be challenging when nothing works.

Captain Newcome said to the posse, "You can have your horses when we get to St. Johns. There are only seven here. How many are missing?"

Ed Fuller stood up and shouted, "Twenty-two by last count."

Conger cried, "I guess 22's a good clue of how many there are!"

While Conger complained loudly about the Master Potter innocence, he had never seen Rumsey before. Captain Newcome was in no mood to negotiate anyone's release. He replied, "I don't care if he is a minor, he and Rumsey will be processed with all the others. Only the courts can decide their fate."

Two Abenaki Indian scouts had ridden to the edge of town when they heard the gunshots. They didn't interfere, they just watched. Then later, they faded back into the woodland and returned up the hill towards Abbott's Corners.

Total Captured so far

Stanbridge East	4
West Farnham	1
Frelighsburg	<u>6</u>
Total	11

Including Rumsey and Ben

Granpappy McGrorty, Jim Doty, Bill Moore, and Bill Huntley were an older group than the others. They didn't talk at all. They just trotted through to West Berkshire.

No one said a word. On entering West Berkshire they were stopped by the same shadow as the first group.

"You aren't from Boston by some chance?"

"No" said McGrorty, "we are not."

"Dammit! Then you must be with the Rebels here before you."

"How the hell did you know that?"

"A posse came this way then headed north for Frelighsburg."

Joe didn't say anything.

"Have a good trip. By the way, I wouldn't go by the low valley road along the Pike River. You might want to avoid Frelighsburg at the moment. Why don't you take the high road? Take the Potato Hill Road north. It joins the old Boston Post Road from Skunk Hollow. Keep straight ahead to the border."

"Why are you helping us?" asked McGrorty.

"We don't want any trouble."

"Right now our only concern is what the hell happened to our tobacco shipment. You can't do much …uh … business when there are posses about."

The trip north was uneventful but tiring for the horses. They took the high road and eventually noticed the pylon announcing the border declared by the Treaty of Washington in 1842. From there they could just see the Pinnacle rising like a giant shadow in the moonlight to the east. Just then a tall scrawny man with bleary eyes, long gray unkempt hair, very poor clothes and an old pair of britches, jumped out from the bushes beside the road and aimed an old smooth bore rifle at them.

"Who are you and what do you want? This is Canada, eh?"

Joe replied quietly, "We just want to pass, we're on our way to Abbott's Corners and Dunham."

"Well, tradesmen's entrance is at the back on Tuesdays! Ha, Ha, Ha, Ha," roared the apparition. "I'm the official greeter to Canada, ya might say."

They just stared at him and asked his name.

"Folks hereabouts call me Muir. Mad Muir! They say I'm always mad at something. Why not stay for a smoke or a chaw on some good genuine plug tobacco."

Teavis frowned and said, "What kind of tobacco is that?"

Muir laughed and cried, "Why, this is a good Virginia blend, born in Virginia and married in White River Junction!"

With Mad Muir in hysterics, the Rebels turned and didn't look back. They just shook their heads, proceeded up the Post Road and took the turn to the village. The land was beginning to level out onto the St. Lawrence River Valley. When they reached Dunham, the four of them broke up into pairs so as not to attract attention. Yet the bailiffs were watching the street and spotted them coming down the long hill into town. They thought they were free. Joe and Jim went straight to a tavern, and were arrested within a few minutes. Bill Moor and Bill Huntley went through town and didn't look around. No one noticed them.

Moor and Huntley continued their travels due north past West Shefford and then east to the train station in Waterloo. Both bought tickets and boarded the 10.30 p.m. train to Montreal. Behold! Sleeping on a bench was Sam Gregg. They didn't waken him. Charlie sat beside him wide-awake. Bill Huntley sat opposite them and fell sound asleep.

Dunham, the former Seeley Hotel

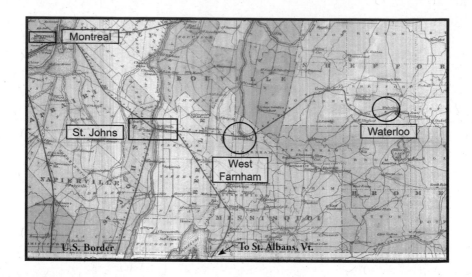

(Smith & Company, 1867.) The Stanstead, Shefford & Granby RR. The track to Magog and Sherbrooke had not been completed in 1867. Note the West Farnham and Waterloo stations, where many of the Rebels were captured and sent to the British fort in St Johns, Quebec, enroute to trial in Montreal, Quebec, to the northwest.

1845 residence, Dunham, Qubec

10

WILL TEAVIS'S RUN

North Enosburg, October 19, 1864

There were six remaining: Will Teavis, Dan Butterworth, John Moss, Louis Singleton Price, Homer Collins, and John McInnis. Teavis was in charge of the group. Dan Butterworth was a quiet man. John Moss didn't say much and little was known about him. Louis Price had style. He dressed well, sat very straight in his horse and looked like General Longstreet. Homer Collins was very impressed with Price and followed closely behind him wherever he went. John McInnis was from Alabama, a seasoned soldier and prisoner. He was not comfortable with these men but got along with them in order to survive.

Watching the other groups leaving for Enosburg Falls left these men with a slightly empty feeling in their stomachs. With 20 men there was a certain feeling of security. Now there were only six of them. There was coldness among this little group that never left them. They all wanted to be left alone to survive.

Young's instructions were to have them turn north on the Boston Post Road and avoid Enosburg Falls and Frelighsburg altogether. By this means they could enter Canada by staying on the high ground and keeping out of sight.

There was no reason to bury their metal too soon because they weren't going through any major towns. Above all, he told them to remember where they put the coins, so that it wouldn't be too hard to identify the location when they returned. The run to West Enosburg went without a mishap. The village of West Enosburg was quiet. It was mostly farms. Later they turned on to the Tyler Branch Road that followed a narrow and winding creek. Their progress was slowed because the branches of the bushes and trees that kept hitting their faces. In the darkness they had to reduce their travelling to a walk.

Finally after the struggle along the Tyler Branch, they arrived at Enosburg Center. The village wasn't much larger than either West Enosburg or East Enosburg. Yet this village was different. Many of their sons were away in the Civil War and the parents had strong feelings about Rebels. Will Teavis whispered to his men, "Let me do the talking." They walked their horses into the town just as a whoop went up from the town people. They were cheering. Will asked a lady who was watching the proceedings, Madame, what is this festive occasion? I don't recall October 19th meaning much on the Methodist calendar."

The lady replied, "Of course not. It has nothing to do with church but everything to do with the Civil War. We just received a telegram that General Phil Sheridan has defeated Jubal Early and taken the Shenandoah Valley out of the War. This is the big swing in events that we have been hoping for. The Confederacy can't win without the Shenandoah."

Teavis and his men just stood there. Will turned to them and with blazing eyes whispered, "Don't say a word!"

The lady continued, "We have the biggest flag in the State. When the Union is being defeated, we lower the flag to half-mast for the lost soldiers, but when the Union wins, we raise the flag to its full height for the victors. See there it goes up and up. If we had a cannon, we would sound it too." No one invited them to dinner because they were too busy celebrating.

Will motioned his men to turn north on the Boston Post Road that went straight through the village. Not a word was said. They had called their regiment The 'Retributors' to avenge Sheridan's scorching and killing in the Shenandoah. They couldn't believe that anyone would celebrate Sheridan for what he had done

The Rebels were shocked. This was the first time that they had seen such a display against their own cause.

The hills had eased up and the road was clear as the approached the Missisquoi River Bridge at North Enosburg. They didn't talk to anyone. They just kept on going straight up the Post Road. Eventually they arrived in Berkshire, a more active town than they had expected. Being on the Boston Post Road meant that hotels and services were available. No one said anything. They didn't look one way or the other. They just kept going north.

On the Missiquoi River east of Enosburg Falls, Vermont

The Boston Post Road eventually swung west and followed Skunk Hollow Road. Skunk Hollow went over the hills to Potato Hill Road that led to the border. It was getting late and after the supper hour.

Will was having some trouble with his men. They wanted to stop. He insisted, "Wait until we get to Canada. We are so close now. As soon as we get across we'll look for lodging. It won't be a tavern, the way we are going, but a good farm will have straw and food."

After being on Potato Hill Road for a while they passed the border pylon and knew that they were in Canada. What a relief. They had made it. They still knew nothing about the posse in the United States or the Canadian Militia in Canada. If they had listened carefully at the border, they might have heard the gunshots in Frelighsburg. In their case, ignorance was bliss.

Off to their right was the Pinnacle. Just below the south slope was the light from a farm that was on a road that led to Abercorn just above the Canadian border near Richford, Vermont.

The Rebels could have seen each other as they escaped to the border. But the day was late and dark. Young took 108, McGrorty took Potato Hill and Teavis chose the Post Road and Skunk Hollow.

Off to their right was the Pinnacle. Just below the south slope was the light from a farm that was on a road that led to Abercorn just above the Canadian border near Richford, Vermont.

The men never said a word. They just pointed their horses along the road to the east and arrived at this farm within a few minutes. They could hardly wait to talk to the farmer about a meal and a little straw. It was an interesting place. None of the Rebels had seen a 'widow's walk' since they had left the fancy homes of Louisville behind many months ago. A gazebo on a roof was not so common in Vermont or Canada, but this gazebo on a clear day overlooked a panoramic view of beautiful mountains from the Green Mountains in Vermont to the Adirondacks in New York. The farm was rumoured to have been active in the Underground Railway with Franklin, Vermont, according to a local resident. (3)

Farm on Richford Road near Abbott's Corners, Quebec

View of the Vermont border from the farm

In the morning they could check to see if a posse was coming after them from there. Jeremiah Flint ran this farm with his family. Being just off the Boston Post high road and nowhere near the Pike River low road, the Flints seldom had visitors. Yet the farm looked unusually active to the Rebels. Before Jeremiah came out to greet the Rebels, a young black boy came running around the corner and nearly ran into them. When he stopped, he took one look at them, listened to their dialect and ran for Mister Flint as fast as he could. Something happened on the farm after that. People disappeared and Flint came out with a shotgun. The Rebels knew something was up.

Will Teavis was the first to speak. "Good evening sir. We have been traveling all day and are anxious to find food and rest."

Jeremiah Flint was nervous. You could tell he didn't want them around. "You're free to stay in our barn for the evening. There should be enough straw. I think Mrs. Flint can put up some food for you, but I'll have to serve it to you in the barn."

Road sign leading from the US border

They all agreed and Flint returned to the farmhouse. No one could be seen now in or around the house. The only light was in the kitchen. The men didn't argue. They all went straight to the barn. Moss and McInnis were fast asleep by the time Flint arrived with a lamb stew.

Teavis couldn't resist asking Flint, "Who was the young boy that I saw earlier?"

Flint's eyes flamed and he looked closely at Teavis and said, "I'm not asking who you are, so don't you ask who I am or what that little boy is doing here on the farm. I take it you're from the South?"

Will replied after some thought, "Yes."

Flint looked at him again. He raised his gun and said, "And so is that little black boy! I take it you'll be gone in the morning?"

Will just stood there and stared at Flint. Finally he recovered and asked the best way to get to the trains at Waterloo.

Flint replied, "Take the road here to Abbott's Corners. Then keep to the high roads to Dunham." Flint paused then said, "By the way, keep away from the Abenaki Indians. Some of the land on the Pinnacle is sacred land for their religious ceremonies. They even have stone circles that you never walk over. You never know what the Abenakis will do to you, if they get mad."

Will muttered, "Who, pray tell, are Abenakis?"

Flint looked at Will for a few moments, then said, "The Abenaki are Indians who have been living along the Missisquoi River for thousands of years. They call the Missisquoi River, the Crooked River, because it winds back and forth between Canada and the United States. They often travel this way for hunting and religious burials and sacred rites."

Flint changed the subject. "Did you meet anyone at the border?

Will said he didn't.

"Not even an odd duck by the name of Muir, Ethan Muir?"

"No," said Will.

"You should've," said Flint. "He works for me from time to time."

Teavis and his men went to sleep that night still not knowing what had happened to everyone else. They still felt that they were in neutral country.

Jeremiah had just awoken the next morning, when his wife told him she had heard from a neighbour who had been doing some early shopping in Frelighsburg that there had been trouble at the tavern last night. The militia had arrested a whole platoon of Confederate Rebels. They were on the hunt for more as well.

Oh, oh, muttered Jeremiah to himself. Might just have some in the barn. Better get them on their way. Don't want anymore trouble. So he went out to the barn to talk to his guests. He told them about the arrest of the Rebels in Frelighsburg and suggested that they leave quickly.

Teavis met with his men and discussed the silver and gold. They decided to leave and bury their coins as soon as possible. Price, Moss and Butterworth were getting fed up. "When will we ever be back this way? What's in it for us? We're not a bunch of pirates with sunken treasure. Why should we risk our lives for this stuff and have no compensation for what we did?"

When Will Teavis started his reply, he could see an expression in their eyes that he hadn't seen since St. Albans. Dan Butterworth and Louis Price reached for their revolvers but just left their hands on the holsters. They stared intently at Teavis and didn't blink. Nothing more was said until they found themselves approaching Abbott's Corners. On their right was a new red brick Baptist church. Behind the church was a field running up to the first rise of the Pinnacle, called Paradise Hill.

Louis Price was in a bad mood. "I'll be damned if I'll give up these Moroccan satchels that the Mission had given to me. These satchels are valuable and needed for our long trip back south. Don't you dare ask me for my satchel."

Teavis looked around and when no one was looking, he went quickly into the church. He found the church collection box and stole it. Will came out of the church and announced that this box was the answer for their treasure. They would use the box for burying their coins. Moss and Butterworth pressed the issue of how many coins would go in the box. This time they, too, pulled their revolvers out and stared at Teavis. Will started to sweat. He knew the character of these men and knew that they were capable of anything. Will put down the box and started to talk.

"Look, let's be reasonable. We knew the obligation we had made to the Confederacy. If we want their protection, we have to play it their way! Let's make a deal. Each one of us can take a fistful each of silver and gold. That should be enough to help us get back to Richmond."

Old Baptist Church, Abbott's Corner, Quebec

After a few moments they all looked at each other and agreed.

They put their guns away. Each one emptied their satchels into the collection box and then returned for a fistful of silver and gold that was put back into their satchels along with their greenbacks and clothing. They seemed satisfied. The procession then departed up Paradise Hill. Bill Teavis and John McInnis carried the box up the hill followed by Price, Collins, Moss, and Dan Butterworth in what looked like a funeral procession. When they reached the first maple wood on the knoll they stopped and prepared to bury the box. The job was done in about 30 minutes. They returned the way they had come, mounted their horses and talked about where to go from here.

Teavis said, "The further north and east we go the further away from any trouble we will get. I guess Montreal is out of the question. So it looks like Quebec City, Halifax and then Virginia. If we can get to Sherbrooke, on the east side of the Green Mountains, hopefully no one will be expecting us there. The rail line runs from Portland, Maine, through Sherbrooke to Richmond, Quebec, and branches there to Montreal in the west and Levis across from Quebec City on the St. Lawrence River in the east. If we get to Quebec City we can wait until a ship can take us to Halifax or Portland … or maybe even the Chesapeake Bay! Once we make it, we can work our way up the James River to Richmond. The first part of our trip is to move east across the Pinnacle to the town of Sutton rather than north to Dunham and West Shefford. Then we take the valleys that lead north to Knowlton, Brome Lake and Waterloo. If we can get to Waterloo unnoticed we have a good chance of taking a trail over Mt. Orford, then down to Magog at the outlet of Lake Memphremagog and finally down the Magog River east to Sherbrooke. We should be able to do this trip in about two days."

They had thought that once they crossed the border they would be home free. Slowly they were beginning to realize what they had gotten themselves into when they joined Bennett Young.

They moved north out of Abbott's Corners and took the first road east that they were told would take them between the northern slope of the Pinnacle and the southern slope of Le Petit Pinnacle east to the Sutton River valley. This was pristine wooded country with few or no farms.

The two Indian scouts had ridden back to their families who were camping temporarily on the slopes of the Pinnacle. They had reported all the activity that they had seen the night before to their chief. After a meeting with their father it was decided to apprehend any more Rebels who might come this way. They would send six good sons from their families to look for them. Killing was out of the question. The strategy was to take whatever wealth they could steal, take the Rebel's horses, and then leave them alone. Many of the sons were quite opposed to being so lenient.

"Why not kill them and take their money and horses right there?"

The two fathers looked on, smiling and shaking their heads. The bigger picture meant picking favours wherever they could from the white people. Don't cause any trouble! Their battle had been a long one in getting acceptance for their tribe. Locally, they needed to barter with the stores for food and clothing. The sons finally agreed and put their plan into action.

When they returned to the road above Abbott's Corners in the morning, they saw six more Rebels on horseback galloping up the road as they had expected. They moved into the woods and prepared to follow and attack them when the moment was to their advantage. The group turned east between the Pinnacle and Petit Pinnacle. Once the road left the fields behind and entered the deep woods surrounding the Pinnacle, the Indians attacked.

Louis Price was very proud of his Confederate hat, even though no one else seemed to notice. However, there was one Indian who noticed it. He lifted his smooth bore rifle and shot the hat off Price's head. Louis nearly passed out. With that done, the Indians came out onto the road and stopped the Rebels. Both parties just sat there looking at each other. No one wanted to speak first.

Finally the oldest Indian said in stumbling English, "Welcome to the Pinnacle. This is our sacred land and you are being asked to leave."

Will Teavis, blustered, "This is part of Canada East! You can't ask us to do any such thing."

The Indian replied, "Oh, yes, we can."

All six Indians raised their rifles and quietly began to load them. When they were ready they pointed them all at Will and prepared to fire. That their fathers prohibited any murder was not mentioned.

"Since you will not leave," the Indian commented, "my brothers will tie you all up and take you to Frelighsburg. I suspect that some people are looking for you there. Before we do, would you please empty your satchels?" The Rebels did as they were told, the robbery was complete and all their greenbacks and coins were on the ground. While the Indians were gathering up this prize, Will started to weigh their chances for success and escape. They had just been stripped and were now being sent to the Militia. After all this time they had failed. The time had come to negotiate for his life! Will Teavis talked over the situation with his men.

"Maybe you were right about the treasure. Would we ever get back to retrieve it? It looks like the only thing we can do would be to make a deal for our freedom." The others agreed quickly and told Will to do whatever he could. Will turned to the Indians and started to talk.

"If you tie us up and take us down to Frelighsburg, you could be missing the biggest opportunity of your life. See those coins that you are fingering? How would you like so many of them that your hands could not hold them all? We could arrange to give you a full chest of silver and gold coins. See our horses? They are stolen. Take them to Frelighsburg and the Militia will return them to their rightful owners in St. Albans. Where would you be? I'd like to suggest another approach, which would help us both. If you were to take us towards Sherbrooke and dress us up like Indians for the trip, we will give you our horses and a map of where the silver and gold has been buried. We'll need to keep some of our cash to pay for our trip home to Richmond. On the other hand, you could keep the buried coins. After all, we need to travel to Virginia, which is a long, long way from here. Don't be too greedy! You could get so much more otherwise."

Will looked at the oldest Indian. The Indian looked at the others and promptly disappeared into the woods. The Rebels were told to remain where they were. Their leader was going to consult with his father. About 30 minutes later he was back with his father, who was introduced to them all. He couldn't speak English so had to depend on his son for communication. Will was asked to repeat his offer, which was translated for the father. The Indians then had a meeting and the oldest son appeared to speak on their behalf.

"You have made some good points. But how do we know that you have this treasure hidden nearby?" demanded the Indian.

Will shrugged his shoulders and said, "You have my word. I can only swear to my God that the treasure is where we will say it is. It should be worth the gamble. I'll draw you a map. Besides, you'll get the horses as part of our deal with you."

The father agreed and accepted their promise. The Rebels were then led into the woods and over a number of hills before they arrived in a hidden glen of cedars that was the temporary village of the Abenaki.

The oldest son's opinion was valued highly. He had learned some English from the streets of Swanton and was slowly becoming the decision maker for the fathers of the tribe. The squaws were consulted. With much giggling they quickly prepared the dyes for makeup that was made from natural seeds and leaves. They cut and sewed the outfits from their own clothing. By evening they had Abenaki clothing of headbands, leggings, vests, and gloves for each of the Rebels. All six members had beards and long hair, well down below their ears and flowing Victorian mustaches. All this had to change if they wanted to look like Abenaki. Two razors were discovered amongst the Rebels clothing. Louis Price became the barber and cut their mustaches and cleaned their faces of all beards. Eventually, the shaving was completed and their hair combed from the middle and made into braids. The squaws were laughing at the transformation.

Homer Collins urged them to stop. "The laughing may be heard down in Frelighsburg. We're still within earshot, you know. We have two problems that the Indians can't solve. One, the height of John McInnis and myself, both over six feet. We should stay in our saddles and never walk whenever we are in public view. The Abenaki are much shorter."

Then there was their Dixie accent. "Don't talk too much to anyone. Make only brief answers or comments. Never ask a question. It only starts a conversation. Indians are hesitant to talk to white men."

The Rebels were offered an evening meal and straw for sleeping. The next morning the Rebels were feeling a bit more confident. The chief's son asked Will about their plans. Teavis told him that their intentions had been to go overland to the Sutton River, north to Brome and then to Waterloo.

The son pondered this approach. He looked at Teavis closely and said "I hear there are soldiers in Waterloo looking for people. I hear there are soldiers in Montreal looking for people. I suspect that you should take a more southerly path to the east that is further away from these soldiers."

Will was astounded. "What do you mean?"

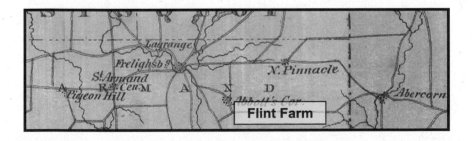

**Teavis's escape: North Pinnacle Road
east to the Sutton River, Quebec**

"If you stay on the west side of the Big Mountains, Yankees call them the Green Mountains, soldiers are looking for people there. Go to the east side of the Big Mountains. Soldiers are not looking there. So take this road east to Sutton River, then turn north to Brome, then take Stage Coach Road east. This road will go through Bolton Pass to Knowlton Landing and the Great Pond Place. In Abenaki we call the place, Lake Memphremagog. At the landing take the ferry to Magog and the stage coach down Magog River to Sherbrooke and the railway."

Teavis looked nervous. "Wouldn't passengers want to talk to us? What about the stage coach?"

The son said, "White men do not talk to Indians. The weather is getting colder and the ferry season will be over soon. Few white men will be taking trips on the ferry. Don't worry. No one will talk to you. We will take you to the ferry and will take your horses. Then you will give us your map." The chief listened and nodded. Will was in the middle of serious negotiations and losing. What could he do? At least they would be protected to the lake. The chief had spoken. This was his deal!

Teavis talked to his men, all who were scared. They had no other idea and didn't know what to do. Dan Butterworth spoke for the group. "Dressing up as Indians, with Collins and McInnis, riding on ferries and stage coaches and passing through a busy town are the furthest things from our minds. We will never make it. We should give up!"

Louis Singleton said, "But could we? Would the Indians let us go?"

In the end the Rebels had to accept. It was crazy. The odds of surviving were remote. Will turned to the chief and quietly nodded. The chief nodded back, it was done!

The chief's son then smiled and told Will, "This meeting is timely. We have been travelling from Swanton to hunt and find spiritual salvation for the next and most important leg of our trip. The Pinnacle is our favorite hunting ground, but up the Crooked River near the western shore of the Great Pond Place is a mountain that we use for our sacred rites. My family is on their way there to make me their new tribal leader. You know, we've hunted and fished in and around Great Pond Place for our existence for many years. After the death of our greatest chief, whose name was Owl, we decided to commemorate his existence and allow his spirit to live forever on the top of this mountain beside the lake.

We believe the mountain's outline resembles our great chief's profile. We have named the mountain, Owl's Head."

He smiled again and whispered to Will, "How would you like to sit in a dark and damp cave for three days alone without food or water?

Stagecoach Road historical marker, Brome Corners, Quebec

This is the ultimate part of the initiation that I must survive in order to be crowned the tribe's chief on the top of Owl's Head. Because the mountain is only a few miles south of Knowlton's Landing, it's convenient for us to take you there. My father and I with our braves will take you by the white men's roads. Our family will continue along the time-worn path beside the Crooked River. That way there are no mountains for them to cross and it leads straight to Owl's Head."

Will cried, "That sounds perfect. The river is the obvious way to escape. No soldiers at all. Why can't we all go that way?"

The son looked closely at Will and said quietly, "My family are very nervous about having you with us. We agreed amongst ourselves that we would look after you but let the family proceed. Life is hard enough for us without your war getting in the way. They will go on alone. We will meet them later at Owl's Head."

Will knew that he couldn't argue the point. There was silence.

Then the chief, with a twinkle in his eye, leaned closer to his son and whispered, "Remember to caution them about the Anaconda, the largest sea serpent ever found in Great Pond Place. It could upset the ferry. Hope they can all swim."

Will listened to the translation, "You can't be serious?"

The chief and his son nodded knowingly. But the chief's twinkle never left him. The squaws were ready to apply the make up. Herbs had been boiling all night and the thickened syrup was ready to be applied. While their faces and necks were covered, the same syrup was added to their hair. Because the Rebel's hair colour was fairly dark, the transition looked reasonably natural. Their hands were hidden by beautiful doeskin gloves, heavily decorated with colourful sky blue, turquoise and cherry red beadwork, a gift from the squaws. While the vests and leggings were from the elders, the Rebels could use their own shirts.

The party left about mid-morning heading east over the northern slope of the Pinnacle on North Pinnacle Road and down to the Sutton River above Abercorn. Then they turned north along the Sutton River to Brome Corners.

At the Village of Brome Corners, they turned east on the Stage Coach Road for the Great Pond Place. After they had travelled a short distance, they noticed a number of riders behind them.

One of the braves told them all not to talk. He claimed that they were militia from Montreal. Oddly the strangers kept their distance.

While they made Bolton Pass that night, they could not stay in the Exchange House at the Pass. Being Indians, they had to eat and sleep off the land. Tonight, there would be no tavern mattress, cider or pork pie. Meanwhile, the militia stayed their distance, but stopped at the Exchange house for the night. One of the braves watched them come and go on to the Inn. They never saw him standing behind some trees beside the road.

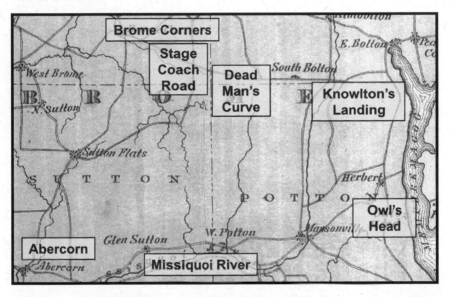

Teavis' run up the Sutton River north to Brome Corners and then east to Lake Memphremagog on Stage Coach Road. Compare their trip to the Abenaki who took the Missisquoi River to Owls Head along the border.

By now McInnis and Collins were becoming hysterical and wanted to be Indians no longer. Will Teavis had been successful in seeing that the others kept their cool, but these two were different. They were the youngest.

Towards morning, McInnis and Collins quietly took off their Indian accessories, mounted their horses and calmly walked out onto Stage Coach Road and down past the Exchange House where the militia were sleeping.

The old Indian chief slowly opened his eyes and watched them go. They would have been problems anyway, he thought to himself.

The Militia had been watching the Indians most of the night and their patience paid off. They were sure that the two were Rebels, but figured that the others would all be real Indians. "No need to get too close to the them," the Sergeant whispered to his men. No one liked to argue with the Abenaki. So after saddling their horses, they went down the road after the two white men.

As Collins and McInnis were climbing the road up the side of Mount Pevee they could look back and see the militia near South Bolton. Unfortunately the militia could see them as well. So waiting for the ferry was out of the question. They would have to continue on to Magog in the hopes of finding a place to hide.

At Lake Memphremagog, McInnis and Collins turned north through Austin hoping to make Magog before dark. However, not long after the turn north, Homer Collin's horse started to limp. The shoe had come off the horse's right front foot. Collins panicked and had no choice but to walk his horse. Local people offered to help, stating that "Matthew Baird's Blacksmith Shop is just a hen's race up the road."

The militia was not far behind. They had forgotten about the Indians, leaving the way clear for Will Teavis, Moss, Price, and Butterworth to take the ferry without being either shot or arrested.

Pretty soon the two Rebels saw the smoke rising from Matthew Baird's shop. Mr. Baird didn't stop forging. He looked up and studied them carefully. "You're strangers."

Homer Collins tried to introduce himself and stumbled badly. Finally, he was so nervous that he said, "Sir, we are members of the Confederate Army and are trying to escape trouble from the Canadian Militia. Sir, we mean absolutely no harm. In fact, raiding the way we have has got to stop. That's one of the reasons why John McInnis here and I have selected Canada East to settle down. We hear that you are neutral in the Civil War."

"That's true enough. What can I do for you?" Matthew Baird was old United Empire Loyalist stock and his sympathies were not with the Yankees whom he feared may some day attack up Lake Memphremagog.

Just then John McInnis who hadn't said anything cried out, "Horses with lanterns riding up the long hill. They could be the militia!"

Matthew thought to himself, These young men look innocent enough. He didn't need any posses waving their guns around his shop, and young men were hard to find these days. Many were down in the War making good money from the Vermont families that had paid them to replace their own sons, as long as they lived.

Matthew spoke out, "Quick, run over to the summer kitchen and I'll let you down into our root cellar. There is no window down there but they won't be able to see you." Leaving their horses, McInnis and Collins ran for the cellar.

The next hour was awful. There was no room to move, no light and especially no air! McInnis and Collins could only tough it out and wait for the posse to leave, but the posse had other ideas.

"Who owns these horses, Smithy?" demanded the sergeant.

Baird looked at the men calmly and quietly replied, "That sergeant, is none of your business. These horses are my business, my trade and my modest earnings. Care to help make some shoes?" He was a big man and he stood his ground, glaring at the sergeant.

The men of the Militia had been casually looking around and had decided not to cause any trouble. "We need some beds and breakfast"

Matthew needed the money. An opportunity is an opportunity, he said to himself. So the Militia bunked out in Henry's outbuilding beside the forge. They were up early, fed and gone just after sunrise.

He then walked over to the root cellar wondering in what condition he would find the two men. They stumbled out exhausted and ravenously hungry. He looked at them carefully and came to a decision.

"We need men like you on the farms here and in my smithy shop. My neighbor Timothy Turner sold his son to the war so that a Vermont family could keep their own son at home. He is living to regret the sale. Apparently, his son is badly wounded and has lost a leg. He desperately needs help on his farm. One of you could make a big difference to him. Also, I could use one of you right here. Why not ride out the War peacefully? Then when you feel confident you could get home safely enough, you could leave either directly on the ferry to Newport or take the stage and rail to Quebec City."

And so Homer Collins and John McInnis stayed at the Baird's and the Turner's, occasionally diving for the root cellar but otherwise sleeping, eating and building their strength for the trip home, which, with luck, would come in the spring.

Knowlton's Landing, October 20, 1864

The next morning William Teavis and his three Rebels walked their horses slowly and carefully to Knowlton's Landing on the west side of the Great Pond Place to wait for the ferry. The *Mountain Maid* left Newport at 7.30 a.m. and returned by 6.00 p.m. each day. There were no white men on shore. When the ferry arrived, there were no white men on the boat.

The Rebels gave the Indians their horses and map then said goodbye. Will Teavis took one last look at the Abenaki on the pier. He asked himself, Will we ever make it to the Chesapeake Bay? What a trip it's going to be. Who knows whether we will ever make it or not. He shrugged his shoulders and turned to join his men out of the wind on the lee side of the boat.

* * *

JAIL

St. Johns, October 20, 1864

There had been a garrison at Fort St-Jean on the Richelieu River since long before the British occupation in 1759. This garrison defended Canada from invasion along the easiest and fastest approach to Montreal - the Richelieu River that drains Lake Champlain into the St. Lawrence. The town of St. Johns grew, was then Saint-Jean-Iberville, and is now Saint Jean sur Richelieu. In 1864, it was St. Johns. In those days, the garrison was used mostly to house British troops whenever the need arose.

Several Militia corporals caught two prisoners, Sam Gregg and Bill Moor, on the train waiting to leave at the Waterloo station. They were arrested and told not to move an inch. On the way the train stopped at Farnham West. Moore and Gregg, were shocked when another member of the militia escorted a sad looking George Scott onto the train.

Much to the surprise of a sleepy conductor, the passenger car was filling up with prisoners and soldiers. No one dared say a word to anyone. When they all arrived at St. Johns, they were marched to the garrison. It was 1.00 a.m.

Bill Huntley, who had embarked at Waterloo with Bill Moore, looked neither left nor right and pretended to be asleep. He even asked the corporals to keep the shouting down because he was a light sleeper! Being an older-looking gentleman from Georgia, the soldiers bowed to his wishes. The soldiers were told to look for young Kentuckians in their early 20s. No one interrupted him. He slept all the way to Montreal and made it to Mr. Goodenough's Exchange House by 2.00 a.m. Mr. Goodenough was not too pleased. He was tired and nearly slammed his window shutter in Bill's face.

The motley group of Captain Newcome, the Company of Canadian Militia, the other prisoners from Stanbridge East, Dunham, and Frelighsburg, bailiffs, justices of the peace and the St. Albans posse all arrived in the early morning after spending the night riding tired horses.

All anyone wanted when they reached the gate was to get some food and sleep. Moor, Gregg and Scott were already asleep when everyone else arrived. The prisoners had to be jailed in the local militia's garrison quarters. This meant that everyone else had to camp out on the parade square or try the inns in town, but at 3.00 a.m., there was no one awake at the inns to receive them.

Considering their sworn duty as soldiers and officers of the Crown, all involved in the arrests tagged along. No one wanted to miss out on the action. The posse from St. Albans was not about to let these Rebels get away. They wanted their horses back and the return of the money and specie.

Captain Newcome wasn't thinking too clearly at 3.00 a.m, but at least he was able to determine who had arrived in St. Johns. A motley group indeed! He couldn't believe how the numbers had added up to an extraordinary large group of people.

Present in St. Johns

Militia	15	Farnham, Dunham, Waterloo, Stanbridge East and Frelighsburg
Bailiffs & Magistrates	4	Dunham, Stanbridge East and Frelighsburg
Prisoners*	13	Young, T. Collins, Bruce, Lackey, Scott, Spurr, Swager, T. Teavis, Wallace, Gregg, McGrorty, Doty and Moore
J. Rumsey & Ben Potter	2	
Posse	15	St. Albans
Total	49	
*Missing:	8	Huntley, Higbee, W. Teavis, Moss, Price, McInnis, Buttersworth, and H. Collins.

The troops all had bed rolls. Since the magistrates and bailiffs had nothing, blankets were issued to them by the garrison. The posse sat, stood and fussed all night watching the magistrates and bailiffs, the prisoners' horses and the money. Captain Conger and Ed Fuller were there 'til hell freezes over! One militia corporal blandly commented that ice was coming in a few weeks and they should look for rooms in town.

Conger just glared at him. He huffed and puffed. "...And don't think they can get away with stealing Master Potter. That is the most ridiculous thing I have ever heard. At least Ben is bedded down, while we have to wander around the parade ground all night."

When the sun came up, rather late the next morning, the garrison was adjusting and had breakfast ready for everyone, even the posse.

Captain Newcome, true to his word, let the posse have the prisoners' horses, but only the 11 available horses. These horses were only part of the 22 that the Rebels had taken from St. Albans the day before. Remaining were the four horses on hitching posts at the stations in Farnham and Waterloo, the six horses from Will Teavis' group that escaped and the one from Bill Huntley, who was still wandering free around Montreal.

Fuller was determined to get the four horses at the stations. With the assistance of the magistrates, he took off on horseback for Farnham West and then Waterloo. Ed Fuller had to ride all day to pick up the four horses and return to St. Albans. No one was more tired, or had legs more chafed than Ed Fuller when he made it back that evening. It had been two days of hard riding. No sooner had he returned, than the whole town wanted to know the story. Ed did his best to explain.

Jasper Saxe said, "Don't move, I want your picture for *The Messenger*. You, sir, are a hero! Now just stand over here for a moment!"

Ed could hardly stand up let alone cope with the attention being forced upon him. "Jasper, thanks, but not now. Maybe in a day or two. I'm going home."

Captain George Conger and his men did not leave St. Johns. They had questions. How neutral is Canada East in the Civil War? The government has taken the law into its own hands, but the Rebels were robbers! Shouldn't they be apprehended? Too many issues had to be resolved.

The Questions

Was the raid a military or criminal exercise?

Can they hold these men prisoners?

Should they be turned over to the American or to the Canadian government?

They have been arrested, but no charges have been laid on them.

What should be the charges?

What will the Canadian government do with the money and specie?

What would the government do with Rumsey and Ben?

Conger demanded answers to these questions. "Newcome, you can't just stand there and do nothing. These are serious international issues involving your government. My country, St. Albans and I want answers to them now!!"

"Captain, I understand. Believe me, I understand! But I have to hold tight and keep the men in the garrison until someone wiser than I can answer these questions."

More people started to arrive in St. Johns from St. Albans after Ed Fuller had told them where the prisoners were being held. One of the early arrivals was Lieutenant Frank Stranahan. He had been involved in forming the posse, and then stayed back to look after the governor's mansion. Mrs. Smith was losing her patience and ordered Frank to start off for St. Johns and represent St. Albans and the State of Vermont.

"Try to take possession of the prisoners, their money and specie. St. Johns isn't really that far. Take the train down Lake Champlain and along the Richelieu River."

Frank arrived on the train later that day to meet with Captain Conger, Captain Newcome and, in particular, with Bennett Young. Governor Smith had ordered Major John L. Barstow, recently retired from the 8th Vermont Regiment to represent him in St. Johns as well. "Find Stranahan and look for Bennett Young."

After Major Barstow had found Frank, he delivered the Governor's message in no uncertain terms to Young. "You don't realize what you have done to the poor citizens of St. Albans and the Missisquoi Valley. When the banks are finished so is the economy. You feel that the silver and gold is yours, do you? Do you feel that the people deserve that kind of treatment? Do you really feel that you are free to kill and wound people and dogs? You have taken their belief in God and thrown it in their faces. Do you really feel that you can manipulate religion that way? As for carting off Master Potter, never come back to St. Albans!"

Young lifted his head and replied that he wasn't impressed. "All nice talk when applied to the northern people, but it has no significance with the northern armies subjugating the south by fire, musket and sword."

Major Barstow rose to leave Young's cell, but first he looked Bennett in the eye and said, "Fie on you, sir! We demand the silver and gold. Otherwise it will go bad for you, I guarantee, Lieutenant Young."

Rumsey, Young's cellmate, whispered, "God, I hope my family doesn't hear about this."

"John, shut up! Sit. Sit! Maybe the Militia will shoot you dead. Humph, might save me the trouble" Life was not so good for Bennett Young.

St. Albans, October 20, 1864

Harold Bellows and Henry B. Sowles, presidents of the two federal banks, offered a $10,000 reward to anyone who could provide information that would lead to the capture of the robbers and the return of the money.

Mrs. Smith wrote to her husband, the governor of Vermont, describing her feelings about the raid.

"We have had to use Cousin Joe's forcible expression a 'Raid From Hell'. For about half an hour yesterday afternoon I thought that we should be burnt up and robbed. But I hope you don't imagine I was one moment frightened, though the noise of guns, the agitated looks of the rushing men and our powerless condition were startlingly enough."

Washington, October 21, 1864

Washington was very concerned about attacks from the British and sent troops, cannon and arms to St. Albans. In addition, it offered a reward of another $10,000 for each captured raider. Secretary of State William H. Seward demanded their extradition and surrender of the securities seized. The Secretary demanded the provisions of the Webster-Ashburton Treaty with Britain be respected. The property must be returned.

St. Johns, October 22, 1864

In several days, the militia had returned to Montreal, the bailiffs and magistrates to their jurisdictions, and the posse back to St. Albans. The prisoners, plus Conger, Stranahan and Barstow, were still in St. Johns.

Young declared: "Canada is neutral. The government can't keep us in prison. We plead *habeas corpus*. I demand we be accused or released."

Montreal, October 23, 1864

Governor General Charles Monck appointed Charles J. Coursol, Judge of the Court of Queen's Bench, to conduct a full investigation into the circumstances of the raid upon Vermont, the flight of the prisoners to Canada and the claims of ownership of the stolen money.

George Sanders of the Confederate Mission engaged legal counsel, J.G.K. Houghton, to represent the Confederacy at the trial. Next morning Houghton met Judge Coursol at the Bonaventure railway station, where they bought their tickets for St. Johns. It was indeed fortunate, because it gave them time on the train to discuss legal ramifications.

St. Johns, October 24, 1864

Judge Coursol and Houghton got off the train at noon and made their way to the garrison. The Judge told Houghton, a man he respected quite highly, that he was moving the trial back to Montreal where he could have the proper facilities. He was sure that Houghton would agree.

The hearing to transfer the trial began after lunch. It lasted for only a few minutes. Judge Coursol instructed the presiding bailiff to transfer the prisoners to the Montreal city jail where they would be incarcerated properly. Judge Coursol met with the other bailiffs and officially received the monies they had taken from the prisoners, which he planned to deliver to the Montreal Chief of Police in a local bank.

Collin's boys from Stanbridge East	$35,195
George Scott from Farnham	2,000
Joe McGrorty and James Doty from Dunham	13,825
Bill Moor from Waterloo	930
Total	$51,950

The entourage started off all over again, the 13 prisoners, Rumsey, Ben, the military officers, the bailiffs, Judge Coursol, Mr. Houghton, Captain Conger, Lieutenant Stranahan, and Major Barstow.

Montreal, October 24, 1864.

The prisoners were taken off at the Point St. Charles Station hoping to avoid all the crowds waiting at the Bonaventure Station.

But the word was out and crowds were everywhere. The town had not seen such an occasion since the arrival of the Prince of Wales a few years before.

Montrealers were still nervous about the American threat of invasion. When some southern Rebels from the Civil War arrived in town, sympathies were for these poor southern farmers. When these boys arrived in chains, the people on the streets were more vocal than ever. The prisoners were treated as heroes. They were led, with their entourage, in carriages along Wellington Street until they reached the center of town and then took Notre Dame Street to the market square. In 1809, Britain had erected a large monument of Lord Nelson to celebrate the great naval battle at Trafalgar. Nelson stood and looked down upon the market square of the city to the immediate south.

Across Notre Dame Street to the north lay the jail, the courts and the garrison for the British troops. The prisoners were placed in the officers' quarters of the Montreal garrison, which were equivalent to the good hotels of the city.

Payette's Hotel, October 27, 1864

Bennett Young, referred to their jail as 'Payette's Hotel', named after Louis Payette, the officer in charge. If the officer's quarters were used, it would be more appropriate for Victorian ladies and gentleman to visit the prisoners, which they did, rather than having to go into the jail. Bennett Young was in his element, holding court for all sorts of people wanting to talk to him about the raid and the War. He had never slept so well nor eaten so heartily. Being the center of attention is what drove Bennett. On the other hand, while he talked to his men at mealtimes, he normally stayed alone and continued to read his Bible, much to the consternation of his jailers.

His home life in Nicholasville, just south of Lexington, had been a struggle. The majority of Kentuckians lived on small farms with one or two slaves. His father cared only for farming, day and night. His mother cared only for feeding and raising the children.

Young learned to accept the values of other young people from Central Kentucky who believed in the Confederacy and the slave issue. This belief led to accepting the actions of war in 1861, such as looting and killing. It wasn't too long before he joined 'Morgan's Men' and experienced the most exciting time of his life. He became swept up in the thrill of raiding. Raiding and burning the towns of the midwest was a logical extension of war in Young's point of view, even raiding Union Kentucky towns.

His personal family values never caught up with his thrill of riding and raiding. No social issues would ever stand in the way of the six-gun and using religion to achieve these actions was normal, he felt. He used his Bible to deceive and influence people. After all, church services were the only diversion from farming. It was popular to be religious, he thought. Standing there with a Bible in his hand, a straight back, his chin up and wearing a broad smile, he looked like a man who would never find himself in a Canadian prison.

Young began each day after a hot breakfast, by writing letters to his father, to President Davis, to Secretary of War James A. Sedden, to Secretary of the Navy Stephen Mallory, the press of Richmond, and finally to the 'friends' that he had made in St. Albans. One morning when the weather was clearing and the sun was a little warmer, his thoughts turned to Sarah Stark, the blonde schoolteacher whom he had met in St. Albans. In another life, he would have asked her to marry him. He sent the Tremont Hotel a five-dollar St. Albans Bank banknote to settle his hotel bill. Then, as an afterthought, he apologized for leaving so suddenly and asked to be remembered to the young lady he had befriended at the hotel, Miss Sarah Stark.

At lunch, Tom Collins approached Young with a question that brought him back to reality, "Lieutenant, where are the soldiers that got away?"

The Escapees

1. Charlie Higbee and Bill Huntley, 2
2. The group that took the Boston Post Road; Will Teavis, John Moss, Louis Price, John McInnis, Dan Butterworth and Homer Lean Bean Collins, 6

Bill Huntley had been free to move about town after he had reported to Agent Sanders at the Diplomatic Mission in the St. Lawrence Hall Hotel. He moved out of Mr. Goodenough's Exchange House on St. Peter Street and moved into the St. Lawrence Hall Hotel on Great

St. James Street, all paid for by the Mission, of course! He shaved off his beard, wore spectacles, carried his loot of $10,000 in Franklin County Bank greenbacks and sported his two loaded, navy sixguns that the Mission had provided him before the raid. However, several days later, Huntley's visibility, while strutting along Great St. James Street, got him into trouble. Jasper Saxe often travelled from St. Albans to Montreal. It was convenient to take the train to pick up supplies. He never trusted the shipping for his film and development chemicals. Being a keen commercial photographer. Jasper recognized Huntley from the raid on the Franklin County Bank where he was a witness to the robbery.

* * *

MINNIE'S RUN

Green's Corners, October 27, 1864

Charlie slept, sweated, swore, drank Minnie's Green Mountain corn chowder soup, ate more of her apple pie, and slept again. Finally after a week, Charlie opened his eyes and asked where he was being hidden. He looked around and said, "Where is my holster and pistol? I must have lost it on the run up here." Charlie felt particularly vulnerable. He simply didn't have a gun anymore. How do you behave without a gun? He would have to find out! While his shoulder wounds were slow in healing, he had started to gain his appetite back and wanted to get going somewhere.

In the meantime, Minnie travelled into St. Albans, sold her soup and vegetables, bought some bread, and in particular purchased copies of the *St. Albans Messenger* daily newspaper to keep up with the current news of the Rebels. She picked up her mail and talked to everyone. The town had been turned upside down by the raid. Every town along the Missisquoi River had been affected.

The day after the raid, the troops started to arrive from Burlington. While they were a little late, their presence made the citizens feel more comfortable. The troops camped just below town.

When Charlie awoke, Minnie told him all the affairs of the town and the destiny of the Rebels who, it seemed, were all in court. What shocked Charlie were the arrests in Canada. Young had promised them that they would be protected in there. The opposite seemed to be true.

"Minnie, what should I do? If I go to Canada I'll be arrested. If I stay here they'll hunt me down and shoot me dead!"

"There must be a solution, Charlie, let me think about it."

Charlie went to sleep that night a troubled man. Minnie didn't sleep well either, not knowing what to do. One thing was clear. "The time has come, Charlie. You have to leave as soon as possible. People here know something is up! Besides, I've received a letter in response to my advertisement for a roomer." Minnie stared intently at Charlie.

The next morning, Minnie served Charlie some coffee and beans that she had made especially for her son, Charley, whom she expected to be home on leave from the Wilderness by Christmas. Charlie started to complain about the parlour cook stove. "My ma would never own one of those contraptions. You could die from the fumes. That's what she says. Don't you freeze to death in these northern winters? I can't believe you have no open hearth! How does your family gather round? There is no focus for everyone, and how do you roast chicken, or bake bread, for goodness sake?"

"I agree, that being near a cook stove, the heart builds no alters."

Wanting to change the subject, a thought came to Minnie. "Charlie," she said, "listen to this. You are old enough to be my son who is fighting you Rebels down in the Wilderness. Guess what? His name is Charley, too. What if we climbed aboard my wagon and set off for Richford? I could say that you are a friend of my son, Charley, who has been wounded in the Wilderness. You lost your family at Harpers Ferry and my son had sent you here to rest and recover. People would not be suspicious. They would sympathize. We could say that I'm helping you find a job in Richford. The town is starting to really grow these days. People would understand. It would make sense. We'd have to clean you up, shave off your beard and mustache, cut your hair to a soldier's level and get rid of your southern accent! Charlie, I've been very patient with you," Minnie stated. "You were injured and needed rest more than anything else, but now you have to smarten up.

"You have to rise up to the challenges ahead. That means you have to look, act, and above all SMELL the part of a gentleman! You can't continue looking and smelling like a robber! If that's what you want, then get out! I won't have anything more to do with you. You know what, though? I see a good man underneath all that dirt. So we, I repeat, we, have to do certain things if you want to survive. Do you realize how dirty you are? All that dirt, sweat, alcohol, tobacco, blood, horse sweat, gunpowder, and dirt again? Then, look at your clothes; vest, pants, shirt, socks, underclothes, and long johns. No change for months and with your internal problems...."

"Yeah, but what was I supposed to do with the War on everywhere?" He growled. Minnie realized that she had touched on a sore point and tried to change the subject. Charlie was standing taller and taller.

"You get in the tub and I'll wash your clothes for you. But you need new clothes, because your vest, shirt and underclothing are finished."

Charlie couldn't believe that a lady was demanding he take a bath and get his clothes washed. Internal problems indeed! Minnie doesn't understand war! So Charlie stripped, turned his back to Minnie and tried to get into the tub. There he was, stripped down to a hairy ape. Embarrassed? Yes! What a way to start over. The more he tried to get into the tub, the smaller the tub seemed to get. He just couldn't get his legs in the tub. He was too big. So he thrashed for about 30 minutes leaving soap and suds all over the floor and little on him.

Between his thrashing and swearing, Minnie left the house. "To hell with washing his back," she said to herself. When Charlie finished his bath, Minnie returned and poured out the filthy water and started boiling a new batch for his clothing. She washed and scrubbed everything. The trouble was that now it all had to dry.

Charlie stood there naked except for an old towel. All he could do was get back in bed and wait for his clothes to dry. That meant waiting until the following morning if he was lucky! In the meantime he went back to Minnie's son Charley's bed. All of a sudden Charlie felt vulnerable. His whole mindset had been violence, guns, fire, robbing, and killing. Always running away from burning houses. He was getting conditioned to this life. Now here was this woman who wanted to change him.

Not much you can do when you're standing there in the altogether, he complained to himself. Wouldn't Lieutenant Young laugh ? From the Fifth Confederate State Retributors to the Reverend Christian Clement Clyde's United Christian Circuit! All I need is a Bible. My God, could I do it ... do I want to do it?"

Charlie paused and admitted that Young had walked the streets impressing and influencing people. He radiated all sorts of images and was able to switch roles with a blink of the eye. Could I do that? he asked himself. If I could get home, the War were to cease and if peace were to come ... what would I do? Practice law? It seems so long ago that I went to law school. So much has happened since then.

Minnie had mentioned railway security as a growing item these days in railway expansion to the west. "One of the newest problems of the railways seemed to be train robbers and Indians. That is serious stuff and needs experienced people. Remember, you don't just ride the rails toting a shotgun from the roof of the caboose, you investigate and inspect people, shipments and animals," said Minnie.

Charlie knew Minnie was watching him closely. He had to make a decision. Sitting down he said, "Well, Minnie, what do I have to do?"

Charlie, we have to change your roots. Let's make your last name Higgins, Charles Higgins, Harpers Ferry, West Virginia, a Union garrison town."

"You can't be serious," he growled.

"No matter, Charles Higgins!" Minnie shouted, "it's all behind you now. You can't continue to be a Rebel, not when you are fighting for your life here in Vermont! Say you fought for the north ... and above all remember your name is Charles Higgins not Charlie Higbee."

After having Minnie nagging him for a couple of days, Charlie was growing tired of pretending. He finally sighed and grinned, "You mean I love Phil Sheridan, my general?"

"Yes," insisted Minnie. "What you do next year is your business. You are paying me $5,000 to save your life. I'm trying to do it! Right now, the border is a hot place to be, especially directly north of Highgate Springs on Lake Champlain. Both the U.S. Army and the Canadian Militia are encamped all over the border areas. Everybody was surprised and embarrassed by the raid. So, neither side, U.S. or Canada, wants to see anything like it happen again. My advice is to stay clear of the border until next spring. Winter is fast approaching. In fact all the leaves are down. Now would be an awful time to start a long trek to the south. Why don't you stay in Richford until spring?"

Charlie couldn't believe what he was thinking. Staying in Vermont for six months? After Quantrill's Irregulars and his hatred of the north, now he was thinking of settling down here. What a turn of events! While Charlie knew about the Rebel's arrests, he didn't know about the silver and gold that was buried all over the Missisquoi Valley. He finally agreed with Minnie that he should leave Greens Corners, but stay in Vermont. He should try to fade into the hillside, get a job and wait until spring. Minnie was right, the War was not going well. Especially, the fortunes of Sheridan in the Shenandoah and Sherman in Georgia made the southern position a very weak one. His side was losing! He looked up at Minnie and said, "I agree. What do we do next?"

Minnie laughed and said, "Next? Your dialect must go. Southern dialects are all drawls. You emphasize your vowels too much. You stretch out words terribly. You have to practice flattening your voice by emphasizing the consonant and reducing the emphasis on the vowels in the middle of your words. Now 'Charles', look at me. Look at my mouth!

Y'aaaaall - you   Raaaaaight - right
        Laaaaike - like   Naaise – Nice

For several hours before lunch Minnie sat in front of Charlie and made him repeat after her all sorts of words. All he would say was, "The southern drawl is so much fun. Your dialect isn't romantic at all. When I say peanut bowl, guess what I mean?" he asked with a grin.

"I have no idea … a bowl of peanuts?" posed Minnie.

"It means peanut boyell " laughed Charlie.

"A what???"

"A peanut boil … we boil green peanuts in a salty brine until they are sauwft. Then yew shucks 'em and eats 'em. Ahhhh eat 'em with sweet potato pa."

"Pa??"

"Pie!

"Your sound is no fun at awl. I really don't laaaaike it."

"Like it."

"Like it."

"You want to live or die? Shut up and start learning," stated Minnie.

"Raaaaight"

"Right"

"Right"

And so it went. Charlie worked hard at his dialect. Eventually, he sounded like a Vermont farmer, but not a happy one. Later, they looked at his clothing. Charlie tried wearing Minnie's husband, John's, clothing. Some of it fit, some didn't. Finally, he was ready to pass the test.

He could look, act and talk like a Vermonter. At least he could talk like one who had come from the northern part of the south or was it the southern part of the north? Harper's Ferry was always in the middle of the action.

'Charles' stood clean-shaven with fresh clothing talking like a neighbor. He passed, but because it was late October, he would need a coat or a cloak. Very early the next morning, before the sun had risen and the fog had lifted from the land, Charles and Minnie set out as any family would to go shopping. They had rehearsed and rehearsed how Charles would answer questions about himself and the War. He was pretty impressed with himself.

They came out onto the Plank Road and didn't look back. They were on their way to Richford. By the time they had travelled a few miles down the Plank Road to Sheldon Springs, St. Albans seemed very far away. Charles's shoulder was still taped and the pounding of the wagon hurt. Charles practiced being Charley's friend, working on his dialect and rehearsing stories of the Wilderness. How he hated being on the other side.

Before long they had passed North Sheldon, South Franklin and were entering Enosburg Falls. There didn't seem to be any way around the town, so they were forced to go straight through it.

The first order of business was to buy Charles some new clothing. Minnie gave Charles the money and they entered a gentlemen's shop to buy Charles his new clothes and underclothes. The widow was even able to use some of her new coins. No one noticed.

The folks in Enosburg were kindly folk who hadn't suffered too badly from the raid and liked to talk to strangers; "Where are you from? Where are you going? What are you doing here? When are you coming back? Have you any family in the valley?" When they heard Charles Higgins was a veteran, they really wanted to know much more than Charles was capable of telling them. He started to get nervous. When he got nervous, his accent started to return. When this happened, Minnie quickly took over the conversation. Charles was uncomfortable talking about his injuries and battles, so he tried to change the subject. Minnie helped him along, but they were terrified. The folks were none the wiser and kept offering them lunch. Charles was always willing to eat, but Minnie kept refusing and moving on.

With a name like Green, everyone wanted to know the connection to Greens Corners and the Green farm. Minnie said, "It was sheer coincidence. There is no relation. My husband and I came over the pass from White River Junction right after our son was born. We had heard about this very fertile valley outside of St. Albans near the shore of Lake Champlain. Folks said that it was good land to homestead."

People kept pressing Minnie and she was getting nervous. The more nervous she got, the more she tried to leave, the more Charles wanted to talk and the more Minnie urged her horse, old Alf, to get going. They ended up by rushing out of town with her old wagon rattling and old Alf wheezing, while the kindly folk of Enosburg Falls just stood and stared after them. The townsfolk had overwhelmed them with kindness.

The Plank Road had followed the Missisquoi River the whole way, winding its way between the hills. Very seldom were they out of sight of the 'Pinnacle', as the locals called it. They could even see the Green Mountains to the east. The harvesting had been done by then. Corn was a new industry and was grown along the valley from Sheldon Springs to East Berkshire. When they arrived in Richford it was dark, and they hadn't thought about lodgings. This would mean passing some of the Rebel's money over. This terrified Minnie. She thought that she would be discovered and arrested. She wasn't. They took a room at the Union House Inn by the falls.

Charlie cried out, "The Union House? This is too much, Minnie! Surely they have another hotel here in town? We're taking my dialect and this Higgins thing too far … Union be damned! That's as bad as Mrs. Davis, our President's family, living on Union Avenue in Montreal. This 'Union' business has got to stop."

Minnie never said a word. She led old Alf to the stable in the rear. She watered and fed him then saw to it that he was properly stalled before they went to bed. No one thought anything of a mother and a son's injured friend travelling together. Folks on the street made the odd comment. "They seem like nice people. Apparently, he is a veteran of the War and wounded. Wonder if she is related to the Greens of Greens Corners?"

* * *

THE TRIALS

Montreal, Court of Queen's Bench, November 5, 1864
The attorneys for the prisoners submitted an application for a Writ of Habeas Corpus to the Court of Queen's Bench before Judge Coursol, claiming that he had exceeded his powers of jurisdiction and ordered that he bring the Rebels to court to determine whether or not they were imprisoned lawfully and whether or not they should be released from custody. Unfortunately for the Rebels, the writ was denied and the request for release refused.

A few days later on November 7th, a warrant was received by the Montreal Court from the Justice of the Peace for Franklin County dated October 20th, to apprehend the prisoners and to deliver them to St. Albans to answer for their actions in assaulting the teller of the St. Albans Bank and for stealing money. No mention of the shooting, wounding and murdering of innocent people was made.

The submitting of evidence started in the morning. It included statements from Bennett Young. He claimed "I am a commissioned officer of the Confederacy and that whatever was done at St. Albans was done with the authority of the Confederate Government."

He went on to describe the atrocities that were conducted by Yankee officers in the land of the Shenandoah and throughout the State of Georgia. "On behalf of my fellow soldiers, I'm asking for thirty days in order to secure documentary evidence from the Confederate States."

The only problem was delivering the message through to Richmond and securing their written answer. The prisoners were ready for a long battle and felt that Richmond's assistance was the only answer to being released.

An imposing lady stood up and demanded that she be able to speak. The judge hesitated and then thought the better of it. "Yes, madame."

"My name is Mrs. Ann Eliza Brainerd Smith, wife of Governor John G. Smith of the Green Mountain State of Vermont. This dialogue today is pure hypocrisy. I have never in my life heard such meaningless statements by the court and the defense. Military action? How can you claim that St. Albans is a battlefield? We are a defenseless community living as peaceful a life as we can in light of the Civil War conflict. The Green of St. Albans is not the Wilderness where both armies are trying to destroy each other. This act was purely a criminal act by some young Kentucky boys who robbed and pillaged a town that could offer no resistance. They wounded and murdered people. Mr. Huntingdon was badly wounded and Mr. Morrison was killed. They were shot at close range by Colt pistols. As for Lieutenant Young, what an absolute farce! Reverend Clement Christian Clyde indeed. Can you imagine, your honour, this man reading his Bible one minute and then killing someone the next! You call that a military action? No man with an ounce of intelligence would let these men free. I can assure you that if you do, you'll hear from the banks in St. Albans who have lost over $200,000. May the Lord have mercy on your soul, your honour!"

With that said, Mrs. Smith opened her parasol, motioned for her maid to follow and marched out of the court without looking back to the rising cheers of the audience from St. Albans. As Mrs. Smith left, Ethan and Elizabeth Potter stood up as the cheering continued from their neighbors in St. Albans. Ethan stood erect and shouted at the judge. "My son was captured by Bennett Young as a hostage, my fourteen-year-old defenseless son. I demand his release!"

The court rose as one to protest with the Potters. Judge Coursol found himself being very embarrassed. How had this happened? How come he didn't notice Master Potter before? Without any further hesitation he released Ben to his parents and apologized to them.

After embracing, Ben babbled to his parents, "Boy, do I have a story to tell you." Ethan replied, "Let's get back to the railway station first, then tell us all about it. I think we can still catch the afternoon train home. We haven't slept in days."

The Potters left, arm in arm, with Elizabeth weeping all the way to the Bonaventure Station as the crowds cheered them on.

Just as the hearing was coming to an end, a lady jumped up and addressed the court. "Your honour, I implore you to release one of the prisoners, Doctor John Rumsey, an innocent bystander who had been enlisted by Young at gunpoint to attend to a wounded raider."

Judge Coursol asked the lady her name and who she represented.

"My name is Minnie Green, a resident of Greens Corners and I represent many of the St. Albans citizens who claim that Doc Rumsey has been wronged. He was not part of the Rebels and with his dog, Chester, sold patent medicines on the Green. He's from England. In fact the leader, Bennett Young, was seen shooting the dog and at point blank range!"

With that outburst, a number of St. Albans citizens jumped up and cheered Minnie and demanded Rumsey's release. Judge Coursol then asked Doc Rumsey if these statements were correct. Under oath, Rumsey stood and confirmed them as true. The Judge didn't hesitate. The shooting of a dog enraged him. John Rumsey was released immediately. The spectators stood and applauded at the decision. John Rumsey rose up in the prisoners dock and edged his way past the raiders and Bennett Young.

Bennett whispered to Rumsey, "Don't you dare go for the silver and gold. So help me, I'll hunt you down and shoot you dead if you do!"

Rumsey turned to Young, smiled at him and said, "I hear that my dog, Chester, may live. Imagine anyone's shooting a loyal dog." He smiled at them all in the dock and slowly left the courtroom with his head held high.

* * *

14

RUMSEY'S RELEASE

Notre Dame Street, 10.30 a.m., November 7, 1864

The crowd was pushing from as far back as Notre Dame Street and climbing all over Nelson's Monument, trying to hear about the events as they were occurring at the courthouse.

"Oh, John, I'm so happy to see you. I was frantic. We just missed the Potters. They all took off for the railway station. Ethan shouted to me that they'd see us in St. Albans."

"Minnie, I'm not sure how to thank you, but I've never felt better in all my life. I think back to those hungry times in this town when I couldn't find work and no one seemed to recognize that I even existed. Now here are all these people from St. Albans standing and cheering for me, led by Minnie Green! I've never had a town behind me like that before. It is an awesome feeling. Thank you. Thank you. There is only one problem, now, what do I do?"

Minnie looked at John and slowly grinned. She replied, "Let's celebrate! I don't think you know that Charlie Higbee left me some coinage that is negotiable, not just useless old Franklin County Bank greenbacks. John, it's a long story. Much has happened that you should know about. Why don't we take our time and walk over to Great St. James Street. We could have lunch at the St. Lawrence Hall Hotel and think about what you might like to do next."

Minnie took John's arm and together they pushed through the crowd. "You must be starved," Minnie whispered in John's ear.

"They did look after us pretty well. The army has their own kitchen, we could have had anything we wanted, but I'm hungry for lunch."

Minnie looked at John, "Your clothes look awful! Haven't you ever changed?"

"Minnie I don't own anything but what I have on my back. Ever since I arrived in Montreal last year I've only been able to buy the odd shirt and trousers. My frock coat has suffered from wind, snow and rain. I don't know what it's like to change into fresh clothing."

"How long ago was that? No, don't answer." Minnie was shocked. She thought to herself, Patent medicines may be the way to change his life. With my husband dead, I need someone to live with me and to tend to the garden. This one is vulnerable. He seems gentleman-ly enough. Obviously John comes from a good family background in England. Maybe this could be an investment.

Turning to John she said, "We have some time before lunch. There's a gentlemen's shop on Great St. James Street that looks worthwhile, it's owned by Giovanni Primo, and isn't too far from the hotel. Let's see what we can purchase. Maybe we can buy a set of long johns, socks, a shirt, cuffs, and links. Your pants and jacket are close to the size of my husband, so let's pass on them for now. But your boots have little soles left. How do you walk?" John didn't reply. He just kept walking and looking straight ahead. It had been a long time since anyone had fussed over him like this.

It took only a few moments before they saw Primo & Sons, Custom Tailors & Designers of Gentlemen's Attire, Masters of the Sartorial Art. Below the shingle hung a smaller sign that said Tailor in Residence, Luigi Primo.

They looked through the beautiful bay window that allowed the in-terior of the shop to be bathed in bright natural sunlight and marvelled at the new woolens on display for the coming winter. Minnie took John by the arm and moved into the shop. Giovanni was quick to greet them and take them on a tour of his clothing, ready-made and bespoke suits for clientele, bolts of new woolens and haberdashery. Giovanni was a big portly man who held himself very erect and tended to look down at everyone. He was always properly dressed to meet his customers. His shirts always had mother of pearl buttons. His pants were always pearl gray with pinstripes. Many businessmen in town nicknamed Giovanni as the 'Pearl of St James Street'. With a slight Italian accent he would modestly claim 'A little village in Tuscany', as his family home.

When they had completed their tour Giovanni had persuaded Minnie that her gentleman friend really needed to be made over. "I suggest a bespoke suit to ensure that you get your money's worth with a proper fit. When a full front frock coat hangs properly, it lasts for years."

Minnie hesitated, "But when would it be ready?"

"Well, when do you need it?"

"Tomorrow?"

"Oh, then why not a frock coat that I have made for showing? With a few alterations tonight we could have it for you tomorrow.

"Let's move on to shirts. You will need a proper white pleated front collared dress shirt with drop shoulders, gathered sleeves and cuffs. The collar is attached in a stand and fall pattern, just what the gentlemen of today are wearing. Mind you, for everyday wear I recommend also the collarless detachable collar pull-over shirt. I notice, sir, that you are wearing a linen collar?"

"Yes," replied John, "I purchased it here last spring."

"Ah, I knew it was a good collar! Have you cleaned it lately? Now, sir, to complement your shirts, I have a most exciting notched collar vest with a seven button front closure that would fit for all occasions."

It wasn't long before John was looking at matching wool trousers and finished off with a newly-made frock coat of bankers gray. John paused.

"Minnie, the long winter underwear, sock and shoes?"

"Oh, John, I know, but why don't we wait and drop into Breck and Weatherbee's. It would not be right to buy everything in Montreal. Everyone at home would notice it."

"I still need new long winter underwear, Minnie."

They met Giovanni's son, Luigi the tailor, who brought their selections to be viewed by the natural light of the bay window before final decisions were made. The clothing was then fitted and measured by Luigi. The trousers, vest and frock coat would be ready tomorrow by lunchtime. With the wait, John and Minnie had to decide where to stay in Montreal that night. The St. Lawrence Hall Hotel was the only choice to Minnie.

The noon bell was ringing on the Notre Dame Church steeple and it was time to move along to the hotel. John Rumsey was starting to feel like his old self again. His reassurance and British demeanor were returning. He was feeling like a lawyer again. It felt terribly good!

The hotel proprietor's calling card said:

One day while walking along Great St. James Street, Chester Goodenough had tried to introduce John to Henry Hogan, the owner of the St. Lawrence Hotel, the most prestigious hotel in town. The man was terribly proud of his position in town as a major proprietor, colonel of his militia regiment and friends of Dickens, the Prince of Wales, the officers of the Grand Trunk and the members of the Montreal Hunt Club. Goodenough was not in Henry's circle. Normally, Hogan would barely respond by tipping his high topper to them, but today, seemingly years later, was different.

Henry was up on the news of the trial and welcomed them profusely. John arranged for a room and he and Minnie retired to freshen up. Then with John's new shirt they went downstairs for lunch. John selected the fish, a salmon in shrimp sauce, with small boiled potatoes and carrots that was the specialty of the house. While they waited for their turtle soup, John ordered the wine. "I've ordered a foxy little thing from New York that I think you will like. I hear that the European harvests are a disaster from disease these days." John was trying to impress.

By the main course the wine was starting to make John mellow. He became quite morose. "Minnie how do I thank you. You've given me back some self-respect again. I haven't felt this way in years."

By dessert, he decided he had better get upstairs. Minnie rose from the table and excused herself for a few moments. She went straight to the main desk in the lobby and reserved a hot bath for her husband. After the apple pie, she walked upstairs with John. She sat him down on the bed and said, "First, you need a bath and your hair and beard washed. I've reserved a tub down the hall that is being filled with hot water this very moment." Minnie laughed to herself, First Charlie ... now John!

John just looked at her bleary eyed. Minnie looked at him closely.

"You can rub and wash your own back. They have long brushes for that occasion." Once in the bathroom Minnie said, "Now take off your clothes and step into the tub," and went back to the room.

After some time had passed and John had not returned, Minnie was worried. Quietly she walked down the hall to the men's bathroom door.

"John. Are you finished?"

"John?"

Silence. Minnie burst in. John was sound asleep in the tub. Minnie said, "John!!" He awoke with such a start that he didn't know where he was.

"You're in Montreal, for God's sake!" cried Minnie. "Now get up!"

After he had dried off, Minnie had to direct him in the altogether down the hall and into their room without anyone seeing them. Poor John couldn't even hold a towel around his waist. He kept dropping it! He was led to the bed where he promptly fell face down and went to sleep. It was 2.30 in the afternoon. Minnie covered him with a blanket and left the room.

I've never seen Montreal, thought Minnie. I've never seen such a beautiful church as Notre Dame. So many bells! The harbour, the noise, the smells. The fine stores and banks along Great Saint James Street look so impressive. There is a new store at the corner of McGill Street, Henry Morgan & Son, dry goods that I'd like to come back to sometime.

By evening, she had returned to find John still asleep. John had not slept in a good bed with fresh linens in months. Usually sleeping had been in a common bed with another heavy-set man who sweated and snored. So the luxury overwhelmed him and he slept … and slept. John never felt Minnie slide in beside him. She slept quietly, lost in her own thoughts of returning to St. Albans.

By morning, Minnie had risen early and walked next door to the Grand Trunk railway office to buy tickets for St. Albans. John awoke with a slight pain over his left eye. Otherwise, he could feel a new day and a new life. There on top of the dry sink were his new shirts. He couldn't believe how fresh and clean he felt. When Minnie returned, they went down for breakfast. Since they had not had any supper, the breakfast buffet was a marvelous welcome. All the meat, eggs and coffee you wanted. When breakfast was over, John took some coins from Minnie and paid their bill. With the tickets for St. Albans in hand, all they had to do was walk along to Primo's shop, pick up John's new clothes and catch a carriage for the station.

With John wearing his new suit, shirt and cravat, he became a different person. You could see it in his face. He stood taller. He began taking control of the situation, much to Minnie's relief. In this day and age a man should be in charge, she said to herself.

The Bonaventure Station, 10.00 a.m. November 8, 1864

They were recognized as heroes as they rode in their carriage up Great St. James Street to the railway station. The response was very heartening. The folks on the street were all anxious to wish John and Minnie well. At 10.00 a.m., the train's steam engine blasted the high ball and the train for St. Johns left Montreal. When would they ever be back? That was a question John wasn't too anxious to answer. He had a funny feeling that St. Albans had more of a future for him than he had ever realized. As the train rattled over the Victoria Bridge across the St. Lawrence River, John rose to shake the coal in the potboiler. There was a chill in the early November air despite the sun and clear sky.

"By the way, in all the hustle today, I had forgotten about Chester and ... and oh, how is Charlie Higbee?"

"Well, John, Chester has been improving with the whole Potter family attending to his every need. I think you'll be surprised at how well he has come along. As for Charlie, he was pretty sick. But eventually he was better and I took him to Richford. The town has a big new grist mill. Despite his sling, Charlie was able to get work. Once I had Charlie settled down, I left. We agreed that I'd be back in the spring. Right now is a bad time on the border. The number of troops on both sides would astound you. Charlie's strategy is to lie low."

John laughed and then paused. "Charlie is a Rebel! A bank robber! Was his salvation worth the money he had given to you? Bank money?"

Minnie looked at John and didn't say a word. Then after a few moments she said, "At the end of the day, as they say, we'll see. If his money helps us find the silver and gold ... it's worth every penny!"

John had forgotten about the satchels. "We should think about talking to the banks."

Minnie smiled at John and said, "Let's not hesitate. Remember, never plough a field by turning it over in your mind! The two St. Albans Banks have offered a reward of $10,000 for information leading to the recovery of their money. You've met Mr. Bellows at the First National and I have an account at the St. Albans Bank and a small mortgage at the Franklin Bank."

"Minnie, then we should talk to Bellows and Sowles right away. Can you imagine keeping the Rebels' silver and gold? I couldn't live with that on my conscience, and besides all the new greenbacks are hand-numbered in ink. If the banks were smart they would have recorded the number of every bill that was taken."

"I doubt if Mr. Burton, President of the Franklin County Bank, would redeem his bank's greenbacks that Charlie gave me."

John looked long and hard at Minnie and said, "Then we had better get to St. Albans, see the banks and organize a posse to find the coins. I never saw them bury the silver and gold, but I can lead the posse, to where two of the caches are generally located, North Sheldon and Enosburg Falls."

Minnie replied. "Good idea. By the way, the City of St. Albans is suing the Canadian Government for the full amount of the banks' losses. Apparently, Canada had no right to arrest and detain the Rebels."

They transferred at St. Johns and then at the border for the ride to St. Albans. Entering the Champlain Valley brought back memories to John of his first trip. It was then that Rumsey started to think of Chester, Ben, Ethan, and Elizabeth Potter. It seemed like months since he had seen them all. John and Ben had been kept apart in the escape, arrest and jail and hadn't talked to each other since the raid. The views of the Green Mountains, the Adirondacks and Lake Champlain were as breathtaking as the first time, making John realize what a special place this was for him.

He turned to Minnie, "Last night, I uh, I uh, I'm sorry. I slept through the night and never ... said anything to you."

Minnie just laughed and took John's hand.

John looked at her. "Today is such a different day for me and I know that things have moved awfully fast, but I can't see myself living without you in the future. Minnie, I...."

"Yes John?" Minnie said softly.

"I mean, you need someone around your place. The garden, you know? Well maybe you might like to uh, to uh - get married?" John sat back, shut his eyes and sighed. He had done it. He had actually proposed to Minnie. He was perspiring into his new shirt!

Minnie said to herself, Is now the time to talk about it? I think I'll make John wait just a bit. On the other hand, I could try a bit of fly-fishing. Renting my room has proven difficult, being out of town.

"I'm a Baptist, John," whispered Minnie shyly.

John replied, "Oh, I'm an Anglican. Actually, that means the Episcopal Church here in America. That makes me an Episcopalian. We stand a lot. You'd love it!"

"John, I'd miss the singing."

"You mean you wouldn't switch?" asked John, a bit shocked.

"Oh, John, I'd miss 'The Lord Be Willin' and the Creek Don't Rise', it's a marvelous hymn. You'd love it."

"I'd miss the 'Jubilate Deo'."

"We could join the Methodists, they sit, stand and sing"

Silence.

"John, how good are you at laying bricks?"

"Who me? Why back in High Wycombe we always had our man do that sort of thing. Why?"

"I was just thinking about a nice open hearth fireplace where we could sit in comfort and warmth. We need to spend more time together, John. A cook stove isn't quite what I had in mind," whispered Minnie.

Silence.

No, I guess this isn't quite the time, she thought to herself.

Both paused and became thoughtful. No more was said for a while. The train had passed through Swanton and was approaching St. Albans. When they got off the train, it looked as if the whole town was there to welcome them.

Election Day, St. Albans, November 8, 1864

The Union had gone to the polls to elect their President. The Republicans made a significant political move by renaming their party 'The National Union Party' for the 1864 election to accommodate the Democrats who wanted to vote for Lincoln.

After casting their votes, the people of St. Albans moved on to the railway station at 2.00 p.m. to welcome John and Minnie back to town. The mayor gave Minnie a bouquet of flowers. Ben was carrying Chester in his arms. Ethan Potter had just put up a big sign in the station.

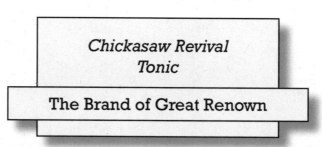

Chickasaw Revival
Tonic

The Brand of Great Renown

What a change from the 19th of October. So much had happened that John was overwhelmed. He turned to find Chester barking loudly. He jumped out of Ben's arms and hobbled over to John. Chester even stopped to sing a few notes.

Then Ed Fuller, the bankers, Mary Beatty and Alice Butters came by to greet them home. John asked Messrs. Bellows and Sowles if they had a few minutes. "Master Ben and I have a pretty good idea where everything is buried."

The two bankers eyes popped out and both said, "Where?"

John called Ben over and they started to explain. "While we were kept away from the actual digging, we know the general areas of the digging.

"Tom Collins led the first group across the Missisquoi River at North Sheldon and up past Elinos Taylor's farm. I'm sure that they buried their loot at the top of the hill behind the farm," said Ben.

"Then Young's group went to Enosburg Falls and buried their loot in the hills on the south side of the river."

The bankers listened carefully. Both were willing to pay them if they could get their hands on the specie. Harold Bellows had high hopes that the Canadian government would co-operate with the City of St. Albans in their lawsuit.

Ed Fuller was listening. His eyes gleamed and he interrupted, "Let my men go after it for you. 'Doc' Rumsey and Master Ben can show us the way." They all agreed to meet again the next day.

Ethan and Elizabeth Potter could hardly wait to make a deal with John Rumsey and his medicines. If John was willing to market the products, Ben could produce the tonic and Ethan could warehouse everything. John's bank, The First National, was very willing to listen to their proposal regarding inventory.

Governor and Mrs. Smith stood up on Church Street and watched all the commotion down on North Main as John and Minnie returned to a hero's welcome. Mrs. Smith turned to her husband and said, "You should have seen it here when the raid occurred. What a sight looking down on the Green - the smoke, the noise, the shooting, and the people. What a relief to see such a joyous moment now. You know, John, we should invite the Potters, Master Ben, John Rumsey, especially his injured dog, Chester, and the widow Minnie Green for a big dinner. I think they deserve some recognition for what happened to them. Tomorrow I could go down to the Potters shop and invite them all."

"Of course, Ann, why not make it for Saturday night? With all of the elections over after today, I don't have to be back in Montpelier until next week."

Washington, D.C., November 9, 1864

The public went to the polls on November 8th, and the counting of all the ballots from across the United States was completed the following day. Abraham Lincoln, Republican, was re-elected President, carrying 55% of the vote, defeating former General George McClellan, Democrat. Vermont voted overwhelmingly for Lincoln, 76%.

The Governor's Mansion, November 12, 1864

Mrs. Smith received everyone in a lovely hoop skirt and matching bodice. While Elizabeth Potter and Minnie were a bit nervous about their own humble, somewhat time-worn skirts and bodices, at least they were matching. The Smiths certainly didn't notice. They were the perfect host and hostess. Even Chester was welcomed and sent discreetly to the kitchen where he was fed enthusiastically by the kitchen staff.

The Governor made a splendid speech recognizing what everyone had done. Then he made a special tribute to those who couldn't be there, in particular, William Morrison who was killed and Charles Huntingdon, who was still recovering.

The Governor said grace. "May we rejoice in our great harvest festival, the busy growing of the food and the sustaining of it during the cold months ahead. May we rejoice in each other's warm companionship and enjoy the bounteous table before us. Amen."

The pea soup came first followed by battered oysters and pumpkin chips as the appetizers. The main course followed - roast turkey, with side dishes of sweet potato pudding, green beans and beets.

Ben whispered to his mother, "May I have the merry bone?"

The governor who was busy carving heard the remark and laughed, "You mean the wish bone? Of course you may."

"Ben," his mother whispered, "the Merry Bone is often called the Wish Bone. You take one end of it while someone close to you takes the other. You pull and break the bone. Then you make a wish."

"Doctor Rumsey, would you pull with me," Ben asked. John did and the bone broke. Ben closed his eyes and made his wish while everyone watched expectantly.

Elizabeth Potter leaned over, "What did you wish, Ben?"

"That's a secret! Then again, if you really want to know, I wished that the Chickasaw Revival Tonic would do well. Then I made a wish for Mom, Dad, Chester, Doc Rumsey, and Mrs. Green."

Mrs. Smith smiled and a glisten came to her eyes as she said, "Master Ben, don't you mean 'God bless us everyone?' Mr. Dickens would be pleased."

Everyone smiled and fell silent for a moment.

Then John Rumsey smiled and said, "Governor, may I have lots of stuffing, it looks marvelous."

The Governor laughed again and said, "Mr. Rumsey, you may have anything you want!" Then he paused and lifted his glass of wine. "We have this *vitis labrusca* Catawba wine from the Jacques Brothers in the heart of the Catskills. It's a gift from my friend Reuben E. Fenton who has just become Governor of New York. I hope you will like it."

Minnie leaned over to John and whispered, "Don't you dare say anything about a foxy little thing!"

John lifted his nose and winked.

The Governor stood and proposed a toast, "Master Ben, you forgot about yourself. May you do well, too."

Then, the Governor proposed a toast to Abraham Lincoln. He followed with a toast to General Sheridan for his recent win at Cedar Creek and General Sherman who was just starting his march to Savannah. A short while later, Ethan slowly stood up and proposed a toast to the Governor for his second win last September with 71.5% of the vote.

During the dinner Mrs. Smith and the two ladies talked about Mrs. Smith's new Oberlin 6 plate stove. Imagine ovens that bake bread! Minnie kept saying how much she loved the dinner. After the pumpkin pie and coffee had been served and consumed, the ladies went into the kitchen to look at the stove. It was during this visit that Minnie expressed her love of cooking to Mrs. Smith.

Eventually they all repaired to the drawing room where the Governor was anxious to discuss their future. "Mrs. Green, have you applied for your widow's pension yet? Remember you have to ask for it."

Minnie just looked at him. "No, I haven't. I wouldn't know where to start."

Rumsey looked up and stated, "Minnie I'm a lawyer, you know. That's the kind of thing I'm very good at doing!"

The Governor look surprised, "Mr. Rumsey, you amaze me. I didn't know you were anything but 'Doc' Rumsey, a seller of patent medicines." He looked at Rumsey thoughtfully.

"That, sir, is quite wrong. I am a graduate of Cambridge and had a successful law practice in High Wycombe. Mind you, I fell on hard times and was transported to America because of my debts, but that doesn't mean I'm not a good solicitor!" John stuck his chin out then realized he was talking to the Governor of Vermont and started to laugh at himself.

The Governor looked at John and said to himself, "A Cambridge solicitor right here in St. Albans? Well, isn't that something!"

Then he turned to John sympathetically, "Mister Rumsey, my family has owned the Central Vermont Railroad since its inception. We suffered through the failure of the railroad a few years ago and had to start over again. We moved the operation here to St. Albans and plan to change the name from the Vermont Central to the Central Vermont. So I know what you have been through. I know what it is like to change names, images and places. I also recognize the courage and strength that it must take to stand on a street corner and solicit a patent medicine to strangers."

John was very flattered. He sat up straighter and straighter in his seat. With his new suit, Minnie, the Potters and Chester supporting him he became the old John Rumsey, solicitor. High Wycombe was behind him now. Somehow or another he would bring his two daughters to America. The strength of his Cambridge education and upbringing was returning.

The Governor looked at his wife and they smiled knowingly at each other. He spoke first. "Mr. Rumsey, I have a couple of thoughts that you might consider. Firstly I am in desperate need of a contract administrator for the Central Vermont Railroad. Between shipping agreements and working with all the other independent railroads in New England I am far behind in preparing, executing and managing these contracts. I can't grow without this kind of help. How would you like to consider working from time to time for the Central Vermont?

"My other thought is that you and Mrs. Green should consider expanding your market garden and getting into the catering business. I hear your Green Mountain corn chowder and apple pies are famous, Mrs. Green. If you can sell that every week in the market, I'm sure that you could sell a variety of foods."

The Governor then turned to his wife, " Mrs. Smith, you have an idea as well?"

"Mrs. Green, my husband and I have been concerned about our cook. While she and her kitchen staff can handle the daily activities, she is finding it increasingly difficult to handle banquets. Alice Butters has a fine future here but she needs time and experience. She has little experience in the kitchen. You know, being a Governor brings with it certain responsibilities. We have to entertain. Mrs. Green, I observed your interest in my stove. How would you like to manage it from time to time? You and Mr. Rumsey could cater our dinners for us. In fact Mr. Rumsey, your English background, etiquette and manners would be perfect for those moments when we are trying to impress. The perfect English butler."

John's jaw dropped. "I'm a solicitor, Madame. I would have to think long and hard about being a butler."

Mrs. Smith laughed and said; "Now Mr. Rumsey, remember you are in America. It's different over here. If you can do it for patent medicines, you can do it for us."

John laughed, "I've heard that said to me before, Mrs. Smith. You have a good point - never pass up an opportunity, as an old Irish friend used to say. Let Mrs. Green and me think about all of this. We are extremely flattered. Governor, I would love to talk about contracts with you. It is just the right thing for me." Rumsey was beaming.

Minnie looked at Mrs. Smith, "Catering sounds excellent. I had never thought of that before!"

Eventually the evening came to an end, so Ethan, Elizabeth and Ben made their farewells followed by John, Minnie and Chester. Everyone was very satisfied with the dinner. John and Minnie had a lot to think about. As they turned up North Main, John smiled, "I think a little Tennyson would be nice about now.

Who can say?

Who can say
Why To-day
To-morrow will be yesterday?
Who can tell
Why to smell
The violet recalls the dewy prime
Of youth and buried time?
The cause is nowhere found in rhyme.

Minnie looked over to John and said quietly, "You never told me that you were a solicitor." John replied with a blank look. "I just forgot!"

As the Potters walked across the Green, Elizabeth turned to Ben. "Did you know about Doc?" "Sure," he said.

And you didn't tell us...."

"I forgot."

* * *

185

THE QUEEN'S DECISION

The Court of Queen's Bench, Montreal, December 13, 1864
Some weeks later, former Solicitor General of Canada East, William
Kerr, acted on behalf of the prisoners. He began the session with a mo-
tion that the warrants on which the prisoners were held were defective.
Judge Coursol opened the hearing and read a lengthy decision:

> "I therefore declare that having no warrant from the Governor General
> to authorize the arrest of the accused, as required by the Imperial Act,
> I Possess no jurisdiction. Consequently, I am bound in law, with justice
> and fairness, to order the immediate release of the prisoners from custody
> upon all charges brought before me. Let the prisoners be discharged."

Judge Coursol also discharged the prisoners from five other separate offenses and warrants on which no hearings had been held.

He ordered that the money and securities seized when the prisoners
were arrested should be returned to them. Coursol turned to Guillaume
Jean-Baptist Lamothe, the Chief of Police, and instructed him to give
back the funds immediately. Chief Lamothe led the Rebels out of the
court and down the hall towards an anteroom.

Suddenly a Mr. Porterfield, Special Agent for the Confederacy,
burst out of the crowd in the hallway and demanded that the monies be
returned to the Confederacy. He said that the Mission would look after
the released prisoners.

Lamothe looked the agent straight in the eye. "That's fine, here is
the order for the release of the funds and securities. As you can imagine such funds are in safekeeping. I suggest you go immediately to the
Bank of Montreal at the corner of St. Francis Xavier and Great St. James
Streets."

Porterfield didn't even look at the Rebels. He went out to a sleigh
that was waiting for him and took off. Lamothe turned to Young and
smiled knowingly. "That man was in quite a rush, wasn't he? Too bad

most of the money is sitting on a table right through that door. If you will all follow me...." Nobody asked any questions. Lamothe promptly distributed the money to the 14 Rebels. There was $51,000 American or $3700 each. Huntley's Franklin County Notes of $10,000 were worthless due to the bank's closing, and were not distributed to them. "That should be enough to get you home," Lamothe smiled.

The Rebels stood for only a second outside the courthouse. They thanked Lamothe and left quickly. Most took sleighs down Great St. James Street, straight to the railway station and booked passage due east for Quebec City.

Despite Lamothe's hints about leaving quickly, Bennett Young, Bill Huntley, Squire Teavis, Marcus Spurr, and Charles Swager returned to their rooms to gather up their belongings and to celebrate.

REV. CAMERON   SCOTT   TARVIS
HUTCHINSON   SAUNDERS   YOUNG
Some of the captured raiders. Picture taken in the
Jail office, MONTERAL, P.Q.

Bernard Devlin, representing the United States, demanded the prisoners be re-arrested, charged and tried for criminal offenses, so that they could be extradited back to the United States to stand trial. Such charges could invoke the conditions of the Webster-Ashburton Treaty regarding the extradition of prisoners.

Devlin, with much sarcasm, spoke out. "Apparently, the prisoners and their friends knew in advance of the decision that the discharge was going to be granted."

Just as Devlin was arguing with Justice Coursol, Justice James Smith of the Superior Court stood up in the lower court and ordered the prisoners be re-arrested. Mr. Devlin was most pleased. When Chief Lamothe was given Justice Smith's judicial order, the Rebels were racing down Great St. James Street. He stood on the sidewalk of the Palais de Justice and pondered over the Order for about 15 minutes. During that time, nearly all the prisoners got away. When Secretary Seward in Washington, heard about Lamothe's delay, he was speechless and complained to the Canadian Government. The newspapers accused Coursol and Lamothe of complicity. The City Council of Montreal asked their Police Committee to get answers.

"Bribery!" shouted the townspeople. Those who were sympathetic kept quiet. Others who sided with the Americans shouted long and loud for the heads of two such corrupt officials. Coursol and Lamothe were in a difficult position. They followed the letter of the law, sort of. Under heavy pressure from the United States, the Canadian Government fired both Judge Coursol and Chief Lamothe.

The St. Albans banks promptly sued the Canadian government for their losses of approximately $200,000 American. This action did not stop the Commanding General of the U.S. frontier, General John A. Dix, from issuing orders to shoot down any such predators who cross the border and to pursue them wherever they might take refuge. President Lincoln disapproved of this proclamation. Through Secretary Seward, he issued an order directing no traveller, except immigrants, directly entering an American port by sea, should be allowed to enter the United States from a foreign country without a passport. Enforcing the order would be interesting because few travellers had passports.

Superior Court, Montreal, December 13, 1864

Bennett Young, Bill Huntley, Squire Teavis, Marcus Spur, and Charles Swager had returned calmly to their rooms. They had not heard the judicial order and weren't rushing anywhere. They were re-arrested on the spot. The raiders were charged with only the robbery of Samuel Breck's $393 by Marcus Spur, which Mr. Breck was going to deposit in the St. Albans Bank. The trial began on Dec. 27th. With only the one charge it was believed that the trial would not last very long.

Bennett Young testified at length as to the military aspect of what they had done. With no remorse he said he owed his allegiance to the State of Kentucky and not the United States. He stood and held his chin high but his eyes were blinking. He would look no one in the eye.

All the five prisoners stood and claimed innocence, being soldiers of the Confederacy. Young finally asked the Judge for continuance to prove his documents valid, in order to counter Devlin's claim. The continuance was approved. The trial was held up and reconvened on February 15th.

The Mission's chaplain, Stephen Cameron, went to Richmond to secure the proper documents from President Davis. Justice Smith's decision was rendered upon his return:

"A hostile expedition by the Confederate States against the United States was an Act of War and not an offense for which extradition can be claimed. Furthermore, they were not robbers but soldiers and subjects of a belligerent power, engaged in a hostile expedition against their enemy. Though the Confederate States are not recognized as independent, they are recognized as a belligerent power ... it cannot be robbery because open war exists between the two parties and the law of nations does not regard the acts as murder or robbery. It is a political or military act."

The United States government agreed to drop all charges and appeals if the prisoners would accept the charge of violating Canadian neutrality laws because the raid was planned in Canada. The prisoners agreed and were released on April 5th. After all the cheering, the prisoners were re-arrested under warrants from the Superior Court of Toronto. It was alleged that the prisoners planned the raid in St. Catharine's, Ontario, Canada West - not Canada East. The prisoners were transported by rail to Toronto the following day.

16

CHARLIE'S ESCAPE

Richford, Vt., April 6, 1865

Minnie arrived just before lunch and went straight to Charlie's boarding house. It wasn't long before she saw Charles Higgins sauntering up the street for his lunchtime break from the mill by the falls. After embracing warmly, Charlie had quite a bit to say about Richford. He found the people of the town to be no different than his hometown folks of Fayette City, Kentucky.

"I could live here. The potential from waterpower and lumber is tremendous. Lots of jobs are opening up and I hear that the railroads are coming!"

"Charles," Minnie looked closely at Charlie, "I think you should go home now. You've heard about your capital, Richmond, Virginia? Three days ago nearly the whole city was set aflame. Two days ago President Abe Lincoln entered the city and walked the two miles from quay on the James River up to Capital Square to find everything had burned to the ground, and now General Grant's army is chasing General Lee's all over Virginia. It's only a matter of time, Charles. Peace has to come soon. I've heard that Lincoln wants amnesty for everyone. He wants peace and reconciliation in the south. He wants to start reconstruction immediately. Grant's troops won't be shooting or imprisoning any of the Rebels. Lincoln says, "Let 'em up easy.""

I suppose you're right, Minnie. What a terrible future. I just hope Kentucky is saved from such destruction, but you're right, I should go." The next morning, Charlie quit his job, met Minnie, and hitched the horse to the wagon. They started up the hill for Canada, a mile away.

They made their way past the hamlet of Abercorn, took the road along the Sutton River, then turned up onto the Brome Road to Brome Corners. The road passed through low land and was very muddy. Minnie cursed her decision to avoid the higher and drier Echo Road.

Eventually they turned east on the Stage Coach Road at Brome Corners and headed for Lake Memphremagog. Half the trip was over.

They had driven 15 miles from Abercorn and had 15 more to go. Because of the mud, old Alf, Minnie's beloved horse, found the road slow going, and they missed lunch.

As they reached the junction with Sugar Hill Road that led down to Knowlton, Charlie said, "Minnie, I read in the Richford paper that Alfred Kimball has a pretty good inn near Brome Lake called the Knowlton Stage House. We could stay there tonight. It's the middle of the afternoon and we don't know what's ahead of us."

"Well," Minnie said, "with the mud the way it is, we couldn't make Lake Memphremagog today, anyway. Let's do it!"

They turned down to the Exchange House where Mr. Kimball greeted them himself. Charlie asked, "We're moving on to Lake Memphremagog tomorrow, Mr. Kimball. Which would be the better way to go, the Stage Coach High Road or the low road over Bolton Pass?"

Old stone house on Echo Drive above Knowlton near where Minnie and Charlie passed on their way to the ferry

"It's spring so don't take any low roads when a high one is available. Stay on Stage Coach Road. There is still a 300-foot drop back to the Bolton Pass Road, and mud can break wheels and axles. We call it the 'Big Hill'. Fatal accidents have occurred at the bottom of the hill from time to time. There is a very dangerous section we call 'Dead Man's Curve' to remind the stage drivers to slow down! Be very careful. You may have to stay at the exchange house at Dead Man's Curve in Bolton Pass and go on to the ferry the following morning."

Knowlton, April 7, 1864

The following day, they set off and reached the Big Hill by noon. Then poor old Alf needed help from Charlie. Pulling a wooden wagon up a long hill was one thing, but having the wagon push him down the hill was another. Minnie sat on the hand break and held on! When they reached Bolton Pass, and then Dead Man's Curve, they called it a day. They were covered in sweat, dust and mud.

Arriving at the Dead Man's Exchange House Charlie complained to Minnie, "What an odd looking place. I swear the building was planned as a general store. Someone must have changed their mind and built that curved arch that is recessed into the front of the building making a small porch. Very few customers could squeeze onto the front porch and sit, like I want to do right now!"

The proprietor of the exchange house, Jake Baker, or 'Jake the Bake', couldn't match Kimball's stew, but his bread was excellent. Minnie and Charlie didn't mind sharing a bed. "Provided you have a bath, Charles!"

Dead Man's Curve, April 8, 1865

The next morning they asked Mr. Baker about the final leg of the trip. They thought the lake was just around the corner.

Mr. Baker grinned and said, "Oh sure, once you get over the long hill beside Mount Pevee. Remember, you're in the middle of the Appalachians!"

Charlie looked puzzled. "Don't you mean the Green Mountains?"

"Yes, the Appalachians!"

"How high is the hill?"

"Oh, 300 feet."

Just like the day before, the mud and the hills took their toll. Minnie and Charlie arrived at Knowlton Landing exhausted. They had missed the ferry by three hours.

Charlie was back to sweat, dust and mud. He looked sorrowfully at Minnie and cried, "Now don't ask me to have another bath. That sort of thing has got to stop!" For the third night in a row they stayed in an exchange house, the Pine Lodge at Knowlton's Landing. Yet they still couldn't see the Lake!

That evening while sitting in front of the hearth, Minnie pressed, "Charles, now that the war is pretty well coming to an end, don't you have a sense of guilt for what you have done over these last few years?"

Charlie thought for a while, then turned to Minnie and changed the subject, "I hear that the Franklin County Bank closed for good. That means that some of the greenbacks I have aren't worth anything."

"You can't use the Franklin money," Minnie agreed. Then she paused and thought about her Franklin mortgage. The money wasn't any good to anybody. Maybe the Franklin Bank president, Orville Martin would forgive the debt. Mind you, she had just scolded Charlie. Now here she was talking out of the other side of her mouth!

Minnie smiled to herself, Well, it's a bad hen that won't scratch itself. So she looked at Charlie and said, "If you like, I might be able to use some of it."

"How much?" asked Charlie?

"$152?" responded the widow Green, thinking of the outstanding balance of her mortgage. "You never know! It's Franklin money. Why shouldn't the president be practical about the payment?"

Charlie reached inside his portmanteau and pulled out a fist full of bills. He peeled off $200 in Franklin notes and gave them to Minnie and said, "That's the least I can do for you, Minnie. The other $5,000 was for hiding and helping me. I'm also very aware that you could have turned me in!"

Minnie just smiled warmly and turned to another subject, "Charles, I have news for you. John Rumsey and I plan to marry in May."

Charles laughed and congratulated her. "Well," he said, "John is no spring chicken, but I guess the older the fiddle the sweeter the tune, as you would say, Minnie!" Charles leaned over to Minnie and whispered, "You know what they say about old widows?"

Minnie flushed and glared at him. "What's that?"

Charles laughed and laughed for the first time in months. He giggled and answered, "Uh, uh, I forget!"

"Goodnight, Charles."

Knowlton's Landing, April 9, 1864

The next morning Minnie and Charles left the Pine Lodge and took the road down to the pier on Lake Memphremagog where they waited for the *Mountain Maid* to arrive. Slowly, the ferry came into view

Charles said, "Gawd, it's going to be a long trip." Then he looked at Minnie and smiled, "I think Charlie Higbee is a nice name."

Minnie leaned close and whispered, "Yes, I like Charlie Higbee, too."

For a moment they shared a brief silence. Then Minnie turned to Charlie, "Now Charlie, remember one thing, once you get on that ferry you have a decision to make. You can go to Newport, Vermont, at the bottom end of the lake and pick up the Grand Trunk Railroad over at Island Pond for Portland, Maine, or you can go to Magog, at the top end of the Lake, take the stage to Sherbrooke and work your way by rail to Quebec City. Both routes will take you to the sea ... one on the American and the other on the Canadian coast."

They said their good-byes. Charlie got on the ferry, stood on the leeward side and waved. Minnie waved back. The *Mountain Maid*, eased away from the dock, picked up steam and turned for the islands across the Lake.

When the ferry was slowly approaching the pier at Georgeville, he could hear people cheering and waving, "Lee has just surrendered to Grant. The war is over. Thanks be to God!"

Charlie lowered his head, I wonder if I can ever settle down. It may be difficult after running with Quantrill and then Bennett Young. We did have a cause, but now I'm just a Rebel with some useless money.

William H. Bartlett. **Lake Memphremagog at Georgeville, Quebec, with Owl's Head in the distance. 1842**

* * *

EPILOGUE

Appomattox, Virginia, April 12, 1865

Lee formerly surrendered to Grant, officially ending the Civil War. It was four years to the day from the beginning of the war when the South bombarded Fort Sumpter.

Toronto, April 12, 1865

After a Confederate agent posted a $10,000 bond, the prisoners were released, but the United States did not grant Bennett Young amnesty until two years after the war was over, so he couldn't enter the United States.

He walked out of the court slowly, a free man in a neutral country. The wind was completely knocked out of him. Had he committed a crime? Had he been a robber? With General John Hunt Morgan's death last September, Bennett Young had 'come down off the mountain'. His ride was over. Young left the halls of the Upper Canada Law Society and moved aimlessly along Queen Street, not knowing what to do next. He spotted a park bench and quickly sat down. He lowered his head into his hands, shut his eyes and whispered,

"I want to be a cavalryman,
and with John Hunt Morgan ride.
A Colt revolver in my belt,
a saber by my side.

I want a pair of epaulets
to match my suit of gray
The uniform my mother made
and lettered CSA.

I can't go home now so what should I do? Young stood up, sighed and continued walking. He was just a Rebel with nowhere to go.

Young studied in Toronto until the bond was released in October 1865, and then he went to Europe. Young claims to have travelled to Great Britain and Ireland to study law during this period. When he came home after the amnesty period had expired, he married Mattie Robinson of Kentucky. Her father was a Presbyterian minister.

Portland, Maine, April 12, 1864

Charlie found a vessel that was preparing to leave for Hampton Roads in a couple of days, so he decided to leave and take his chances that some rail lines would still be open after the conflict. He could travel across Virginia and be in Central Kentucky shortly thereafter.

Some people claim that it was he who shot Elinus J. Morrison. Others claim that he couldn't, being injured and trying desperately to ride his horse out of town. Some folks claim he stole $75,000 of gold from the sacking of Lawrence, Kansas, the year before and that his wife had hidden the cache in their home. Who's to say?

After his daring rides of the past two years, Charlie wasn't sure that he could go back to law and settle down. Maybe he should ride shotgun on trains.

White House, Good Friday, April 14, 1864

Assistant Secretary of War, Dana, reported to Lincoln that a 'conspicuous secessionist' named Jacob Thompson, who had been operating in Canada and organizing raids across the border, was seen by their intelligence agents to be en route to Portland, Maine, where he was planning to take a steamer to England. Secretary of War, Stanton, wanted to arrest him."

Lincoln replied, "No, I rather think not. When you have an elephant by the hind leg, and he's trying to run away ... it's best to let him run." (4) That night Abe and his wife, Mary, could finally relax, so they went see a play. (5)

The Night of Horrors, April 14, 1865

At 10.07 p.m.   John Wilkes Booth shoots Abraham Lincoln at the Ford Theatre.

At 10.15 p.m.   Lewis Payne stabs and severely injures Secretary Wm. Seward in his bed.

At 10.15 p.m.   George Atzerodt gets cold feet, fails to murder Vice President Andrew Johnson
Later that night Payne and Atzerodt are arrested.
Booth escapes.

Washington, The Petersen Boardinghouse, 7.22 a.m., April 15, 1865

Surrounded by his friends, colleagues and family, Abraham Lincoln's nine-hour struggle with life ended, after being shot at the theatre the night before.

Port Royal, Virginia, 4.30 a.m., April 26, 1865

Booth was shot and killed by Union soldiers at the Garrett Farm.

Quebec, Canada East, December 1865

Governor General Charles Monck issued funds to the three banks equal to the money that was given back to the raiders of $51,950 USD. Based on a severe drop in the price of gold from the year before, the Canadian Government had to pay the current day equivalent of $81,922 USD (United States Denomination).

Washington, D.C. December 1865

The government was still pressing Bernard Devlin for answers regarding the raid. He had tried to figure out where all the money had gone. The banks of St. Albans recovered $51,950 from the Canadian Government in 1864 dollars and Huntley's $10,000 in Franklin Notes. They might have found some of the silver and gold buried in the hills, but not much. Not recovered was $143,050. The total loss was $205,000.

Devlin pondered the destiny of the Rebels. They had all gotten away. Young was denied amnesty and couldn't return for two years, but that was the only punishment.

Devlin then muttered, "They also got away with murder. Imagine robbing banks, killing and injuring innocent people, and saying it was a military operation! Yet both Canada East and Canada West agreed with the Canadian judge that they had no jurisdiction over the actions of the Rebels."

He buried his head in his hands and whispered, "Who the hell won anyway?" He stood up, shrugged his shoulders and laughed to himself, Who's to say?

* * *

HISTORICAL BACKGROUND

Canada East (Quebec) and Canada West (Ontario) were the new names of Upper and Lower Canada in 1841. One capital represented both districts and would rotate between the two every four years. In 1864, the capital was in Quebec City. The two districts were called the United Province of Canada. The constitution was changed again in 1867 creating four provinces: Ontario, Quebec, New Brunswick, and Nova Scotia.

British Troops and the Canadian Militia: After 1759, Britain sent regiments out to settle and integrate with the people. They were a part of the daily scene garrisoning the forts for over 100 years. The Canadian Militia was formed in 1855 and was managed by the British until Confederation in 1867 when the British troops returned to Britain.

Montreal business was dependant upon supplies from ocean ships in spring, summer and fall. During the winter months, the St. Lawrence River was frozen. When the Victoria Bridge, over the St. Lawrence River, was completed in 1859, it connected the railways from the Atlantic to Montreal. Consequently, the City could conduct business over twelve months, not just the ice-free ones.

Commissioners Street or Boulevard de la Commune: from French to English to French over the centuries. As a result, the name 'de la Commune' after the British occupation of 1760, changed to 'Common Street'. Common areas such as like parks and streets are often called 'The Common' or 'Common Street'.

The street was named after the harbour commissioners that removed the walls and fortifications of Old Montreal around the turn of the $18^{th} - 19^{th}$ Century. This name lasted until recent years when the name reverted back to 'Boulevard de la Commune' in the revival of Old Montreal.

Great St. James Street. With the advent of the railways, commercial activity in Montreal began to shift. Commissioners and St. Paul Streets had been serving the harbour. With the completion of the Bonaventure railway station on Great St. James Street West, this street was becoming the principal business street of the city. In the mid-1800s many of the main businesses and institutions of Montreal were firmly established on Great St. James between Victoria Square and Little St. James Street.

The Eastern Townships

Lower Canada opened the Eastern Townships for settlement in 1792, after the Constitutional Act of 1791. The government had given generous land grants to the United Empire Loyalists - Americans who wished to remain loyal to the Crown. While the original French families had settled the lands along the St. Lawrence years before, the new townships south and inland from the St. Lawrence were entirely English.

Roman Catholic parishes were encouraged by Canada East (Lower Canada) in 1850. These parishes had the right to tax Catholic property and build Catholic schools. The first French arrivals were strangers in a part of Quebec where the language had been traditionally English. One of the results of the French immigration was the 'grafting' of a Catholic parish name to an English village's name. Thus it is common to find the names Sainte-Edwidge-de-Clifton, Sainte-Catherine-de-Hatley, Saint-Cyrille-de-Wendover, or Notre-Dame-de-Lourdes-de-Ham.

The Pinnacle that rises just east and above Frelighsburg and the border, is a pristine mountain woodland shaped like a pinnacle, and called as such. The Abenaki have hunted here throughout their history. In some respects it was their 'happy hunting ground'.

Frelighsburg, a village located just above Franklin, Vermont, was named for Abram Freligh, a Loyalist Doctor of Dutch descent. In 1800 he came from Clinton Duchess County in New York with his wife and ten children, his servants, his slaves, and 22 double-harness carriages full of personal effects and merchandise.

Dunham, a village just north of Frelighsburg was founded in 1796. The town was the first in the Eastern Townships to be built by a group of Loyalists, represented by Sir Thomas Dunn.

Stanbridge East, another village north of Frelighsburg was established to serve the new United Empire Loyalist farming community that had settled along the Pike River. Other villages along the border such as Philipsburg, Pigeon Hill, Bedford, Cowansville, Sweetsburg, and Knowlton, had similar origins. Farnham, Waterloo, Richmond, and

Sherbrooke are towns and cities further north from the border that are early railway towns and grew more quickly.

The Township of St. Armand along the border is the one exception that was a seigneury, circa 1700. However it, too, became part of the Townships in 1791.

St. Johns, Quebec (Saint Jean d'Iberville) was the first major center en route to Montreal from the Townships. It is located on the Richelieu River with direct links to Vermont and Lake Champlain.

Magog and Austin are spread along the northern and western shore of Lake Memphremagog. The northern outlet of the lake into the Magog River was called The 'Outlet'. Eventually, the name was changed to Magog in 1855, the shortened form of Lake Memphremagog.

Lake Memphremagog has its origins in the Abenaki, meaning 'Lake of Beautiful Waters' or 'Great Pond Place'. The lake stretches 33 miles (53 km) from below Newport, Vermont, to the south, to Magog, Quebec, in the north.

Owl's Head is a mountain maned after 'Owl', an Abenaki Indian Chief. It is just above the border towards the southwest end of Lake Memphremagog. The silhouette of the mountaintop appears to be the great chief lying in repose. Local history buff, Professor Gerard Leduc, founding President of the Potton Heritage Association, discovered engravings and stone formations near the peak of the mountain. This discovery reinforced his claim that Owl's Head was sacred to the Abenaki. It was used for the initiation and crowning of their new leaders.

Stage Coach Road, originally called the Old Magog Road, was one of the original wagon roads to be built into the Eastern Townships in 1793 after the Constitution Act was passed in 1791 to open up the Townships for development.

The trail leads east from St. Johns and winds its way to Stanbridge East, Frelighsburg, Dunham, Sweetsburg, Brome, and through Bolton Pass down to Knowlton's Landing on the western shore of Lake Memphremagog and then on to Magog.

Today, only part of the Stage Coach Road is in existence. The road starts near the junction of Highways 139 and 104 just east of Cowansville and continues to Highway 243 at the eastern end of Bolton Pass. Just before the road ends at Highway 243, it drops 300' in one half mile of rocks, pebbles and dust.

Inns and Exchange Houses were often private homes, with the exception of Goodenough's and the Knowlton Exchange House that were built as inns. Goodenough's is no more but the Knowlton Exchange Houses is now Auberge Knowlton. The Inns in Frelighsburg and Stanbridge East and the exchange house at Bolton Pass are all private homes today. The blacksmith shop in Austin is today a B&B named Aux Jardin Champetre. One of the owners, Monique Dubuc, claims that the Rebels did hide in her cellar. The root cellar and storm doors are still in existence. The Pine Lodge at Knowlton's Landing is still an inn called Aubergene. Flint Farm was built in 1825 and is now the home of Crawford's Pinnacle Iced Wine. While Flint is an old family in the region, it wasn't the name of the farm in 1864.

Canada East Railway Timeline

1836 - The Champlain and St. Lawrence Railroad opened. This was Canada's first public railroad from Montreal's south-shore town of Laprairie to St Johns.

1853 - The St. Lawrence & Atlantic Railroad reached Richmond and Island Pond and the Atlantic & St. Lawrence Railroad reached Portland.

1853 - The Montreal & Vermont Junction Railroad was completed between St. Johns and the border at Highgate Springs, Vt.. The line connected with the Vermont and Canada Railway which went to St. Albans and points south.

1854 - The Grand Trunk (GTR) completed the Richmond to Quebec line and connected with the future Intercolonial Railway from Halifax on July 1, 1876.

1856 - The GTR opened its line between Montreal and Toronto.

1859 - The Victoria Railway Bridge, Montreal, was completed.

1862 - The Stanstead, Shefford & Chambly Line reached from St. Johns to West Farnham in 1858, to Granby in 1860 and Waterloo in 1861.

Vermont was an independent republic that received statehood as the 'Green Mountain State' in 1791. Shortly thereafter the State was broken up into counties. The population of the State rose from 16,550 in 1860 to 29,000 in 1870 and the proportion of French-Canadians increased to 44.4%. (6)

Franklin County was organized in 1792. The County borders on Canada and has an area of about 630 square miles. The Missisquoi and Lamoille rivers provided waterpower to numerous mills in the County.

Sheldon, chartered in 1763, was known for the Sheldon Springs. Rolling hills and farms form the landscape of this town with Black Creek that runs through it.

Enosburg Falls was named after an early settler, Roger Enos. The falls were the center of industry. Dr. B.J. Kendall, a teenager during the War, put Enosburg on the map when he began making his cure for a common horse ailment.

Franklin was settled in 1789. A civil war veteran, Carmi L. Marsh, donated the famous Soldiers Memorial Monument that was dedicated 'To the memory of those who dared to serve and died … and to those who dared to serve and lived.' The nearby lake was named 'Carmi' in recognition of his contributions.

Berkshire is nestled in between Enosburg and the Canadian border. In 1780 Berkshire was one of six towns to be authorized by the earlier Republic of Vermont legislature, constituted in 1777.

Swanton was chartered during the Revolution and became an important railway junction. 284 soldiers, mostly of the Green Mountain Guard, fought in the Civil War. 28 died. The population of Swanton in 1860 was 2678.

St. Albans is the principal city of Franklin County. While it was chartered in 1763, settlement didn't start until 1785. St. Albans had 4,000 people by 1864.

The Abenaki tribe was the first group to settle in Vermont. Unfortunately, diseases from Europe nearly wiped them out. As the years passed and tribes shrank, they gathered together in ever decreasing communities. Today, the Abenaki are centered in Swanton.

The Old Brigade: In the fall of 1861, Brigadier General William 'Baldy' F. Smith suggested to Major General George B. McClellan that he should form a brigade entirely of Vermont troops. When this brigade was formed it was the only one in the Union Army with soldiers from one state. This distinction was kept throughout the War.

Northwestern Vermont Railway Timeline

1845 - Charles Paine was governor of Vermont from 1841 to 1843. He became president of the newly chartered Vermont Central Railroad.

1848 - The Vermont Central (VCR) opened the first short stretch from White River Junction to Bethel. The next year the VCR opened all the way to Essex Junction and then to Burlington.

1849 - The Rutland & Burlington Railroad (R&B) ran from Bellows Falls through the town of Rutland then north to Burlington.

1851 - A third railroad, the Vermont & Canada (V&C), was chartered by Gov. John Smith to connect one railway line to the Great Lakes and another to the Canadian border.

1853 - The V&C extended to Swanton and the border at Highgate, Vt.-St. Armand, Que. This line connected with the Montreal & Vermont Junction Railroad that ran on the east side of the Richelieu River.

1853 - The VCR and the V&C were placed under receivership by Governor Smith. He moved the head office to St. Albans in 1861, changed the name from the Vermont Central to the Central Vermont and renamed the VCR and the V&C, the Central Vermont Railroad (CVR) in 1873.

The United Empire Loyalists were Americans who preferred to remain loyal to the Crown. Many moved to Canada, settling along the Saint John River valley of New Brunswick, the north shore of the Saint Lawrence River west of Montreal, the Bay of Quinte on Lake Ontario, the Niagara Peninsula, Missisquoi Bay of Lake Champlain, the Eastern Townships and Lake Memphremagog.

Boston Post Roads: During the colonial period, post roads connected New York City to Montreal via the Hudson River-Lake Champlain corridor and Boston across the Green Mountains to the Lake Champlain forts. Part of one Boston Post Road is now the 10th Mountain Division Memorial Hwy #108 that runs up through the Green Mountains at Smuggler's Notch to Canada. Unfortunately the Post Road is broken up and is difficult to follow. In 1864 the Post Road was an alternative 'high' road to Frelighsburg in Canada. The 'low' road, Hwy 108 to the immediate west, is still in active use today. In 1942 the 'high' road was cut off from Canada to limit border access.

The Webster-Ashburton Treaty: In 1842, Secretary of State Daniel Webster met with the British Foreign Minister, Alexander Baring, the first Baron Ashburton. The resulting Webster-Ashburton Treaty reached agreement on the following points: Clearly defined borders to be drawn between Maine, New Brunswick and the Great Lakes and a legal process to be enacted for returning fugitives to another jurisdiction.

Telegraphy was invented in 1843. By 1864, Montreal and St. Albans were hooked up to all points north, south, east, and west.

The United States Civil War in Canada: During the Civil War (1861-1965), Union deserters called 'Skedaddlers', crossed into neutral Canada and approximately 30,000 Canadians went south to serve on both sides of the war. In 1963 the Confederacy sent men to Canada to organize a group to rescue Rebel prisoners near Chicago, but the plan failed. However many prisoners escaped and went to Canada. The South had agents that established diplomatic missions in St. Catharines, Toronto and Montreal. They supported raids into the States, while U.S. government officials appealed to England not to let the Rebels attack from British soil.

20,000 additional British soldiers were sent to guard the frontier. Yet Abraham Lincoln claimed, "There will be no war with Canada as long as I'm President." (7)

Between 1860 and 1870 approximately 100,000 (8) French Canadians left for the New England states. British sentiment was Confederate. Britain had their woolens, but the South had their cottons, much cherished by the British people.

By 1864 the war was not going well for the South. Jefferson Davis sent his mother-in-law, wife and two children to live in Montreal. John Lovell gave up his town house on Union Street for their use. Davis's mother-in-law died there and was buried in the Protestant Cemetery in Cote des Neiges.

The Civil War in America: Nearly one million soldiers were either killed or wounded - 25% of all those who fought in the War.

U.S. Banking: With the advent of the Civil War, in 1861 Congress authorized Demand Notes - the first issue of paper money by the government. These notes were printed in $5, $10 and $20 denominations, redeemable in coins on demand. Being green in color, they were called 'greenbacks'. By 1862, these notes were changed to Legal Tender Notes or United States Notes of larger denominations. These notes were the first national currency to be used as legal tender.

The Treasury stopped redeeming these notes in coin later in the War to save their supply of gold and silver. In addition, from 1862 to 1876, fractional currency was issued to replace the coinage of three to fifty-cent denominations. The 'paper coins' were called 'Shinplasters' because the troops used the paper to line their worn-out boots.

The National Bank Act of 1863 invited the state banks to take out federal charters to become known as national banks. Each bank had to buy federal government bonds equal to 1/3 of its paid-in capital stock. The bonds had to be deposited with the U.S. Treasurer, who would then turn over to the bank, bank notes equal to 90% of the current market value of the bonds. These national banks in the major cities kept reserves of at least 15% and 25%.

The issuance of national bank notes was more secure than the state bank notes whose security was based only on the individual bank's reserves being held at the time. If a state bank closed because it couldn't meet its demand liabilities, the notes were worthless. So having adequate reserves of gold and silver in the vaults of the State banks was vital in 1864.

Counterfeit Money: By the end of the Civil War, it was rumoured that one third to one half of all U.S. paper currency in circulation was counterfeit. Some claimed that the Canadian towns on the U.S. border were busy printing money.

The Morgan Horse: In the Civil War, trains became critical to troop and ordnance movement. But to win a war, breech-loading rifles and good horses were the preferred assets. The Morgan breed originated in 1789 in West Springfield, Massachusetts, with the birth of a bay colt named 'Figure'. At one year of age, Figure was given to a Randolph, Vermont, schoolmaster named Justin Morgan in partial payment of a debt. He was renamed 'Justin Morgan" and became widely known for his ability to pull stumps and logs while clearing the land for new settlers. U.S. General Philip Sheridan's famed Morgan charger, 'Rienzi' (a town in Mississippi) was renamed Winchester (the Battle of Winchester in the Shenandoah) and is immortalized in the Smithsonian Institute. Al Capone may have wanted a Model T but Lieutenant Bennett Young wanted a Morgan.

Writ of Habeas Corpus: Latin, meaning 'You have the body'. Prisoners often seek release by filing a petition for a writ of habeas corpus: a judicial mandate to a prison official ordering that an inmate be brought to the court. The objective of the order is to determine whether or not that person was imprisoned lawfully and whether or not he should be released from custody. During the Civil War, President Lincoln suspended the rule when he felt that Rebel forces threatened Washington.

Civil War Revolvers: Almost all Civil War pistols were single-action revolvers. Colt made several hundred thousand with half as many made by Remington. These revolvers were tediously loaded with either combustible paper cartridges or with loose powder and ball. The soldier inserted the powder and bullet from the front, and a rammer was built into the gun to swage (cram) the bullet into place. The swaging held the bullet from falling out of the gun when fired. Soldiers melted lead and poured it into bullet molds at their campsites before battles. Eventually, a percussion cap would be invented to fit individually to the back of the cylinder with one required for each of the five or six chambers.

Because reloading could take minutes, two or more spare cylinders were carried pre-loaded. The cylinders would be switched much more quickly than reloading a fired one.

Civil War guns used 'Black Powder' that created clouds of smoke. Six shots rapidly fired from a revolver on a windless day could create a smoke cloud so dense as to obscure the targets.

The shooter had to hold the grip of a Colt 1860-44 caliber revolver and cock the hammer without shifting the shooting hand's position on the grip. The shifting up and down of the hand takes time. Two hands are used. One holds the grip and is prepared to pull the trigger as soon as the other has thumbed the hammer all the way back.

None of the Civil War revolvers had good sights by recent standards. When the guns were fired, they were lucky to hit a target consistently at 50 yards, or less.

The Shenandoah River Valley winds its way north between the Blue Ridge and the Appalachian Mountains, serving as the backbone to the State of Virginia, before it finally reaches the Potomac River at Harper's Ferry. During the Civil War, the Shenandoah was strategic to both sides. The Valley was the Confederate's key to attacking Washington and a vital supply route for both armies.

The Union's strategy was to control the Shenandoah and cut off the Confederate capital, Richmond, from their military forces to the south. 'Win the Valley and you could win the War.'

General Jubal Early had led his Confederate forces all the way up the Valley and down into the suburbs of Washington in early 1864. But he lost momentum and retreated to the Upper Shenandoah. General Grant sent Phil Sheridan to defeat Early and take the Shenandoah Valley out of the War.

On August 26th Grant told Sheridan, "Ravage the Valley until a foraging crow would starve there." Then he continued, "Do all the damage to railways and crops you can. Carry off stock of all descriptions, and Negroes so as to prevent further planting. If the war is to last another year, we want the Shenandoah Valley to remain a barren waste." Few campaigns in the War aroused more bitterness than this one. On October 19th at Cedar Creek, Sheridan gave Early his final defeat. The campaign was over. (9)

Kentucky in the Civil War: In 1861, Kentucky declared its neutrality in the Civil War. The State had supplied about 86,000 troops to the north and 40,000 troops to the south. Ironically, Central Kentucky was the birthplace of the Union president, Abraham Lincoln, his wife Mary Todd Lincoln and the Confederate president, Jefferson Davis, further enhancing the state's dualistic role in the War. Early in the War, Kentucky counties started to declare their sympathies and the Confederates tried to set up their capital at Bowling Green, Kentucky. But with increasing military pressure, the Rebel leaders eventually moved to Tennessee to be under the protection of their army located there.

Lexington, Kentucky: When news reached Lexington of the attack on Fort Sumter by Confederate forces in South Carolina, heralding the start of the Civil War, Lexington and the Bluegrass Region, like the rest of Kentucky, became strongly divided.

On the week after the fall of Fort Sumter, an armed body of men bearing the Confederate flag passed through the streets of Lexington, heading south to swell the Confederate army, amidst cheers for Confederate President, Jefferson Davis.

Shortly thereafter, Lexington Unionist David A. Sayer, an aged banker, began receiving shipments of rifles and revolvers and distributed them in secret to his pro-Union friends, using his bank at Mill and Short Streets as a base.

Both sides occupied the town. The Bodley-Bullock House, at 200 Market Street, was at different times the headquarters for either Union or Confederate forces. The Hunt-Morgan House was the home of Confederate Brigadier General John Hunt Morgan. The Mary Todd Lincoln House was at 578 West Main Street in Lexington.

Bennett Henderson Young was born in 1843 in Nicholasville KY, educated at Bethel Academy in Jessamine County and attended Center College in Danville.

John Hunt Morgan was born in Huntsville, Alabama, on June 1, 1825, Morgan had moved to Lexington, Kentucky, and established himself as a successful businessman before the Civil War. Morgan joined the Confederate Army under General Simon B. Buckner of Kentucky, and was promoted to Colonel of the second Kentucky Cavalry on April 4, 1862. He became legendary as a Confederate commander leading raiding parties into Tennessee and Kentucky while being chased by Federal troops, and never being captured. He was considered by Confederate Kentuckians to be a picture of a perfect cavalry fighter and southern gentleman even during battle.

On September 3, 1864, he was killed in a surprise attack by Federal cavalry at Greeneville, Tennessee. General Morgan was buried in the Lexington Cemetery in Lexington, Kentucky.

An Ode to Morgan
(Source unknown.)

Yankee rhyme:
"I'm sent to warn the neighbors, he's only a mile behind.
He's sweeping up the horses, every horse that he can find.
Morgan, Morgan the Raider and Morgan's terrible men,
With bowie knives and pistols, are galloping up the glen.

Rebel rhyme:
"I want to be a cavalryman, and with John Hunt Morgan ride.
A Colt revolver in my belt, a saber by my side.
I want a pair of epaulets to match my suit of gray
The uniform my mother made and lettered CSA

Nicholasville, Kentucky, by Jessamine Woodson 1897: "Nicholasville, the county-seat, is quite an enterprising, up-to-date town of 3,000 inhabitants, in the center of the county, twelve miles south of Lexington and eight from the river which can be reached from five different pikes and two railroads. It has eight or nine churches, several of them quite handsome. Several large dry-goods stores that do an immense business and grocery stores too numerous to mention; the prettiest courthouse and yard in the state; the handsome buildings and grounds of Jessamine Institute and Bethel Academy; a public library, a skating rink, a lake, an unfailing well of purest water; a standpipe and waterworks, a steam laundry, two able weekly newspapers, two or three literary clubs, a first-class hotel, well paved streets and street lamps all in good running order, and sanitary laws are well observed."

Cooking. Until the end of the 18th century, most colonial homes were built with brick open-hearth fireplaces and wall ovens. Often the wall would back onto a 'summer kitchen' that would have the same facilities. In winter everyone, including some of the farm animals, would stay inside. Come summer with the oppressive heat, cooks would move outside to the summer kitchen, a lean-to, and continue preparing meals. With the advent of cast iron stoves, cooking methods changed dramatically. No longer were brick walls and open-hearth ovens being built. Families craved for the old methods of roasting and baking, but they preferred the easier form of cooking with portable cast iron stoves. Open hearths brought warmth and sociability into a home while the cook stoves did neither. Interesting comparisons can be made between the cooking methods of Minnie Green, Elizabeth Potter and Mrs. Smith.

Medicine: The practice of medicine in both Canada and the United States in the Victorian era was quite uncontrolled. Hygiene was relatively unknown and doctors treated symptoms but not the causes. Often immigrants and settlers moving into the remote regions would bring with them old family medicine recipes, using herbs and spices taken from the land.

In those days, Apothecary shops were the drugstores. The apothecaries dispensed herbs and spices, opium, morphine, camphor, and alcohol. Most patent medicines were a combination of these items, in particular alcohol and opium. Apothecaries prepared medicines, dressed wounds, performed minor surgery and amputations.

No schools existed to train apothecaries. No one needed a license, neither doctors nor apothecary shops. Doctors and apothecaries apprenticed under seniors for approximately five years, then branched out on their own.

Settlers learned from the Indian population who for years had used remedies taken from the land. Corn meal was an effective poultice for bruises, sores, boils, and swellings. Itching skin and sores could be treated from the smoke of burning corncobs. Corn silk soothed, and improved gastrointestinal, kidney and urinary problems.

Chickasaw / Chickamauga: These names refer to native Indian tribes in the American south and midwest. The City of Chickasaw is in Oklahoma and the Chickasaw plum tree can be found throughout a number of states of the midwest. *Prunus Angustifolia,* is the scientific name for the plum. Near Chattanooga, Tennessee, lies Chickamauga, where the famous battlefield can be visited.

Neither of the patent medicines, Chickasaw Revival Tonic nor Chickamauga Spiritual Elixir ever existed.

Transportation: In Victorian England, a polite word for 'banishment' was 'transportation'. Prisoners who were convicted of a first time felony (other than murder, coining forgery and arson) frequently had their death sentences commuted to transportation out of the country. Their destination had been Australia but America was becoming more popular because it was less expensive for the counties and less time consuming for the prisoners. While minimum time for transportation was two years, sentences did go as high as 21 years to life with about five per cent of the convicts eventually returning to Britain. Banishment was abolished in 1868.

Propriety: An example of the basic rules of good conduct or propriety in the Victorian era was: Meeting a lady whom you know only slightly, a gentleman waits for her acknowledging bow … then and only then may he tip his hat to her, which is done using the hand farthest away from her to raise the hat. We saw the Victorian behaviour of Bennett Young and Sarah Stark on the Green.

The Widow Green's bedding down with Charlie and the Doc was a matter of necessity and economy. Lifestyles were much simpler then.

Entertainment: There was little entertainment in 1864. Religious services were often daily. Some families would often go to hear very direct and outspoken sermons, 'hell fire and brimstone', every night.

The only other diversion was books, when available. Printing and photography were in embryonic stages and in limited supply. A book was to be treasured. Reciting poetry was a common social activity and the reciter very popular. As a consequence, poet laureates were public figures in Britain and the States.

Greek Fire: Petroleum and sulfur have been used since the Middle Ages, but Greek fire is much more potent. It is believed that the Byzantine Navy created Greek fire in the seventh century. Throughout the Crusades, the Saracens used Greek fire extensively. To extinguish Greek fire, water alone was not enough. Often it took sand, vinegar and urine.

N.B.: From the dark ages, historians have pondered the subject of Greek fire. Suffice to say the Confederates had a bomb that when exposed to air sometimes ignited and at other times turned to smoke. The recipe used in this book is not intended to be an accurate recreation of Young's Greek fire. The final word is that the 'real' fire didn't work in St. Albans, anyway.

SOURCES

(1) Comments of Mrs. Anne Eliza Brainerd Smith in a letter to her husband, John Gregory Smith, Governor of Vermont. Oct. 20th, 1864. Ref. St. Albans Historical Museum. From Johnson, Carl. *The St. Albans Raid, 1864.* p. 44, private, 2001.

(2) © Benjamin Tubbs. *Music of the American Civil War.* John Hill Jewett, 1863.

(3) The farm was rumoured to have been active in the Underground Railway with Franklin, Vermont. Seibert, Wilbur H. *Vermont's Anti-Slavery and Underground Railroad.* Spur & Glenn Co., 1937. Reprint by Civil War Enterprises, Newport, Vermont.

(4) Goodwin. *Team of Rivals.* New York: Simon & Shuster, 2005 p. 733.

(5) Winik. *April 1865.* Harper Collins, 2001, pp. 221-229.

(6) Belanger, Prof. Damien-Claude, *French Canadien Emigration to New England.* Montreal: Marianopolis College, 1999.

(7) Belanger, Prof. Damien-Claude, *French Canadien Emigration to New England.* Montreal: Marianopolis College, 1999.

(8) Hoy, Claire. *Canadians in the Civil War.* McArthur & Company, 2004, p. 7.

(9) Catton, Bruce. *Grant Takes Command.* Boston: Little Brown, 1969, p. 361.

* * *

BIBLIOGRAPHY

Bassett, T.D. Seymour. *The Growing Edge, Vermont Villages, 1840-80.* T.D. Seymour Bassett, 1992.

Belanger, Prof. Damien-Claude. *French Canadien Emigration to New England.* Montreal: Marianopolis College, 1999.

Benjamin, L.N. *The St. Albans Raid.* Montreal: John Lovell, 1865.

Berton, Pierre . *The Invasion of Canada, 1812-14*, McClelland & Stewart, 1980.

Booth, J. Derek. *The Railways of Southern Quebec.* Rail fare Enterprises, 1982-85.

Brewer, Priscilla J. *From Fireplace to Cookstove*, Syracuse University Press, 2000.

Catton, Bruce. American Heritage Publishing, *New History of the Civil War.* Viking, 1996.

Catton. Bruce. *Grant Takes Command.* Boston: Little Brown, 1969.

Catton, Bruce. *Never Call Retreat.* Doubleday, 1965.

Collard, Edgar Andrew. *Montreal's Yesterdays*, Montreal Gazette.

Crockett, Walter Hill. *Vermont, the Green Mountain State.* New York: The Century History Company, 1921.

Davison, Donald J. *Banished.* Private printing, 2004.

Goodwin, Doris Kearns. *Team of Rivals.* New York: Simon & Schuster, 2005.

Historic records: The Missisquoi and Brome County Historical Societies.

Historic records: The St. Albans, Enosburg Falls and Richford Historical Societies.

History of Berkshire, St. Albans Historical Society. L.G. Printing, 1994.

Hoy, Claire. *Canadians in the Civil War.* McArthur & Company, 2004.

Johnson, Carl E *The St. Albans Raid, 1864.* Private printing, 2001. Ref: St. Albans Historical Museum.

Lamb, W.K. *History of the Canadian Pacific Railway.* Macmillan, 1977.

McDonnell, Greg. *The History of Canadian Railroads. 1985.* Footnote Productions, 1985.

Missisqoui Historical Society. *2nd Report.* Stanbridge East, Quebec.

Mitchell, Patricia B. *Northern Ladies Civil War Recipes.* Mitchell

Publications, 1994.

"Mrs. Winslow's Soothing Syrup." *The Mayflower Quarterly,* June 2004.

Notes on Berkshire, Vermont, Post Office and early post roads.

Panzer, Mary. *Matthew Brady and the Image of History.* Smithsonian Books, 1997.

Patriquin, Martin. *The Raid at St. Albans.* Private printing.

Perret, Geoffrey. *Lincoln's War.* Random House, 2004.

Potton Heritage Association. *Yours To Discover, 2002-2003.*

Robinson, B.K. *Once A Lion.* Montreal: Price-Patterson, 1996.

St. Albans Historical Society. *Reflections, 1788-1988.*

Stevens, G.R. *History of the CNR.* MacMillan, 1973. Reprinted Civil War Enterprises.

Trent, J.M. & Edw. *"The Railways of Canada".* Toronto: Monetary Times, 1871.

Tubbs, Benjamin. *The Music of the Civil War.* John Hill Jewett, 1963.

Seibert, Wilbur H. *Vermont's Anti-Slavery and Underground Railroad Record.* Spur & Glenn Co., 1937. Reprinted Civil War Enterprises.

Vinet, Marc. *Canada & The American Civil War.* Proud Productions.

Wilson, Charles Morrow. "The Hit and Run Raid." *American Heritage Magazine,* Aug. 1961.

Winik, Jay. *April 1865.* Harper Collins, 2001.

Yesterdays At Brome County, Vol. 6. 1980.

* * *

Acknowledgements

The personnel in historical museums located on both sides of the U.S.-Canadian border were most helpful in providing information on the Raid. They include: Arlene Royea, Brome County Museum; Judy Antle, Missisquoi Historical Society; Janice Geraw, Enosburg Falls Historical Museum; Marian Kittel and Carolyn Coons, Richford Historical Museum; and Dale Powers and the archival staff, St. Albans Historical Museum.

The most important person was Carl E. Johnson, author of *The St. Albans Raid, 1864*. His book was my primary reference.

Thanks to Norma and Bill Leet of Prinyer's Cove, for timely edits during the final publishing process; Tony O'Connor of Newport, Vermont, publisher of Civil War books and documents; Pamela Dillon of Stanbridge East, Quebec, writer, poet and historian; Professor William Prouty (ret. English, McGill and UNB); Professor Gerard Leduc (ret. Concordia); Colin Barclay and George Morris.

Many other friends offered valuable suggestions: Donald McBride, a retired druggist from Wolfeboro, N.H.; Eden Muir, a retired New York Architect, who lives on the border along the Old Boston Post Road; Barry Dwyer of Knowlton, Stephanie Piercey of Bolton Centre; Monique Dubuc of Austin; Jean Webster of Foster; and Gaston Lafontaine and Carol Smith of Knowlton.

Thanks to my family and 'Chester' a much-loved family dog that is named after his hometown, Winchester, Mass.; to my sister, Diana Hopewell, and her late husband, Bob Hopewell, who was a hawk at finding typos; and to my kids, Jennifer and Peter, for their encouragement and support.

Thanks to Terry McGee for recommending that I consider the Raid as a basis for my story of Rumsey.

My thanks to Shoreline Press for their support of this book. In particular, I really appreciated the enthusiasm of the publisher, Judith Isherwood, my editor, John Vatsis and graphic designer, Robert Kertesz.

The maps in this book were used with permission of the North West Regional Planning Commission of Vermont and the National Library and Archives of Quebec.